A PERILOUS PARDON

"Am I forgiven for my indiscretion of the other night?" Lord Thornhill asked.

Jennifer nodded. "It was as much my fault as yours."

"No," he said. "I am more experienced in these matters than you. I should have known better, Jennifer."

It took her a moment to understand why she felt as if something intimate had passed between them. Then she realized that he had used her given name, as her own future husband still had not presumed to do.

"Ah," he said. "Another indiscretion. It seems that it is impossible for two people of opposite gender to be true friends. There are other feelings that interfere. You have just forgiven me," he went on softly, his mouth only a few inches from her own, "for a sin I am sorely tempted to repeat."

Tension rippled between them. But though her mind knew where it was likely to lead, the rest of her being seemed powerless to break free. Or did not really want to. She wanted—she needed—to feel his mouth against hers again, his arms around her, his body.

She might forgive Lord Thornhill for what he had done—but she could not forget it. . . .

DARK ANGEL

by

Mary Balogh

A SIGNET BOOK

SIGNET
Published by the Penguin Group
Penguin Books USA Inc., 375 Hudson Street,
New York, New York 10014, U.S.A.
Penguin Books Ltd, 27 Wrights Lane,
London W8 5TZ, England
Penguin Books Australia Ltd, Ringwood,
Victoria, Australia
Penguin Books Canada Ltd, 10 Alcorn Avenue,
Toronto, Ontario, Canada M4V 3B2
Penguin Books (N.Z.) Ltd, 182–190 Wairau Road,
Auckland 10, New Zealand

Penguin Books Ltd, Registered Offices:
Harmondsworth, Middlesex, England

First published by Signet, an imprint of Dutton Signet,
a division of Penguin Books USA Inc.

First Printing, August, 1994
10 9 8 7 6 5 4 3 2 1

Chapter 1

London was somewhat overwhelming to the two young ladies who entered it in an imposing traveling carriage late one April afternoon. Instead of talking and exclaiming over it as they might have been expected to do considering the fact that they had chattered almost without ceasing during the long journey from Gloucestershire, they gazed in wonder and awe through opposite windows as the crowded, shabby, sometimes squalid streets of the outskirts gradually gave place to the elegant splendor that was Mayfair.

"Oh," one of them breathed on a sigh, breaking a long silence, "here we are at last, Jenny. At last! And suddenly I feel very small and very insignificant and very . . ." She sighed again.

"Frightened?" the other young lady suggested. She continued to gaze outward.

"Oh, Jenny," Miss Samantha Newman said, turning her head from the window at last to look at her companion, "it is all very well for you to be so calm and complacent. You have Lord Kersey waiting here to sweep you off your feet. Imagine, if you will, what it must be like to have no one. What if every gentleman in town takes one look at me and grimaces in distaste? What if I am a total wallflower at my very first ball? What if . . . " She stopped in some indignation when the other young lady laughed merrily, and then she joined in reluctantly. "Well, it could happen, you know. It could!"

"And pigs might fly south for the winter," the Honorable Miss Jennifer Winwood said quite unsympathetically. "One has only to remember how all the gentlemen at home tread all over each other's toes in their haste to be first at your side at the local assemblies."

Samantha wrinkled her nose and laughed again. "But this is London," she said, "not the country."

"And so the crushed-toe malady is about to spread to London," Jennifer said, looking in affectionate envy, as she frequently did, at her cousin's perfect beauty—short and shining blond curls, large blue eyes framed by long lashes darker than her hair, delicate porcelain complexion saved from even the remotest danger of insipidity by the natural blush of color in her cheeks. And Sam was small without being diminutive and well-shaped without being either voluptuous or its opposite. Jennifer often regretted her own more vivid—and less lady-like—self. Gentlemen admired her dark red hair, which she had never been able to bear to have cut even when short hair became fashionable, and her dark eyes and her long legs and generous figure. But she often had the uncomfortable notion that she looked more like an actress or courtesan—not that she had ever seen either—than a lady. She longed to look and be the perfect lady. And she never really craved gentlemen's admiration.

Except Lord Kersey's—Lionel's. She had never spoken his name aloud to anyone, though she sometimes whispered it to herself, and in her heart and her dreams he was Lionel. He was going to be her husband. Soon. Before the Season was out. He was going to make his formal offer within the next few days or weeks and then after her presentation at court and her come-out ball their wedding was to be arranged. It was to be at St. George's in Hanover Square. After that she would have to be presented at court all over again as a married lady.

Soon. Very soon now. It had been such a long wait. Five endless years.

"Oh, Jenny, this must be it." The carriage had turned sharply into a large and elegant square and was slowing outside one of its mansions. "This must be Berkeley Square."

They had indeed reached their destination. The double front doors were opened wide even as they watched and liveried servants spilled forth. Others jumped down from the baggage coach that had followed closely behind their traveling carriage throughout the journey. One of them lifted two maidservants down while the coachman himself was handling the young ladies down the steps of their carriage. It seemed a great deal of fuss and bustle for the arrival of two rather insignificant persons, Jennifer thought in some amusement. She had spent all her twenty years in the relative informality of country living.

But she was very willing to adapt. Soon she would be a married lady, the Viscountess Kersey, and would be lady of her own London home and country estate. It was a heady thought for someone who was only just now arriving in London for the first time. She was so very old to be doing that, so very old not to be officially out. But two years ago when she was eighteen and her come-out was planned and also the engagement and marriage that had been arranged three years before that by her papa and the Earl of Rushford, Viscount Kersey's father, the viscount had been detained in the north of England by the severe illness of an uncle. Jennifer had shed many a tear that spring and summer, not so much at the lost Season as at the delay in her marriage. She had seen Lord Kersey so few times. And then last year disaster had struck again in the form of the death of her grandmother in January. There had been no question of either a Season or a wedding.

And so here she was, arriving in London for the first time at the advanced age of twenty. The only consolation was that her cousin Samantha, who had been living with them for four years, since the passing of her own parents, was now eighteen and able to come out at the same time as Jennifer. It would be good to have company and a confidante. And a bridesmaid at her wedding.

It had seemed an eternity, Jennifer thought, stopping a moment to gaze up at her father's London house. She had not even seen Lord Kersey for over a year and even then only very briefly and formally in the presence of others at various Christmas parties and assemblies. She had dreamed of him every night since and had daydreamed about him every day. She had loved him passionately and singlemindedly for five years. Soon dreams would be reality.

Her father's butler bowed to them with stiff deference from the doorway and conducted them to the library, where Jennifer's father, Viscount Nordal, was awaiting them, standing formally before the desk, his hands clasped behind his back. He would, of course, have heard the commotion of their arrival, but it would have been out of character for Papa to have come out to meet them.

Samantha rushed toward him so that he was forced to bring his arms forward to hug her. "Uncle Gerald!" she exclaimed. "We have been speechless with the splendor of all we have seen. Have we not, Jenny? All we could do was peer out of the carriage windows and gawk with hanging jaws. Was it not so, Jenny? How lovely it is to see you again. Are you well?"

"I gather the speechlessness was not a permanent affliction," he said with a rare sally into humor. He turned from her to hug his daughter. "Yes, quite well, I thank you, Samantha. It is a relief to know you have both arrived safely. I have been wondering if I should have come for you myself. It does not do for young ladies to travel alone."

"Alone?" Samantha chuckled. "We had a veritable army with us, Uncle. Any highwayman would have taken one look and decided in despair that it would be certain suicide to risk an attack. A pity. I have always dreamed of being borne off by a handsome highwayman." She laughed lightly to dispel her uncle's frown.

"Well," he said, looking closely at both of them, "you will do. You both look healthy and pretty enough. A trifle rustic, of course. I have a modiste coming here tomorrow morning. Agatha arranged it. She has come to stay and take charge of all the faradiddle of your presentations and the rest of it. You are to mind her. She will know what is what so that you are both suitably decked out for the Season and so that you will both know how to go on."

Jennifer and Samantha exchanged rueful smiles.

"Well," Lord Nordal said dismissively, "you will be tired after your journey, I daresay, and will be glad to rest for a while."

"Aunt Agatha!" Samantha said a short while later as she and Jennifer were being conducted to their rooms by the housekeeper. "The dragon herself. I always have difficulty understanding how she and Mama could have been sisters. Will we have any enjoyment out of this Season, Jenny?"

"Far more than we would without her," Jennifer said. "Without Aunt Agatha, who would take us about, Sam, and introduce us to Society? Who would see to it that we receive and accept the proper invitations? And who would see to it that we have partners at the balls we attend and escorts to the theater and opera? Papa? Can you really see Papa so exerting himself?"

Samantha chuckled with her at the mental image of her stern and humorless uncle playing the part of social organizer for their Season. "I suppose you are right," she said. "Yes, she will see to it that we have partners, will she not? She will see to it that my worst nightmare will not be realized. Dear Aunt Aggy. Not that you have to worry about partners, Jenny. You will have Lord Kersey."

The very thought was enough to turn Jennifer's heart over in a somersault. Dancing with Lionel. Attending the theater with Lionel. Perhaps being alone with Lionel for a few moments whenever it could be arranged and exchanging kisses with him. Kisses—her knees had turned to jelly at Christmas last year when he had kissed her hand. Would her knees bear her up if—no, *when*—he kissed her lips?

"But not all the time," she said. "It would be most indecorous to dance with the same partner more than twice at one ball, Sam, even if he were one's betrothed. You know that."

"Perhaps you will meet someone even more handsome, then," Samantha said. "And someone who is not cold."

Jennifer felt the old indignation against her cousin's assessment of Lord Kersey. He was very blond and very blue-eyed and had features of chiseled excellence. And to Samantha he seemed cold—although she shared his coloring. Of course, the warmth of her complexion would always save Sam from such an accusation even apart from the liveliness of her face and the eagerness with which she approached life.

Lord Kersey—Lionel—was not cold. Sam, of course, had never had the full force of his smile directed her way. It was a smile of devastating attractiveness. It was a smile that had enslaved Jennifer ever since at the age of fifteen she had met for the first time the husband her father had picked out for her. She had never resented the arranged match. Never once. She had fallen in love with her intended husband at first sight and had remained in love with him ever since.

"If I do meet someone more handsome," she said as they reached the top of the stairs and were led in the direction of their rooms, "I shall pass him on to you, Sam. If he has not seen you first, that is, and fallen prostrate at your feet."

"What a delightful idea," Samantha said.

"Not that it would be possible to meet anyone more handsome than Lord Kersey, of course," Jennifer said.

"I will grant you that," Samantha agreed. "But maybe somewhere in this vast metropolis there is a gentleman who is equally handsome and who admires blond hair and blue eyes and insignificant stature and a nondescript figure."

Jennifer laughed and turned to enter the room the housekeeper was indicating as hers. "And Sam," she said just before they parted, "do be careful not to call our aunt Aunt Aggy to her face. Do you remember her expression when you did so last year at Grandmama's funeral?"

Samantha chuckled and pulled a face.

"Stubbornness will be your undoing one of these days, Gabe," Sir Albert Boyle remarked to his companion as they rode in Hyde Park unfashionably early in the afternoon. "But I must say I am glad you are back in town for all that. It has been dull without you for the last two years."

"But you will note that I do not quite have the courage to take to Rotten Row at five o'clock on my first full day back," Gabriel Fisher, the Earl of Thornhill, said dryly. "Perhaps tomorrow. *Probably* tomorrow. I'll be damned before I'll stay away altogether, Bertie, merely because I can anticipate being looked at askance and watching very proper matrons draw their sweet young charges behind their skirts and away from my contaminating influence. It is a pity hooped skirts fell out of fashion several decades ago. They would be able to hide their daughters more effectively."

"It may not be half as bad as you expect," his friend said. "And you could always proclaim the truth, you know."

"The truth?" The earl laughed without any trace of humor. "How do you know that the truth has not been told, Bertie? How do you know that I am not the heinous villain I have been made out to be?"

"I know you." Sir Albert said. "Remember?"

"And so you do," the earl said, fixing his eyes on the approaching figures of two young ladies, still some distance away, who were strolling beneath frilly parasols, their maids walking at a discreet distance behind them. "People may believe what they will, Bertie. To hell with the *ton* and their scandalmongering. Besides, it is altogether possible that I will be more in demand this year than I have ever been before."

"Scandal does often add fascination when it attaches to a man's name," his friend agreed. "And of course the fact that you are now an earl whereas two years ago you were a mere baron will help. And as rich as Croesus to boot. At least, I assume you are. That is how you always used to describe your father."

The Earl of Thornhill was apparently paying no attention. His eyes were narrowed. "You will never know, Bertie," he said, "how I have pined during the past year and a half on the Continent for the sight of an English beauty. There is nothing to compare in Italy or France or Switzerland, you know, or anywhere else either. Tall and short. Dark and fair. Well endowed and more delicate. But each exquisite in her own very English way. Will they pretend not to notice us, do you think, and direct their eyes downward? Or will they look up? Will they blush? Will they smile?"

"Or frown," Sir Albert said, laughing as he followed the direction of his friend's gaze. "Exquisite, yes. And strangers, unfortunately. Of course at this time of year London is always full of strangers. After a few weeks one will have seen them a dozen times at a dozen different entertainments."

"Frown? I think not," the earl said softly as their horses took them closer to the two ladies, who really should have waited a few hours if they hoped to be ogled as they deserved to be, he thought. He swept off his hat and inclined his head, almost forcing them to raise their eyes.

The small blonde blushed. Very prettily. She was true English beauty personified. The sort of beauty one dreamed of acquiring in a bride when one's thoughts must eventually bend that way. The tall dark-haired girl did not blush. Her hair, he noted with interest, was not dark brown, as he had first thought. When the light of the sun caught it as she raised her head and the brim of her bonnet no longer shaded it, he saw that it was a dark, rich red. And her eyes were dark and large. Her figure—well, if the other girl could turn the thoughts of even a fancy-free twenty-six-year-old to matrimony, then this one could turn the thoughts in another direction altogether. She was the sort of British beauty he had dreamed through tedious months of duty and a type of self-exile abroad of having naked beneath him on a bed.

"Good afternoon." He smiled, directing the full intensity of his dark gaze, not at the blonde beauty who had first taken his eye and who had stopped walking in order to curtsy, but at the greater challenge of her luscious companion, who was making no response at all beyond a candid stare and a slight pause in her walk. It was a pity, he found himself thinking, that she was very obviously a lady.

"Good afternoon," Sir Albert said beside him while the one girl curtsied, the other waited for her before moving on, and the maids stepped closer.

The two gentlemen rode on and did not look back.

"Eminently bedworthy," the earl muttered. "Lusciously, mouth-wateringly so. I am going to have to set up a mistress, Bertie. I have had no one since leaving England, if you will believe it, beyond one reckless encounter with a whore and then several weeks of terror at what she might have given me apart from an hour of strenuous and moderately satisfying sport. I did not repeat the experiment. And taking a mistress seemed somehow disrespectful to Catherine. I shall have to take a look-in at the theaters and opera houses and see who is available. It will not do to salivate in the park every afternoon, will it?"

"Hair the color of pale moonbeams," said Sir Albert, waxing poetic, "and eyes like cornflowers. She is going to have armies of suitors before many days have past. Especially if she has a fortune to match the face."

"Ah," the earl said, "you fancied the blonde, did you? It was the lady of the long and shapely legs who had my mind turning determinedly in the direction of mistresses. Oh, to have such legs twine about one's own, Bertie. Yes, I must say I am glad to be back in England, scandal or no scandal."

He knew he should be spending the spring at Chalcote instead of postponing his return until the summer. His father had been dead only a little over a year—since his own removal to the Continent with Catherine, his father's second wife. His title and his property were new to him. He should have hastened home as soon as the news reached them, but bringing Catherine back had been out of the question and he had felt himself unable to leave her at that particular time. Staying with her had seemed more important than hurrying home too late to attend his father's funeral anyway.

Now he knew he should go home. But Bertie had been right. There was a great deal of stubbornness in him. Coming to London for the Season was madness when doing so meant facing the *ton*, who believed almost without exception that he had eloped to the Continent with his father's wife after impregnating her. And now, of course, he had abandoned her to live alone in Switzerland with their daughter—or so the story doubtless went. Catherine was indeed living there quite comfortably with the child. He had given her the protection of his company during her confinement and for almost a year following it. Now she was quite capable of living independently—and he had been almost desperately homesick.

It would have been far better to have gone straight home to Chalcote. It was what he should have done and what he had wanted to do. London would be better faced—if at all—next year or the year after when the scandal had cooled somewhat. Except that scandal never cooled in London. Whenever he went there for the first time—whether it was now or ten years hence—it would flare about him.

It had never been his way to avoid scandal or to show that he cared one way or another for what people said of him. He did care as much as anyone, he supposed, but he would go to the devil before he would show that he cared. He had not made any attempt to correct that erroneous conclusion that had been jumped to when he had taken his pregnant stepmother away from his father's fury after she admitted that she was with child. It was as Gabriel had suspected—his father, sickly since before his second marriage, had never consummated that marriage. He had been afraid that his father would harm Catherine or her unborn child or would openly deny paternity and ruin her forever. The old earl had not done so, but gossip had blossomed into a major scandal anyway when her flight to the Continent with her stepson and her condition had become common knowledge.

Let people think what they would, the present Earl of Thornhill had thought. He had been established in Switzerland with Catherine before she told him who the father of her child was.

He should have returned to kill the man, he had thought often since. But as Catherine had explained to him, what had happened had not been rape. The foolish woman had loved the villain who had so carelessly impregnated her—the wife of a man who would know that he had been cuckolded—and had then made himself very scarce as soon as his sins had threatened to find him out.

And so the Earl of Thornhill was back, fifteen months after the sudden death of his father, almost one year after the birth of the child who bore his father's name despite the very public conviction that she was not his father's.

Back and foolishly thrusting his head straight into the lion's mouth. And eyeing British beauties who were obviously in town for the annual spring marriage mart. There would be one or two parents who would be outraged and foaming at the mouth if they knew that the Earl of Thornhill had just made his bow to their daughters—and had imagined one of them naked on a bed beneath him, her long legs twined about his.

He smiled rather grimly.

"Tomorrow, Bertie," he said, "weather permitting, we will come for the fashionable squeeze. And tomorrow I shall send back acceptances to some of my invitations. Yes, I have had a surprising number. I suppose my newly acquired rank, as you say, and even more important, my newly acquired fortune, do a great deal to make some people turn a blind eye to my notoriety."

"People will flock to view you," Sir Albert said cheerfully, "if only to see if you have acquired horns and a tail during the past year, Gabe, and if they can see any signs through your stockings and dancing shoes of cloven feet. I revel in the irony of your name. Gabriel of the cloven foot." He laughed loudly.

What would that dark red hair look like without the bonnet, the earl wondered, and beneath the light of hundreds of candles in their chandeliers? Would he find out? Would he ever be allowed close enough to her to see quite clearly?

He looked back over his shoulder, but she and her companion had passed out of sight.

"There," Samantha said, twirling her parasol, well pleased with life. "We are not to be quite ignored, Jenny. I even read admiration in their eyes. I wonder who they are. Will we find out, do you think?"

"Probably," Jennifer said. "They are undoubtedly gentlemen. And how could they fail to admire you? All the gentle-

men at home do. I do not see why London gentlemen should
be any different."

Samantha sighed. "I just wish we did not look so rustic,"
she said. "I wish some of the clothes we were measured for
this morning had been made up already. Aunt Aggy was a
positive love, poker face or not, to insist on so many clothes
for each of us, was she not? I could have hugged her except
that Aunt Aggy is not quite the sort of person one hugs. I wonder if our Uncle Percy ever . . . Oh, never mind." She laughed
lightly. "I wish I were wearing the new blue walking dress that
is to be finished by next week."

"I am not sure," Jennifer said, "that those gentlemen should
have spoken to us. It would have been more proper if they had
merely touched their hats and ridden on."

Samantha laughed again. "The dark one was very handsome," she said. "As handsome as Lord Kersey, in fact,
though in entirely the opposite way. But I think I liked his
companion better. He smiled sweetly and did not look like the
devil."

Jennifer would not own that the dark gentleman was as
handsome as Lionel. He was too dark, too thin-faced, too bold.
His eyes had bored into hers as if he saw her not only without
her clothes but even without her skin and bones. And his eyes
and his smile, she had noticed, had been directed wholly and
quite improperly on her. If he had deemed it polite to sweep
off his hat and to smile and even pass the time of day, then he
should have made it a gesture to the two of them. Not just to
Samantha, and not just to her. His behavior had been quite unmannerly. She suspected that perhaps they had just encoun-
tered one of the rakes with whom London was said to abound.

"Yes," she said, "he did look like the devil, did he not? As
Lord Kersey looks like an angel. You were quite right to say
they are handsome in quite opposite ways, Sam. That gentleman looks like Lucifer. Lord Kersey looks like an angel."

"The angel Gabriel," Samantha said with a laugh, "and the
devil Lucifer." She twirled her parasol. "Oh, this walk has
done me the world of good, Jenny, even though Aunt Aggy
has strictly forbidden us to show our faces at anything that
might be called fashionable until next week. Two gentlemen
have raised their hats to us and bidden us a good afternoon and
my spirits have soared even though one of them looks like the

devil. A handsome devil, though. Of course, you don't have to wait a week, you lucky thing. Lord Kersey is calling on you tomorrow morning."

"Yes." Jennifer went off into a dream. Word had come during the morning that Lionel was back in town and that tomorrow morning he was to call on her father—and on her.

Sometimes it was very difficult to remember that one was twenty years old and a dignified lady. Sometimes it was difficult not to set one's parasol twirling at lightning speed and not to whoop out one's joy to surrounding nature. Tomorrow she would see Lionel again. Tomorrow—perhaps—she would be officially betrothed to him.

Tomorrow. Oh, would tomorrow ever come?

Chapter 2

Lady Brill, Jennifer and Samantha's Aunt Agatha, was merely a baronet's widow and daughter and sister of a viscount, but she had a presence that a duchess might have envied and a self-assurance acquired during many years of residence in London. It should have been impossible for any self-respecting modiste to produce even a single garment less than twenty-four hours after her first call upon a client. And yet, thanks to the cajolery of Lady Brill, early in the morning after Madame Sophie had spent several hours at Berkeley Square with the Honorable Miss Jennifer Winwood and Miss Samantha Newman, a morning dress of pale green was delivered to the former by Madame's head assistant, who made sure that the fit was perfect before she left again.

Jennifer was to be fashionable when she received her first formal town visit from Viscount Kersey.

And she must be demure and ladylike, she told herself as she brushed cold and unsteady hands lightly over the fabric of her new dress, smoothing out nonexistent wrinkles. Her heart fluttered. She breathed as if she had just run for a mile nonstop and uphill. Samantha had just darted into her dressing room with word that the Earl and Countess of Rushford and Viscount Kersey had arrived.

"You look splendid," she said, stopping just inside the door and gazing at her cousin with mingled admiration and envy. "Oh, Jenny, how does it *feel?* How does it feel to be about to go downstairs to meet your future husband?"

It felt rather as if her slippers had been soled with lead. If she had been able to eat any breakfast, she would now be feeling bilious. She felt bilious anyway.

"Do you think I should have had my hair cut?" she asked, and stared at her image in the glass, amazed that she could think of nothing more profound to say on such a momentous occasion. "It is really very long, yet short hair is all the crack, according to Aunt Agatha."

"It looks very elegant piled like that," Samantha said. "And very pretty too with the trailing curls. I thought you would be bounding with excitement."

"How can I," Jennifer asked almost in a wail, "when I cannot lift my feet from the floor? It has been over a year, Sam, and even then we were never alone together and never together at all for more than five minutes at a time. What if he has changed his mind? What if there was nothing to change? What if he never did want this match? It was arranged by our papas years ago. It has always suited me. But what if it does not suit him?" Panic clawed at her.

Samantha clucked her tongue and tossed a look at the ceiling. "Men are not forced into marriage, Jenny," she said. "Women sometimes are because we are rarely given a say in the ordering of our own lives. That is the way of the world, alas. But not men. If Lord Kersey did not like this match, he would have said so long ago and there would have been an end of the matter. You are merely giving in to the vapors. I have never heard you express these doubts before."

She had had them, Jennifer supposed, suppressed so deep that even she had been scarcely aware of them. Fears that all her dreams would come to nothing. She did not know what she would do if that happened. There would be a frightening emptiness in her life and a painful void in her heart. But he was here—downstairs at this very moment.

"If I am not summoned soon," she said, clenching her hands into tight fists and then stretching her fingers wide, "I shall crumple into a heap on the floor. Perhaps this is only a courtesy visit, Sam. Do you think? After all, we have not seen each other for over a year. There will be a few visits before he can be expected to come to the point, will there not? I am being unnecessarily foolish. In which case, I am doubtless very overdressed and Lord and Lady Rushford and Li—and their son will laugh privately at me. His mama and papa would not have come with him if this was it, would they?"

Samantha tossed a look at the ceiling again, but before she could say anything more there was a knock on the door behind her and a footman announced that Miss Winwood's presence was requested in the rose salon.

Jennifer inhaled slowly and deeply through her nose before being subjected to her cousin's hug. A minute later she was walking downstairs with a quiet dignity that belied the wild beating of her heart.

She was about to see him again. Would he look as she remembered? Would he be pleased with her? Would she be able to behave like the mature woman of twenty that she was?

Three gentlemen rose to their feet when she was admitted to the salon. A lady remained seated. Jennifer curtsied to her father and then to the Earl and Countess of Rushford when her father presented her to them. The earl was large and as haughty looking as she remembered him. Samantha had once remarked that he was an older version of his son, but Jennifer had never been able to see any likeness. Lionel could never grow into someone so—unappealing. The countess was dumpy and placid-looking. It was hard to believe that she could have produced such a handsome son.

The earl inclined his head to her and looked her over appraisingly from head to toe, his lips pursed, rather as if she was inanimate merchandise he was considering purchasing, Jennifer thought. But she saw approval in his eyes. The countess smiled reassuringly at her and even rose to hug her and set a cheek against hers.

"Jennifer, dear," she said. "As lovely as ever. What a very pretty dress."

And then her father indicated the third gentleman in the room and she turned her head at last and looked at Viscount Kersey as she curtsied to him. On the rare occasions she had been about to see him in the five years since their marriage had been arranged, she had always wondered anxiously if he would be as splendid as she remembered him. And each time she had been jolted by the fact that he was even more so. The same held true now.

Viscount Kersey was not only handsome and elegant. He was—perfect. There was no feature of his face, no part of his body that could possibly be improved upon. It was the impression Jennifer had again now as her eyes took in the silver blondness of his hair, the deep blue of his eyes, his chiseled features and perfectly proportioned body beneath the immaculately fashionable clothes. He was still a few inches taller than she. She had been terrified that she would grow beyond him, but the danger was now past.

He bowed to her, his eyes on her the whole while. Cold, Samantha always called him. It was the uneasy impression Jennifer had of him now. He did not smile, though he said all that was proper and took his part in the conversation that followed when they had all seated themselves. But then she did not smile either. Doubtless she appeared cold to him. It was difficult to smile and to look and feel comfortable under such circumstances. She sat with stiff and straight back, mechanically taking her part in the conversation, aware of the critical appraisal of his parents.

It was merely a social call after all, then, she thought after a few minutes. It was foolish of her to have expected the event to have greater significance when they had not met for so long. Ridiculous of her. She hoped her appearance and her manner would not cause them to realize that she had expected more. How rustic they would think her.

And then her father got to his feet.

"I'll show you the new section of my library I mentioned at White's last week, Rushford," he said, "if you would care to come and see it now. It will take but a few minutes."

"Certainly," the earl agreed, rising and crossing the room to the door. "My own library is sadly out of date. I shall have to set my secretary to it."

His countess followed him. "And I shall call in on Lady Brill while I am here," she said. "It is always a pleasure to see Agatha when I am in town. Jennifer, my dear, perhaps you will entertain my son for a short while?" She smiled and nodded at both of them.

Jennifer had lulled herself with the conviction that she had been wrong about the purpose of this visit. She felt now almost as if she had been taken unaware. Panic threatened. But gazing down at her hands, which rested in her lap, she was relieved to find that they were neither trembling nor fidgeting.

Viscount Kersey stood up when the door closed behind their parents. It was, Jennifer realized, startled, the first time they had ever been quite alone together. She looked up to find him gazing down at her. She smiled.

"You are very lovely," he said. "I trust you are enjoying London?"

"Thank you." She blushed with pleasure at the compliment, though the words had been formally spoken. "We arrived only two days ago and have been out but once since, for a walk in the park yesterday afternoon. But yes, I intend to enjoy it, my lord." Her mind grappled with the realization that the moment had finally come.

"Is it an encumbrance?" he asked. "This match that was forced on you when you were far too young to know quite what was being arranged on your behalf? Do you wish yourself out of it now that you are here for the Season? Do you wish you were free to receive the attentions of other gentlemen? Do you feel trapped?"

"No!" She felt her flush deepen. "I have never for a moment regretted it, my lord. Apart from the fact that I trust my father to arrange for my future, I . . . " . . . *fell in love with you at first sight.* She had been about to say the words aloud. " . . . I find that it also suits my own inclination to accept his plans," she said.

He inclined his head in a half-bow. "I had to ask," he said. "You were but fifteen. I was twenty and the circumstances for me were a little different."

And then she remembered her earlier doubts. He had been twenty. Only twenty. Now at the age of twenty-five did he regret what he had agreed to then? Had he been hoping that she would answer his questions differently? Had he been hoping that she would offer him a way out? He still had not smiled. She had.

"B-but perhaps," she said, "this planned match is an encumbrance to you, my lord?" Now it was not the soles of her slippers that felt as if they were made of lead, but her heart. It seemed so altogether likely suddenly. He was so very handsome and—fashionable. He did not know her at all. He had not set eyes on her since Christmas of last year.

For a moment he looked at the door through which his parents had just passed and half smiled. Then he took a few steps closer to her and leaned down to possess himself of her right hand. "It was my pleasure when it was first suggested," he said, "to consider you as my future bride, and it is my pleasure now. I have looked forward impatiently to this moment. Shall we make it official, then? Will you do me the honor of marrying me?"

All doubts fled. She looked up into his blue, blue eyes and knew that the moment had come when all her dreams were being realized. Lionel was standing close before her, holding her hand, gazing into her eyes, asking her to be his wife. And then he smiled, dispelling any fear there might have been of coldness in his addresses, revealing perfect white teeth. She felt the old welling of excitement and love.

"Yes," she said, "Oh, yes, my lord." She got to her feet, not having planned to do so, not knowing quite why she did so.

"Then you have completed the happiness that began in my life five years ago," he said, and raised her hand to his lips.

She knew suddenly why she had stood up. They were standing very close. They were alone together for the first time. He had just proposed marriage and she had just accepted. She wanted him to kiss her lips. She blushed at the realization of just how improper her unconscious wish had been. She hoped he had not guessed.

He behaved with the utmost propriety. He returned her hand to her side and took a step back. "You have made me the happiest of men, Miss Winwood," he said.

She wanted him to call her Jennifer and wondered if she should say so. But perhaps it would be too forward. She wanted him to invite her to use his given name as she had used it in her dreams for five years. But she realized suddenly that the stiffness and formality of his manner must be the result of embarrassment. It must be so much more of an ordeal for a man to make an offer than for a woman to receive it. The woman's role was passive while the man's was active. She tried to imagine their roles reversed. She tried to imagine how she would have felt earlier this morning waiting for him to arrive if she had known that she must take the initiative, that she must speak the words of the offer. She smiled at him in sympathy.

"And you have made me happy too, my lord," she said. "I shall devote my life to your happiness."

They were saved from further conversation by the return to the salon of their parents, expectant looks on their faces. In all that followed, Jennifer held on to her happiness, to her knowledge that now, after so long, it was finally official, irrevocable, that her happiness had been signed and sealed.

They were to be married at the end of June. In the meanwhile they were to spend a month enjoying the activities of the Season in company together—or as much in company as propriety would allow—before their betrothal was officially announced and celebrated in a grand dinner and ball at the Earl of Rushford's mansion. And then another month would follow before the wedding would actually take place.

The end of June. Two months. In two months' time she would be the Viscountess Kersey. Lionel's bride. And during those two months she was to dance with him at balls and assemblies, sit with him at dinners and concerts, attend the theater and the opera with him, drive out with him, walk out with him. Get to know him. Get to feel comfortable with him. Become his friend.

And then his wife forever after. His lifelong companion. The mother of his children.

It was too much like heaven, she thought, glancing across the room at him while their fathers talked. He was looking back, unsmiling again. Two months during which to dispel the slight discomfort that made this morning just a little less than perfect. Except that it was perfect, she told herself determinedly. The awkwardness was to be expected. They scarcely knew each other despite the fact that for five years they had been intended for each other. They had not even met for over a year. And a proposal of marriage would be a strained occasion even in the most ideal of circumstances.

Oh, yes, everything was perfect. Except that perfection was an absolute state, and she knew that what had begun this morning was going to get better during the following two months and even better at the end of June.

She was the happiest woman alive, she told herself. She was in love with the most handsome man in the world and she was betrothed to him—officially betrothed at last. He had smiled at her and told her she had made him the happiest of men. She was going to see to it that that held true for the rest of their lives.

He kissed her hand again when he and his parents took their leave a few minutes later. So did the earl. The countess hugged and kissed her again and even shed a few tears.

Jennifer, dismissed by her father, refused to feel flat and depressed. How ridiculous! But how natural when she had just been offered for and had just accepted and had no one at the moment with whom to share her joy. She forgot herself as far as to take the stairs two at a time to Samantha's dressing room.

The Earl of Thornhill put into effect his promise to ride in the park at the fashionable hour the day after he had ridden there early. He was accompanied by Sir Albert Boyle, as before, and by their mutual friend, Lord Francis Kneller.

This time the park was as crowded as it always was at such an hour during the spring. He was not as embarrassed as he had half expected to be, though, he found. Many of the gentlemen he now saw, he had met at White's yesterday or this morning. Men tended not to be swayed greatly by scandal when it concerned one of their own.

Many of the ladies in the park did not know him—yet, anyway. It was a long time since he had been in London. Those who did—mostly older ladies—looked haughtily at him and would have given him the cut direct if he had given them the opportunity, but they were far too well bred to make a scene.

It all went rather well, he thought, and he was glad after all that he had come to town first before going to Chalcote. The next time he came he would be old and stale news. Other scandals would long ago have supplanted the one in which he had been involved.

"A shame," Sir Albert said, looking around the crowd carefully. "Not a sight of her, Gabe—of *them*. The most delightful little blonde you have ever set eyes on, Frank. And her companion had long legs that Gabe admired. Fancied them twined about his own, or something like that. But they are not here."

Lord Francis guffawed. "I hope you did not tell her so, Gabe," he said. "Maybe it is common courtesy to a Swiss miss to tell her such things, but an English miss would have twelve fits of the vapors and her papa and all her brothers and male cousins and uncles would separately challenge you. You would have appointments at dawn for a month of mornings."

"I kept my thoughts to myself," the earl said, grinning, "until I was foolish enough to confide them to Bertie. They must be otherwise engaged this afternoon, Bertie. Or perhaps they have not been presented yet. That would explain yesterday's solitary walk."

He too had looked about hopefully for them—in particular for the redhead. He had surprised himself by dreaming of her last night, but she had been telling him, alas, that he should go home where he belonged.

And then his grin faded and he completely missed the witticism of Lord Francis's that set Sir Albert to laughing. Yes, he thought. *Yes!*

There had been another reason for his return to London. He had hardly acknowledged it to himself and it might very well have come to nothing. But yes. He felt something strangely like elation. He had come at just the right time. He could not have timed it better if he had tried.

He had always known that he must confront Catherine's former lover somehow. The Gothic notion of challenging the man to a duel and putting a bullet between his eyes had passed long ago. But there had to be something. His father was dead. He was the head of the family that had been dishonored. More important, he had always been fond of Catherine, and he had been with her through much of her pregnancy and confinement. She had had to bear the whole burden alone, not the least part of which had been a deeply bruised heart. And though she was now passionately devoted to her daughter, nevertheless all the responsibility and stress of bringing up the child was hers alone and would be for years and years to come.

The father, as was the nature of things, had suffered nothing but physical pleasure from the affair.

The least he could do, the Earl of Thornhill had decided some time ago—the very least—was inform the man that he knew. Catherine had kept his identity a closely guarded secret for a long time and even then had told only her stepson.

And now the father of Catherine's child was riding in the park, bowing gallantly over the hand of a lady in a phaeton and flashing the whiteness of his handsome smile at her. He had not a care in the world. The earl amused himself for a moment with the mental image of his fist shattering those white teeth into a million fragments.

"You are blocking the path, Gabe," Lord Francis said.

"What?" he said. "Oh, sorry." Catherine's former lover had

tipped his hat to the lady in the phaeton and was riding away from the crowd into the more open spaces of the park. "Excuse me, will you? There is someone I must talk to."

Without waiting for their answer, he maneuvered his horse around vehicles and pedestrians and other horses until he was clear of them and could close the gap with the other rider.

"Kersey," he called when he was within earshot, "well met."

Viscount Kersey turned his head sharply, a slight frown between his handsome brows, and then smiled. "Ah, Thornhill," he said, "you are back in England, are you? Facing the music and all that?" He laughed. "Sorry about your father. It must have been a shock to you under the circumstances."

"He had been ill for several years," the earl said. "Your daughter is going to be blond like you, though she does not have much hair to speak of at the moment. Did you know, by the way, that it was a daughter, not a son? So much better, I always think, when the child cannot be acknowledged as one's heir anyway."

It was as if a curtain came down just behind the blue eyes, he noted with interest.

"What are you talking about?" Viscount Kersey asked, his voice both chilly and haughty.

"Lady Thornhill is now established comfortably in Switzerland with her daughter," the earl said, "and is in a fair way to recovering her spirits. I do not suppose you are much interested in hearing about her, though, are you?"

"Why should I be?" Lord Kersey frowned back at him. "Beyond the fact that I met the countess once or twice while I was attending my uncle during his sickness. I rather gather that you are the one who should be most concerned with her wellbeing, Thornhill."

The earl smiled. "I have no desire to prolong this exchange of civilities," he said. "And I am not about to slap a glove in your face. Suffice it to say that I know and that for the rest of your life you will know that I know. If I can be of any disservice to you, Kersey, it will be my pleasure to oblige. Good day to you." He touched his whip to the brim of his hat and turned to ride unhurriedly away in the opposite direction from that taken by Kersey.

He was satisfied, he thought. He had accomplished what he

had always planned to do. Perhaps Kersey would suffer some discomfort from the knowledge that his secret was not quite so secret after all.

And yet, the earl thought, there should be more. His father had been cuckolded and his stepmother dishonored and he himself had had his reputation ruined. A child was to grow up unsupported and unacknowledged by her real father.

There should be more.

For the first time in a long while the urge really to hurt Kersey burned in him. He should be made to suffer—just a little. He could not be publicly exposed without stirring up the old scandal for Catherine again. Lord Thornhill would not do that to her even though she was far away. No, he would have no satisfaction from hurling mud at Kersey and watching him as like as not ducking out of its aim.

But there should be some way.

He would watch for it, the earl decided. If there was anything he could do to see Kersey suffer, then he would do it.

Without the slightest qualm.

Chapter 3

Although he had broken the ice, so to speak, by riding in the park and facing the *ton*, two weeks passed before the Earl of Thornhill attended his first social function. He considered not doing so at all. He had proved a point to both himself and them, and he had confronted Kersey with his knowledge. He was very tempted to leave London and go home to Chalcote. But he supposed that since he had made his stand, he might as well complete the process. Riding in the park was not quite the same as attending an entertainment of the Season.

He decided to attend a ball. He had plenty of invitations to choose among. It appeared that his title and wealth were of greater significance after all than his notoriety. Every hostess during the Season liked to grace her ballroom with as many men of fortune as possible and as many titled gentlemen as could be persuaded to attend. Young, unmarried gentlemen were particularly courted, especially where there were young daughters or nieces or granddaughters to be brought out and married off. The Earl of Thornhill, being twenty-six years old, had every required attribute.

He decided on Viscount Nordal's ball in Berkeley Square for the simple reason that both Sir Albert Boyle and Lord Francis Kneller were going there. Nordal had a daughter and a niece he was bringing out—though it would be more accurate, probably, to say that his sister, Lady Brill, was doing the bringing out. She was one of Society's dragons. But the earl, seated in his carriage on the way to Sir Albert Boyle's rooms to take him up before proceeding to Berkeley Square, shrugged his shoulders. Her brother had invited him, and if she chose to snub him, then he would put on an armor of cold haughtiness and make free with his quizzing glass.

He did not really want to be attending this ball, but it seemed the wise thing to do.

"What do these girls look like?" he asked Sir Albert when the latter had joined him in the carriage. "Does Nordal have a difficult task on his hands?"

Sir Albert shrugged. "I've never seen 'em," he said. "They must have made their curtsy to the queen this week and it is Society's turn this evening. Five pounds say they are not lookers, though, Gabe. They never are. Every maidservant in sight tonight will have oceans of beauty, but every lady will look like a horse."

The earl chuckled. "Unkind, Bertie," he said. "Perhaps they will not like the look of us either. One is supposed to look beyond outward appearance, anyway, to the character within."

Sir Albert made an indelicate noise, rather like a snort. "Or to their papas' pockets," he said. "If they are well lined, the girl's looks are insignificant, Gabe."

"You have become a cynic in my absence," the earl said as his carriage slowed to join the line of carriages outside the house on Berkeley Square.

The hall, when they entered it, was brightly lit, and both it and the staircase were crowded with guests and humming with sound. The two gentlemen joined the line on the stairs. The earl fancied that several raised lorgnettes and several poker faces and outright frowns and whispers behind hands and fans were occasioned by his arrival. But there was nothing openly hostile.

Viscount Nordal, at the beginning of the receiving line, was affable, and even Lady Brill, playing the grand lady as her brother's hostess, nodded graciously before presenting her nieces. Lord Thornhill had an impression of two young ladies of *ton* dressed in virginal white, as was to be expected. The white gown was an almost obligatory uniform for unmarried young ladies.

And then he recognized the one standing beside Lady Brill. Miss Samantha Newman. Looking tonight more the personification of English beauty than ever. She positively sparkled with blond loveliness and was refreshingly free of the pretense of ennui that so many young ladies affected in order to make themselves appear more mature.

The Earl of Thornhill bowed to her and murmured some

platitude before turning his head expectantly toward the other young lady. The Honorable Miss Jennifer Winwood.

Yes. Oh, yes, indeed. He had exaggerated nothing in memory. He was a tall man, but her eyes were on a level with his chin. And fine dark eyes they were too, more amber than brown. All the glorious dark red hair he had merely glimpsed beneath her bonnet in the park was now piled on her head with cascades of curls over her neck and temples. And she was as shapely as a dream, though he did not lower his eyes from her face to confirm the impression. Her coloring and her figure made her look as vivid as if she were dressed in scarlet. And every bit as enticing.

He bowed over her hand, murmured that he was charmed, looked deeply into her eyes to be sure that she had recognized him—how mortifying if she had not!—and moved on into the ballroom.

"Well, Bertie," he said, coming to a pause inside the doors and raising his quizzing glass to his eye to survey the scene about him, "you owe me five pounds, my dear chap. The Season has at least two lookers to offer."

"I had convinced myself," Sir Albert said, "that they must have been a figment of our imagination, Gabe. I am smitten to the heart."

"By the blonde, I suppose," the Earl of Thornhill said. "I intend to dance with the other. We will see if I have been invited merely as an aristocratic ornament, Bertie, or if I am to be allowed within striking distance of one of Society's daughters."

"Five pounds say you will be allowed close, Gabe, and encouraged to stay close," his friend said. "I'll win my money back easily."

"Ah," the earl said. "Here comes Kneller. Wearing lavender. You look too gorgeous to be real, Frank. You are out to slay the ladies, not singly, I see, but by the dozen."

It had been an exciting and a frustrating fortnight. Exciting in the sense that they had prepared for their presentation at the queen's drawing room and, amidst great trepidation, had accomplished the task. And exciting too in that there had been their come-out ball to look forward to and a dizzying number of invitations to read and choose among—though that had usually meant agreeing to the events that Aunt Agatha approved and rejecting others that they might have found more tempting. And there had been fittings to enjoy and newly delivered garments to try on and exclaim over.

But it had been frustrating too. At long last they were in London and the Season had begun and all around them the *ton* were enjoying themselves with furious determination. Yet they must remain in seclusion until they had been presented and then until their come-out ball. It was enough to give even the cheeriest of mortals the dismals, Samantha had declared on more than one occasion.

It had been frustrating for Jennifer in another way too. Viscount Kersey had been to tea once. Once! He had come with his mother and had sat drinking tea and conversing for half an hour—with Jennifer, Samantha, and Aunt Agatha. He had smiled just for Jennifer as he took his leave and had kissed her hand.

But that was all she had had of the first two weeks of her official betrothal. Yes, it was all very frustrating. And all very proper, of course. And there had been the excitement of everything else that was happening.

But at last the evening of the ball had arrived and Jennifer felt almost sick with excitement. She despised herself heartily since she was twenty years old and long past the age for such girlish reactions. But she was excited and there it was. She was not going to pretend otherwise.

She had not realized there could be so many people in all London as the numbers who passed along the receiving line into the ballroom in a seemingly endless stream. Young ladies all in white, like Samantha and herself, older ladies in brighter colors with turbans and nodding plumes, older men who bowed and smiled and paid lavish compliments, younger men who bowed and murmured all that was proper and looked assessingly. Oh, she could understand why all this was known as the marriage mart, Jennifer thought, and was glad anew that she was not really a part of it. Lord Kersey had arrived early and was already in the ballroom. He had solicited the opening set with her as was only right and proper.

There were very few people Jennifer recognized. A few of the girls and ladies who had been at the queen's drawing room. One or two of her father's friends who had called at the house during the previous two weeks. Two younger gentlemen—the two who had ridden past them and greeted them in the park that first afternoon.

Yes, he did indeed look like the devil, she thought when her eyes alit on the dark gentleman and she recognized him instantly. He was very dark and very tall and, unlike any other gentleman she had seen, he was dressed in black—coat, waistcoat, and knee breeches. His shirt and neckcloth and cuffs and stockings looked startlingly white in contrast. He made a perfect Lucifer to Lionel's Gabriel, she thought, remembering her conversation with Samantha in the park.

He was the Earl of Thornhill. A very exalted personage indeed. He looked at her very boldly with his dark eyes—as he had done that other time. Perhaps gentlemen of his rank felt justified in taking greater liberties than other gentlemen did. She felt doubly grateful for Lord Kersey's presence in the ballroom and for the official nature of their betrothal. The Earl of Thornhill made her feel—uncomfortable.

The gentleman who had been with him in the park—Sir Albert Boyle—came after him. He smiled and bowed and went on into the ballroom. He behaved as all the other gentlemen guests had done.

But Jennifer quickly forgot about the only two young gentlemen who had been familiar to her. For actually they were not the only two. There was Viscount Kersey, who surely outshone every other gentleman in the ballroom enough to make it seem that the light from the hundreds of candles in their chandeliers shone only on him while every other gentleman stood in the shade.

It was a fanciful and ridiculous thought, she knew. She smiled at it and at him as he bowed finally over her hand and led her onto the empty floor to signal the formation of the opening set. Lord Graham, one of her father's younger acquaintances and one who had received a nod of approval from Aunt Agatha, was leading Samantha out, Jennifer knew, but she had eyes for nothing and no one except her betrothed.

He was all ice blue and silver and white. And blond. He made her heart turn over and beat with uncomfortable rapidity. She savored the moment with all her heart. It was the moment she had so long awaited. She would remember it for the rest of her life, she decided quite deliberately.

"You look extremely lovely tonight," he murmured to her

as they waited for the sets to form around them and the music to begin.

"Thank you, my lord." She smiled, realizing that she had been about to return the compliment and stopping herself just in time. Though the thought struck her that she should be able to say such a thing to her betrothed. But she had seen so little of him. They would grow more comfortable in time. Now that she was out and could move freely in society, they would be together almost daily. Soon they would be comfortable together. They would be friends. She would be able to speak her thoughts to him without having first to stop to consider if they were proper.

Now, at this moment, she was in awe of him and despised herself for being so. She was being gauche and rustic. She was behaving like a seventeen year old fresh from the schoolroom. She consciously put on her cloak of quiet dignity, and decided to enjoy the moment for what it was worth. Everything else that she longed for would come in its own time. She must not spoil the present by longing for what would come if she but gave it time.

They danced the steps of the opening country dance in silence. Jennifer was partly glad of it. Although she had attended numerous assemblies at home and was an accomplished dancer, nevertheless she had never before danced in such surroundings and in such company. And she felt eyes on them, as was only to be expected since this was her come-out ball, and Samantha's. She was thankful for the absence of conversation so that she could concentrate on her steps. And of course the intricate patterns of the dance separated them frequently so that any sustained conversation would have been impossible.

As she became accustomed to the steps and relaxed a little, her eyes sometimes strayed beyond the confines of the set in which she danced. All these grand and richly clad lords and ladies were gathered in her honor and Sam's. It was a heady thought. And a wonderful one. At last. At last she was in London and out and officially betrothed. Her betrothal would be publicly announced in two weeks' time, and in six weeks' time she would be married.

She glanced again at the splendid blond god who was to be her bridegroom. How all the other young ladies must envy her.

She wondered how general was the knowledge that they were betrothed and guessed that it was very general. Not many things remained secret for long in London society, she had heard. And this was no little thing.

And then beyond her betrothed her eye was caught by that one point of incongruity in the ballroom—by the black-clad figure of the Earl of Thornhill, who stood alone on the sidelines. No, not really alone, she saw when she focused her eyes on him. Two other gentlemen were standing with him, including Sir Albert Boyle. He just appeared to be alone because he looked so different from everyone else around him. So tall and so dark. He was watching her quite steadily, she realized. She lowered her eyes hastily and returned her attention to the dance.

He was the very antithesis of Lionel. It was so remarkable that she wondered foolishly why others were not exclaiming about it. Day and night. Summer and winter. Angel and devil. She smiled again and again wished that she was comfortable enough with her betrothed to share the joke with him.

Kersey! The Earl of Thornhill noticed him a few moments after he had finished teasing Lord Francis Kneller about his lavender and silver evening clothes and then could not understand why he had not noticed the man immediately. His eyes narrowed on the viscount and he felt an unexpected surging of hatred for him.

Perhaps, he thought, he should have left London for the North and home after all. Perhaps London was not big enough for the two of them. But he would be damned before he would allow himself to be driven away by the likes of Kersey.

He forced his attention away from the man and continued his light, bantering conversation with his friends.

But his attention did not remain diverted for long.

"The devil!" he muttered when the whole assembly seemed finally to be gathered and the members of the receiving line entered the ballroom and the orchestra began its final tune-up. The first set was about to begin and the two young ladies whose come-out ball this was were being led first onto the floor by their partners. He spoke another obscenity beneath his breath.

"I could not agree more, Gabe," Sir Albert said, mock

gloom in his voice. "Graham has cut me out and broken my heart. But that is not what ails you, is it? Kersey has done the like for you. Perhaps we should go home and put bullets in our brains."

Viscount Kersey was leading out the delicious redhead—Miss Jennifer Winwood. The devil himself, looking rather like an angel in his pale splendor, was bending over innocence, murmuring something into her ear. Lord Thornhill found that he had clamped his teeth together. He wondered what Nordal would do if he knew. Probably nothing. It was, after all, merely a dance, even though Kersey had been chosen to partner Nordal's daughter in perhaps the most important dance of her life. Anyway, there were not many men who would condemn another for making sport with someone else's wife. To say it was common practice was hardly to exaggerate. It was not even uncommon for one man to impregnate another man's wife. The only unpardonable indiscretion would be to do so before the wife had presented her husband with a legitimate male heir. Kersey had not been that indiscreet, although Catherine herself had borne no other child. And of course, far more unpardonable was to make sport with one's own father's wife. Kersey had not done that either.

"They look rather like something come straight down from heaven, do they not?" Sir Francis Kneller said at Lord Thornhill's side. He nodded in the direction of Kersey and Miss Winwood. "While the rest of us ordinary mortals have to settle for what is left. A lowering thought, eh, Gabe? Though there is nothing ordinary about you, it must be admitted. The choice of black tonight was inspired, old chap. You look positively satanic. The ladies will think it very appropriate—and will doubtless be panting all over you." He chuckled merrily.

"One wonders," the earl said, his eyes following the couple as they began to dance, "what Kersey has done to be so in favor with Nordal that he has been granted such an honor. Apart from being rather beautiful, of course." He did not try to hide the contempt in his voice. It really was not difficult to understand why Catherine, married to his elderly and infirm father, had fallen so recklessly in love with the viscount.

Sir Francis laughed again. "You have not heard?" he said. "It is a crying shame, if you were to ask me, when she is one of the few beauties in this year's crop. But it is ever thus, is it not?" He sighed and raised his quizzing glass the better to watch Miss Winwood dance.

"What is ever thus?" the earl asked. "Never tell me she has the pox, Frank. What a waste."

"Betrothed to Kersey," Sir Francis said gloomily. "Wedding to take place some time before the end of the Season, if gossip has the right of it. At St. George's with the flower of the *ton* present, I would not doubt. Of course, there is still her cousin, the equally delectable Miss Newman. More delectable, in fact. I have always had a soft spot for blondes, as what red-blooded blade has not? She has a more than respectable dowry too, so I have heard. It may be just a lure, of course, and will dwindle alarmingly as soon as one has committed oneself to showing a definite interest."

"The blonde is spoken for," Sir Albert said. "I spoke her name—though actually I did not know it at the time—in the park two weeks ago, did I not, Gabe? Do you think I should slap a glove in Graham's face at the end of the set?"

"Why wait until the end?" Sir Francis asked and the two men chuckled with hearty amusement.

The Earl of Thornhill was not listening to them. Betrothed! Poor girl. He pitied her deeply. And felt a certain anger on her behalf. She deserved better. Though perhaps not. He did not know her, after all, and had been given the impression of a certain haughty reserve both in the park and in the receiving line tonight. Perhaps possessing Kersey's title and fortune and beauty would be enough for her. Perhaps she was in love with him. *Probably* she was in love with him. There was something in the way she looked at him that suggested it.

And perhaps he loved her, the earl thought cynically, or the dowry that would come with her. Nordal was reputed to be wealthy enough. Perhaps Kersey was now ready to settle into a dull and blameless married life. It would not be difficult to settle for the redhead of the long legs, the earl thought, his eyes watching that last feature as she danced. Long and obviously shapely as outlined against the soft silk and lace of her high-waisted gown. And surely it would not be difficult to be satisfied with such loveliness and such voluptuousness for a lifetime.

Yes, perhaps it was appropriate, he thought, as he continued to watch them dance. They matched each other in beauty and in a certain icy aloofness.

And then his eyes met the girl's across the room as she danced. She did not immediately look away and he deliberately held her eyes with his own until she did. Lord, she was a desirable woman. There was a certain incongruity between that glorious red hair and well-endowed body on the one hand and the virginal white and the air of aloofness on the other. Miss Jennifer Winwood did not look either virginal or cold. At least, she did not look as if she should be. That hair should be loose and spread over a pillow. Those breasts should be bared and lifting from a bed to touch a man's chest.

Of course, she would not be virginal for much longer. That hair would indeed be released and those breasts bared and those legs twined—about Kersey's. There was something almost obscene in the thought, and definitely unseemly. His mind was not in the habit of wandering into other men's beds.

He wished Kersey and Miss Winwood happy in their forthcoming marriage, he thought, his eyes narrowing on them. Or rather, to the contrary, if he was to be more honest with himself, he wished their marriage to the devil. Unwilling hatred festered in him as he watched them dance and his two friends continued to chuckle over the witticisms they were exchanging.

What he would really like was to see Kersey suffer as Catherine has suffered, Lord Thornhill thought. Or even a fraction as much as she had suffered. He would like to see the redhead break his heart or otherwise make his life miserable. Though that hardly seemed fair to her. His eyes rested on her again. He did not know her at all and should take his own advice about looking beyond outward appearances to the character within, but she was gloriously beautiful. Kersey did not deserve the happiness of possessing such beauty.

The earl watched the girl for the rest of the set, his eyes narrowed in speculation. He was certainly going to dance with her himself before the evening was out if it could possibly be arranged. The beginnings of an idea were niggling at the corners of his mind.

Yes, he thought, revenge would be sweet. Even just a little revenge. And there just might be a way to get it.

"Is this not the most heavenly night you have ever lived through?" Samantha asked Jennifer later in the evening during

one of the rare moments when they were able to exchange a private word. "Four sets and four different partners apiece. Mr. Maxwell is going to dance with me again later. He is not the most handsome gentleman here, Jenny, but he does make me laugh. He says the most outrageous things about everyone around us."

She was glowing, Jennifer saw, and looking even lovelier than usual if that were possible. Only someone with Samantha's modesty could possibly have doubted that she would take the *ton* by storm, as the saying went. There was not another lady present to match her in loveliness.

"Yes, so is Lord Kersey," she said with a sigh. "Going to dance with me again, that is. I hate this rule that one can dance with the same partner no more than twice. It was the first dance and I was nervous and watching my steps. I feel as if I have spent no time with him at all." In imagination, in her dreams of what tonight would be like, she had danced the night away with Lionel, both of them aware only of each other. It had been an enchanted night—in her dreams. But of course she had known that propriety would keep them apart much of the evening. Sometimes she almost hated propriety.

Viscount Kersey had danced with Samantha and then had disappeared, presumably to the card room, which everyone knew no one but the dowagers and elderly gentlemen were meant to use. But even if he had stayed in the ballroom, he could not have danced with her again. Or if he had, she would have nothing left to look forward to for the rest of the evening.

In her dreams too she had pictured them alone together. Just for a short while. Just long enough so that they could smile into each other's eyes quite privately and exchange their first kiss. Ah, it had been a wonderful dream—and a rather silly one, she supposed.

But perhaps it really would happen later in the evening. Perhaps he would claim the supper dance—surely it would be strange if he did not, and the supper dance was next. And perhaps he would contrive to lead her from the dining room a little sooner than everyone else.

She had looked at his mouth as they danced. She had imagined his lips touching hers and had felt hot all over at the thought. It was ridiculous. By the age of twenty she should at least know what a man's lips felt like.

And then her thoughts were very effectively distracted. A gentleman was bowing before her and soliciting her hand for the next set—for the supper set. A tall gentleman dressed all in black and white. The Earl of Thornhill. Jennifer looked around, startled. Her aunt had brought all her other partners to her. But Aunt Agatha was some distance away, her attention monopolized by a very large and imposing elderly lady in purple.

This was the supper dance. Where was Lionel? She had set her heart on dancing it with him. But he was nowhere in sight. How mortifying!

"Thank you, my lord," she said, dropping a slight curtsy. "It would be my pleasure." She wished there had been a way of refusing. There must have been a way—but she did not know it.

She did not enjoy the dance. He was very tall, far taller than Lionel, and somehow—threatening. No, not that, she told herself when the word leapt to mind. *Disturbing* was perhaps a better word. He watched her constantly, and his dark eyes somehow compelled her to look back so that for several measures of the dance, when they were face to face, she found herself gazing into his eyes and feeling somehow enveloped in something to which she could not put a name at all. He spoke occasionally.

"I was beginning to believe," he said, "that I had imagined you."

He was referring to that afternoon in the park, she supposed.

"Until tonight," she said, "I have not been out and have been unable to attend parties."

"I gather that after tonight," he said, "you will be seen everywhere. I must make sure, then, that I am everywhere too."

Perhaps she should tell him that she was betrothed, she thought uneasily, but she stopped herself from doing so. His words were the typical gallantry that she must expect in London. He would be amused if he thought she had misunderstood.

"That would be pleasant," she said.

He smiled suddenly, and his severe, satanic features were transformed into an expression that was undoubtedly attractive. "I can almost hear you saying the same words to a tooth-drawer," he said. "In just the same tone of voice."

The idea was so ludicrous and unexpected that she laughed.

"I was wrong," he said softly. "I thought that perhaps you had never been taught to smile. But better than that, you know how to laugh."

She sobered instantly. He was flirting with her, she thought. And she found him a little frightening, though she had no idea why. Perhaps because at heart she was still just a gauche little schoolgirl and did not know how to handle gentlemen who had a great deal of town bronze.

Soon after they had started to dance, she caught sight of Lord Kersey, who had returned to the ballroom. Their eyes met briefly and she fancied that he looked annoyed. Indeed, that was perhaps an understatement. For one moment he looked furious. But he had no right to be either. He had not asked for this set and had come late to claim it. Surely he must know how she longed to be dancing it with him. Oh, surely he knew. She tried to tell him so with her eyes, but he had looked away.

A few moments later she saw that he was dancing with Samantha—again. She could have cried with frustration and disappointment. And quite unreasonably she hated the dark gentleman—the Earl of Thornhill—though he could not have known that she had been waiting hopefully for just this set with her betrothed.

He led her in to supper when the set came to an end. She had hoped against reason that somehow he would excuse himself and Lord Kersey would come to take his place. But Lionel, of course, was obliged to lead in Samantha, having danced with her. She could stamp her foot in bad temper, Jennifer thought, but fortunately the foolishness of the mental image of herself doing just that restored her sense of humor and she had to struggle with herself not to laugh aloud.

The Earl of Thornhill found her a seat at a table in one corner that was so crowded with flowers that there was not really room for anyone but the two of them. Indeed, it seemed that the table had not been intended to be sat at at all. Aunt Agatha had intended that she sit at the central table with Lord Kersey and Samantha and her escort, Jennifer knew, but somehow the plan had gone awry. Her aunt was frowning at her now, but what was she to do? Aunt Agatha should have been attending to her duty before the last set and then this would not have happened. Samantha and Lord Kersey sat together at the central table.

"I gather," the Earl of Thornhill said, "that a presentation to the queen is easily the worst ordeal of a young lady's life. Is it true? Do tell me about your presentation."

Jennifer sighed. "Oh, the ridiculous clothes," she said. "I will never know why we are not allowed to wear the sort of clothes we would wear to—well, an occasion like this, for example. All those fittings and all that expense for a few minutes of one's life. And the curtsy, practiced over and over again for months on end and all over and done with in a few seconds. Perhaps it was the worst ordeal of my life, my lord. It was also the most ridiculous."

He looked amused. "You may find yourself in a closely guarded cell in the Tower awaiting execution at the chopping block if you shout that opinion into the wrong ears," he said.

She felt herself coloring. What on earth had possessed her to speak so candidly?

"Tell me about it," he said. "I have always wanted to know what happens at those drawing rooms, and I believe I have always been rather thankful that I am male."

She told him all about it and he told her that he had been traveling for the past year and more and described parts of France to her and Switzerland. There could be no part of the world lovelier than the Alps, he told her, and she believed him, listening to his descriptions.

She was unaware of what she ate or did not eat during supper. And she was unaware of how much time passed or did not pass before the people around them began to leave their tables and wander back in the direction of the ballroom.

It was not fair, she thought as the Earl of Thornhill conducted her back there and then bowed over her hand before removing himself both from her presence and from the ballroom, that that time and that splendid opportunity for conversation should have been wasted with him when she might have been with Lionel. She grudgingly admitted that she had enjoyed both talking and listening to him. But it was what she had dreamed of doing with Lionel. And now the opportunity was gone for the night. Lord Kersey would dance with her again, but there would be no chance to talk with each other, to laugh together, to get to know each other a little better.

The evening was spoiled. The Earl of Thornhill had spoiled it for her, though that was an unfair condemnation. It was not his fault that Aunt Agatha had been delayed by the lady in purple and that Lord Kersey had been late returning to the ballroom. And he really had made an effort to make himself agreeable to her. Under any other circumstances she might have been gratified by his attention, for he was without a doubt as handsome in his own way as Lionel was in his.

Devil and angel. No, that was not fair.

Oh, but she had so longed for a conversation of just that nature with Lionel. He was approaching her now with Aunt Agatha. She smiled at him and felt her heart flutter.

Chapter 4

How could she possibly be feeling depressed? She was not, Jennifer told herself firmly late the following morning. It was just that she was still a little tired. The downstairs salon was almost laden with flowers, roughly half of them hers and half Samantha's. But despite all the excitement of the day before and the very late night, Sam was bubbling with exuberance.

"So many gentlemen sending us flowers, Jenny," she said, her arms spread wide eventually so that she looked as if she were dancing in a garden. "Some of the names I can scarce put faces to, I must confess. This is so very wonderful. I know it is the thing to send ladies flowers the morning after their come-out, but at least some of them must have come from genuine admiration, must they not?"

"Yes." Jennifer touched her fingers lightly to a leaf on the largest bouquet of all. She felt a little like crying and could not at all understand herself—or forgive herself. She had every reason to be gloriously happy. The evening had been a wonderful success—for both of them. There had not been enough sets to enable them to dance with all the gentlemen who had asked them.

"That one, for example." Samantha laughed. "Lord Kersey must have ordered the very largest bouquet the shop was able to provide. You must be ecstatic. You looked very splendid together, Jenny. Everyone was saying so. And everyone knows that you are betrothed. The announcement might as well have been put in the papers already."

"He looked marvelously handsome, did he not?" Jennifer asked wistfully, thinking back to her disappointment of the evening before—though she would not openly admit anything had been disappointing. As she had expected, Lionel had danced with her again after supper, but there had been little opportunity to talk. Dancing was not conducive to conversation, except perhaps the waltz. But there had been no waltzes last night because she and Samantha and many of the other young ladies would not have been allowed to dance it. There had been no chance yet for them to be approved by any of the patronesses of Almack's. A lady was not allowed to waltz until one of them gave the nod.

"And he even sent me a nosegay," Samantha said, lifting one and smelling its fragrance. "Was that not kind of him? I am sorry I ever called him cold. I shall never do so again. A gentleman who sends me a nosegay cannot possibly be cold." She laughed once more. "Do you suppose we will have callers this afternoon? Aunt Aggy said it is to be expected. I keep wanting to pinch myself to prove this is all real, but then I stop myself from doing so in case it is not."

Jennifer touched one of her own nosegays but did not pick it up. Roses. Red roses. It must not be easy to find roses at this time of year.

He had not returned to the ballroom. He must have gone home after supper or else spent the rest of the evening in the card room. She still resented the fact that the half hour or so she might have spent with Lionel during the supper break had been spent with him instead, that the conversation she might have been having with her betrothed had been had with the Earl of Thornhill instead. But then, if she had been with Lionel they would have been at the central table and would still have had no chance for private conversation. And Viscount Kersey had not been traveling in Europe for the past year and more and would not have been able to entertain her with all those stories and to fill her with longing to see it all for herself.

It had not been the earl's fault. She knew that. But she resented him anyway. It was unfair, but it was sometimes impossible to be fair when the heart was involved. She touched the tip of one finger to the petal of a rose and bent her head to breathe in the scent.

Actually she did have positive reason for feeling resentment—against both him and Aunt Agatha. Aunt Agatha had told her at the end of the evening that she ought not to have danced with the Earl of Thornhill and that she certainly ought not to have allowed him to maneuver her to a table in the dining room where no one else could join them.

"I cannot understand my brother's inviting him," Lady Brill had said. "He is an earl, of course, and has a vast fortune besides being the owner of one of the most prosperous estates in England. But even so he is not a suitable guest at a ball with young and innocent ladies. I would have discouraged him quite adamantly if he had asked you or Samantha to dance in my hearing."

"I did not know, Aunt," Jennifer had said. "And he did ask most politely. How could I have said no?"

"He has an unsavory reputation," Lady Brill had said, "and should have had the grace to stay away from you. You must have nothing more to do with him, Jennifer. If you see him again, you must nod politely but in that way all ladies must acquire of indicating that you wish no further acquaintance. If he persists, you will be obliged to give him the cut direct."

She would not say what had given the earl an unsavory reputation and appeared shocked that Jennifer had even thought to ask.

He should not have asked her to dance. He should not have steered her to that particular table. But it would not happen again. She would do what Aunt Agatha had directed if he should approach her again. In less than two weeks' time her betrothal would be announced and then she would be quite safe from any other gentleman, however savory or unsavory his reputation.

"It is a fine day," Samantha said, wandering to the window and staring upward, "even though the sun is not shining. Do you suppose we will have invitations to drive in the park, Jenny? If any gentlemen call on us this afternoon, that is. Oh, I do hope so. On both counts. Of course, you need feel no anxiety. Lord Kersey is bound to call and he will take you driving. But I must live in suspense."

Jennifer linked her arm with her cousin's and they left the room together. "Before you complain further," she said, "think back one month, Sam, and one year and two years. Then the most exciting thing we had to look forward to was a walk to the village to change the floral arrangements on the altar in church."

"Oh, yes," Samantha agreed. "Yes, that is true, is it not? If there are no visitors this afternoon and no drive, there is still tomorrow, of course, and the Chisleys' ball."

And Lionel would surely come, Jennifer thought.

He had sent her a nosegay during the morning. Nothing too lavish, merely what any gentleman might be expected to send the morning after attending her come-out ball. But he did send roses, exorbitantly expensive at this time of year, and he did deliberately neglect to send flowers to the little blonde although normal courtesy would have prompted him to do so.

He did not pay a call at Berkeley Square during the afternoon, though he pondered the idea and was very tempted when he discovered that Sir Albert was going to do so. Attending a ball at the house among hundreds of other guests and attending a drawing room among perhaps only a dozen or so were vastly different matters. He might be made to feel actively unwelcome in the drawing room. At the very least he would be frozen out by the dragon who was the girl's aunt and who had let down her guard over her charges for only that one moment of which he had taken full advantage the night before.

No, he would not call at Berkeley Square. But he would ride in the park at the fashionable hour and hope to see her there. She was almost sure to be there the day after her come-out ball. It was, after all, the fashionable thing to do. Kersey would doubtless take her driving there. It would be perfect.

He would take things slowly, Lord Thornhill decided anew this morning as he had decided last evening when the idea had first come to him. The woman was reserved and neither silly nor emptyheaded. Indeed, he had been amused by her wit as she had described the queen's drawing room. He guessed that she was older than most of the young girls currently making their come-out. She seemed older. She would not be easily led astray. Especially from Kersey. Even sensible ladies would not find it difficult to fall in love with Kersey, he guessed. Catherine had done so and she had always appeared to him to be a woman of sense.

But lead her astray he would, the long-legged, voluptuous redhead. The fact that it would not be easy made it a more exhilarating challenge. She was betrothed even though no public announcement had yet been made. Probably it would be made soon. According to Kneller, the wedding was to take place before the end of the Season. It would be better if the announcement had been made. A public scandal, a broken engagement in the middle of the Season—it would be a nasty humiliation for Kersey. It would not be exactly an eye for an eye. But it would be satisfying enough.

Revenge—even a small amount of revenge—would be very sweet. And the desire for it at the moment was so consuming him that it was even drowning out conscience.

Viscount Kersey had come to call at Berkeley Square, along with an amazingly large number of other gentlemen—and some ladies. It was very gratifying, especially for Samantha, who still had not learned that her beauty and vitality would draw gentlemen like bees to flowers. Jennifer was pleased for her, and both pleased and frustrated for herself. Pleased because several of the visitors made a point of sitting close to her and conversing with her, frustrating because Lionel stood back and let others monopolize her attention.

But he had asked soon after his arrival if she would drive with him in his curricle to the park later. And so during the hour or so when her father's drawing room was crowded with visitors she could console herself with the sight of him, as splendid in elegant day clothes as he had been in silk and lace the evening before. And with the knowledge that at last—oh, at last—they would be alone together afterward for an hour or more, driving out in the fresh air and the beauty that was Hyde Park.

It was a naive hope. She realized it quite early in the outing. Hyde Park at five o'clock in the afternoon was not the place one went to in order to be alone with someone or to enjoy some private conversation. Rotten Row proved to be an even greater squeeze than her father's ballroom had been last evening. All the fashionable world was there, strolling or riding or driving in a variety of fashionable conveyances.

But it was wonderful, nevertheless, to be riding up beside Lionel, almost shoulder to shoulder with him, to be seen there, to know that most people were well aware of the connection between them.

"This is amazing," she said. "Samantha and I walked here a couple of weeks ago but earlier in the afternoon. There was no one here." Except for two gentlemen on horseback, one dark and bold-eyed.

"There is a fashionable time for taking the air," Viscount Kersey said. "There is no point in being here at any other time of day."

"Except really to take the air and exercise," she said with a smile and a twirl of her parasol.

He looked at her uncomprehendingly and she felt foolish. One always felt foolish when one made a joke that the other person did not understand. But it had admittedly been a feeble joke.

"Do you ever find at the end of the Season that you long to return to the country in order to see and enjoy nature without all the distractions?" she asked.

"I prefer civilized living," he said.

It was almost the extent of their conversation. One came to Hyde Park, Jennifer soon realized, not in order to drive or ride or walk, but in order to bow and wave and smile and converse and gossip. It was amazing, considering the fact that she had been officially out for less than twenty-four hours, how many people she now knew and how many of them stopped to exchange pleasantries with her and Lord Kersey.

He was a great favorite with the ladies, of course. It became quickly apparent to Jennifer that those who stopped did so more to gaze at and talk with him than to converse with her. But the realization amused rather than annoyed her. She felt a wonderful possessive warmth, knowing that he was hers, knowing that all these women must be green with envy because he had chosen her as his bride.

And if the ladies stopped for his benefit, several gentlemen stopped for hers. It was flattering to know that she had attracted notice even though it must be common knowledge that she was betrothed. Unlike Samantha, she had not wondered incessantly for the last several months and even years if she would be attractive to gentlemen. She had been concerned only with being attractive for Lord Kersey. She had assumed that no other man would afford her a second glance knowing that she was not part of the great marriage mart.

The Earl of Thornhill was riding in the park, looking less satanic than he had last evening in a blue riding coat and buff pantaloons and Hessians. But he had a powerful presence. Even amid the crush of fashionable persons she saw him when he was quite a distance away. And hoped that he would not come close so that she would not have to treat him with the chill courtesy Aunt Agatha had directed. She wished she knew what had given him an unsavory reputation. Though it was unladylike to want to know any such thing.

Her attention was distracted by Lord Graham, Samantha's first partner of the evening before, and another gentleman, who stopped to pay their respects. When they rode on, Jennifer found that the earl was close by and looking directly at her—as he seemed always to be doing. She inclined her head to him, hoping that he would ride on past.

He stopped and touched his hat. "Miss Winwood, Kersey," he said. "Fine day."

"Thornhill," the viscount said stiffly and made to move on with his curricle. But the earl had laid a careless arm along the frame below the seat on which Jennifer sat.

"I trust you are rested after your success last evening," he said, looking directly into her eyes, ignoring the viscount.

"Yes, I thank you." How did one maintain the proper chill when such dark eyes gazed into one's own and when they were the type of eyes it was almost impossible to look away from? "Thank you for the nosegay," she said, without having intended to mention it. "It must have been difficult to find roses at this time of year. They are lovely."

"Are they?" He did something with his eyes so that they

smiled though the rest of his face did not. It was quite disconcerting, Jennifer found.

"Yes," she said lamely, and wondered if she was blushing. She hoped not, but her cheeks felt hot.

He withdrew his arm from the curricle and sat upright in the saddle again. Jennifer wondered idly if it was just that his horse was larger than anyone else's or if it was his superior height that made it seem that he towered over everyone else in the park.

"But not more lovely than their recipient," he said, his voice making it sound as if they were quite alone together, and he touched his hat again and inclined his head, without looking at all at Lord Kersey.

It had all happened in a few seconds. Several other people had spent longer beside their curricle. And yet she felt ruffled, disturbed, conspicuous. She felt that everyone must be looking at her and wondering why the Earl of Thornhill should be showing a particular interest in her when she was betrothed to Viscount Kersey. She was being foolish, she knew. She twirled her parasol and looked about her. Samantha, riding up beside Mr. Maxwell in his phaeton, was laughing gaily at something a trio of young riders were saying. Mr. Maxwell was laughing too.

"I do not believe it is wise," the viscount said beside her, his voice stiff with something that sounded almost like fury, "to allow the Earl of Thornhill to make free with you, Miss Winwood."

"What?" She turned her head sharply to look at him. "Make free, my lord?" She bristled.

"I was surprised and not altogether pleased that your father saw fit to invite him to your come-out ball last evening," he said. "I was even less pleased that your aunt allowed you to dance a set with him and accompany him in to supper."

"Aunt Agatha did not allow it," she said. "She was otherwise engaged when he asked me. I did not know there was any reason to say no. He was an invited guest in Papa's house, after all."

"You must have known," he said, "that I would come to claim your hand for the supper dance."

"How was I to know?" she asked. "You had not mentioned it. And you were not in the ballroom when the set was about to begin. It was what I had hoped for, but you were not there. It would have been unmannerly not to have accepted Lord Thornhill or anyone else who asked at that particular moment."

"Now you know that he is not respectable," he said, "you will be able to avoid him in future. It is my opinion that he should not be admitted anywhere with respectable people. I especially do not like him to be in company with my betrothed."

Jealousy. The irritation Jennifer had been feeling melted instantly. He was jealous. And possessive of her. He did not want her exposed to an influence that he felt to be less than proper. Or to the attentions of a gentleman who was undoubtedly handsome. She gazed at him and wished that he would turn to her and take her hand in his or show some definite sign of his affection for her.

And then he did both. And smiled. "You are such an innocent," he said.

She winced inwardly. She was twenty years old and did not like being treated as if she were still a child. But she did like to be the object of his solicitation. Her eyes strayed downward to his mouth. They had driven away from the crush on Rotten Row and were almost private together—a rare moment. Would he have found the opportunity to kiss her last night? she wondered. He really had intended to dance the supper dance with her. There would have been the opportunity—if they had lagged behind everyone else on the way to the dining room or if they had left it ahead of everyone else.

"What has he done that has put him so far beyond the pale?" she asked. She was not so naive that she did not know it was fairly common practice for young unmarried gentlemen—and some married ones too—to consort with women of a certain type. Perhaps even Lionel—but no, she could not think that of him. She would not. He was too proper a gentleman. But she could not believe it was just that with the Earl of Thornhill. It must be something more unusual, something worse—if there was anything worse.

He looked at her and frowned. "It would not be seemly for you to know," he said. "Suffice it to say that he is guilty of one of the most heinous sins man is capable of. He should have been forced to stay on the Continent where he was instead of contaminating England's shores by returning."

Exile? It had been exile, then, that had driven the Earl of Thornhill to his almost two years abroad? And what was one of the most heinous sins? *Sin* was the word Lord Kersey had used, not crime. What had he done? It was not seemly that she know. But curiosity gnawed at her.

The viscount lifted her down when they returned to the house on Berkeley Square, his hands at her waist. For a moment his hands lingered there and when Jennifer looked up into his face she thought that he was going to kiss her. In full view of the houses across the street and of the footman who had just opened the doors into the house. But he released her and raised her hand to his lips instead.

"Until tomorrow evening," he said. "You will reserve the opening set for me at the Chisleys' ball?"

"Yes, of course," she said.

"And the supper dance?" His smile had never failed to make her insides somersault.

She smiled back. "Yes," she said. "And the supper dance, my lord."

She was still smiling as she entered the house alone and ran lightly upstairs to her room. Tomorrow night. Tomorrow night he would kiss her. Everything in his look and his smile had said so. She felt a surging of renewed happiness. She could scarcely wait for tomorrow evening.

It was quite by accident that the Earl of Thornhill saw Jennifer entering the library with her cousin and a maid late the following morning. He was with two acquaintances but excused himself and followed the ladies inside. It was too good an opportunity to be missed.

A few people were reading the papers. Some of them looked up to see who the new arrival was. A few more people were browsing over the shelves of books. Miss Winwood was among them, at a different shelf from her cousin. The maid stood quietly inside the door, waiting for her charges to choose books.

The earl waited until Jennifer turned a corner and paused to look at a case of books that conveniently hid her from the front of the library.

"Ah," he said softly, stepping up behind her, "a fellow reader."

He had startled her. She whirled about to face him so that her back was to the bookcase. He was glad that he had stood so close. Even amidst the semidarkness of the shelves and the dust of books she looked startlingly lovely. He still had not satisfied himself as to the exact color of her eyes. But they were wide and beautiful eyes.

"Good morning, my lord," she said. "I am borrowing a book."

He smiled and waited until she realized the absurdity of her own words and smiled unwillingly back—he guessed that it was unwillingly. He guessed too that she had been warned against him. She had looked guilty and almost terrified when she first turned. He wondered what they had told her of him. In particular, he wondered what Kersey had told her.

"So I see." He took the book that was tucked under her arm and raised his eyebrows. "Pope? You like his poetry?"

"I do not know," she said. "But I mean to find out."

"You like poetry?" he asked. "You have tried Wordsworth or Coleridge?"

"Both," she said. "And I love both. Mr. Pope is quite different, I have heard. Perhaps I will love him just as well. I do not believe that liking one type of literature means that one will not like another type. Do you? It would give one a very narrow scope of interest."

"Quite," he said. "Do you like novels? Richardson, for example?"

She smiled again. "I liked *Pamela* until I read Mr. Fielding's *Joseph Andrews*," she said, "and realized how he had made fun of the other book and how right he was to do so. I was ashamed that I had not seen for myself how hypocritical Pamela was."

"But that is one purpose of literature, surely," he said. "To help us see aspects of our world that we had not thought of for ourselves. To broaden our horizons and our minds. To make us more critical and more liberal in our thinking."

"Yes," she said. "Yes, you are right." And then she blushed and looked around her and licked her lips and he guessed that she had just remembered she was not supposed to be talking with him.

"I do not attack young ladies in dark corners of libraries," he said. "But I understand that you must go."

"Yes," she said, looking warily at him. He had not stood back to enable her to pass.

"You will be at the Chisleys' ball this evening?" he asked.

She nodded.

"You will reserve a set for me?" he asked. "The second, perhaps? Doubtless you will dance the first with your betrothed."

"You know?" she said.

"Perhaps you have not been in town long enough to realize how impossible it is to keep a secret," he said. "And I do not believe your engagement is even meant to be an official secret, is it?"

"No," she said.

"You will dance the second set with me?"

She hesitated and swallowed. "Thank you," she said. "That would be pleasant."

"It would," he agreed. "But I wish you would not keep looking at me when you say so as if you saw me as an executioner with his hood on and his ax over his shoulder."

He held her eyes with his until she smiled.

"Until this evening," he said, stepping back at last. "Every minute until then will seem an hour long and every hour a day."

"How absurd," she said.

"Most things in life are," he agreed.

She hesitated and then whisked herself past him.

"Your book," he said.

She looked back at him, mortified, and held out one hand for it. He placed it in her hand, making sure that his fingers brushed against hers as he let it go.

A very fortunate encounter, he thought. Luck was on his

side. He had no doubt it would rattle Kersey to see him dance with Miss Winwood this evening. It would be a pleasure to rattle Kersey.

He just wished, the earl thought as he left the library five minutes later, after the ladies had already done so, that it was a different lady. He had the uncomfortable feeling that beneath the vividly beautiful and desirable body that housed Miss Winwood was a rather likable person. An intelligent one with a sense of humor. Someone whom in other circumstances he might have liked to befriend.

But he shut his mind to conscience. He did not want to be deflected from his purpose. The prospect of making Kersey look a fool was just too tempting for the present.

Chapter 5

The day had been unseasonably warm. The evening was cooler, but the indoors still held the heat of the day. The French windows along the length of the Chisley ballroom had been thrown back to admit as much air as possible and to allow the guests to dance or stroll on the wide balcony beyond and even to descend to the lantern-lit garden below if they so chose.

It was a great squeeze of an event, it being the come-out of the middle Chisley girl. The Earl of Thornhill made his bow to her in the receiving line after passing by her mother, whose manner dripped ice almost visibly. It was quite unexceptionable for his lordship to attend and add luster to her ball, that manner said quite audibly, but let him not expect to dance with Miss Horatia Chisley. Not this evening or any other evening of the Season.

"Well, I am for dancing," Lord Francis Kneller said as they looked about them in the ballroom. "I promised my sister that I would lead out Rosalie Ogden—younger sister of her particular friend, you know. The girl has not taken well." He grimaced. "Nothing for a dowry and nothing much for a face either."

"It is admirable of you to be willing to do your civic duty, Frank," the earl said, raising his quizzing glass to his eye. Yes, they had arrived already, and were being closely guarded by Lady Brill. He wondered if he would after all be able to get past the redoubtable old dragon. Would she agree that a promise given at the library this morning must be honored? "And how about you, Bertie? Have you come with the intention of tripping the light fantastic?"

"Not all night long," Sir Albert replied. "One does not mind being seen to be browsing at the marriage mart, Gabe, but one would not wish to be thought to be shopping in earnest. The very prospect makes me nervous. Point out Miss Ogden to me, Frank, and I'll dance with her too. I like your sister. Miss Newman promised me a set when I called at Berkeley Square yesterday afternoon. I had better claim it early. She is going to be beseiged."

"And you, Gabe?" Lord Francis asked as their friend strolled away to join the group of young men beginning to gather about the little blonde beauty.

"Later," the earl said. The ball was about to begin. Miss Horatia Chisley was being led onto the floor by a young gentleman whose shirt points looked in imminent danger of piercing his eyeballs, and sets were beginning to form. "I intend to stand here and ogle the ladies for a while."

Lord Francis chuckled and moved away.

She was wearing white again—of course. She would wear it all through the spring. And yet she had a way of making white look like the most vivid of colors. Tonight's gown was rather lower in the bosom and more heavily flounced at the hem. It shimmered with lace overlaying satin. She was dancing with Kersey, who was looking startlingly gorgeous in silver and pink. The earl surveyed the viscount through his glass with some distaste. Pink! There was something distinctly feminine about the color. It was worse even than Frank's lavender at the Nordal ball. And yet Kersey was drawing female admiration as he always did.

Jennifer Winwood had eyes for no one else. She smiled with unfashionable warmth at her betrothed. Despite the intelligence and sense and wit that Thornhill had seen in her, she was not immune to the beauty and charm of Kersey, it seemed. She was very probably in love with the man. He hoped not. Not that he would balk at the challenge if she were. He just hoped she was not.

He just wished that, having decided upon some small measure of revenge, he did not have to involve a third person. Especially an innocent.

It would be as well for this particular innocent in more ways than one if her feelings were not deeply engaged. Persistent enquiries over the past few days had revealed that Kersey kept two mistresses, one a dancer of recent acquisition, the other a former seamstress who had already borne him two children.

He was also known to frequent brothels more often than one would expect of a man who had established mistresses on whom to slake his appetites.

It seemed unlikely that such a man would suddenly become a model husband on his marriage. It would be as well if Miss Winwood, like most wives, did not expect either fidelity or devotion. It would be disastrous for her if she loved Kersey.

Though that would be her problem, not his, the earl thought grimly, turning his glass on her for a moment before lowering it. But good Lord, how could any man, betrothed to such a woman, contemplating marriage with her within the next few months, need anyone else? And how would any man after marriage with her have energy left or desire to expend on another woman?

The Earl of Thornhill waited with some impatience and some trepidation for the set to end and for the second to form. Though trepidation waned after Miss Newman, dancing the intricate steps of a vigorous country dance right before his eyes, had her hem stepped on by some clumsy oaf and a ruffle dragged too awkwardly to enable her to continue the dance. A few moments later, just as the music was drawing to a close, she left the ballroom with Lady Brill, obviously bound for the ladies' withdrawing room and a quick repair there by the maids and seamstresses who would be kept on hand for just such an emergency.

The fates appeared to be on his side, the earl thought. And Kersey, aware that his fiancée's chaperone had disappeared, was remaining at her side like a true gentleman and watchdog. It was perfect!

Jennifer was not able to enjoy the opening set even though she was dancing it with Lord Kersey and he had smiled at her and complimented her on her appearance and reminded her that she was to save the supper dance for him. And even though, as usual, he was looking quite splendidly handsome in pale colors that made his blondness dazzling.

She could not draw her mind free of the foolish promise she had given at the library. She had been warned against the Earl of Thornhill by both Aunt Agatha and Lord Kersey. Lionel had said that the earl was guilty of some heinous sin. And her own instinct warned her against him. She did not like the way he looked at her so directly and so boldly with his dark eyes. She did not like the look of him, handsome as he undoubtedly was. He was so very different from Lionel. Besides, she had no interest whatsoever in any man but her betrothed.

And yet she had allowed herself to be drawn into conversation with him at the library. She had allowed herself to laugh with him. It somehow seemed unseemly to laugh with another man—almost intimate. And worst of all—a brief conversation was quite unexceptionable, she supposed—she had agreed to dance the second set at the Chisley ball with him.

The knowledge of her foolishness had weighed heavily on her ever since. And to compound her foolishness, she had not even told anyone. Not even Samantha, who should have been easy to tell since she had seen him in the library and had commented on his presence there. She had not told Aunt Agatha or Lord Kersey. She positively dreaded the moment when he would come to claim his dance. If Aunt Agatha tried to steer him away, then Jennifer was going to have to admit that she had promised the set to him during what was now going to seem to have been a clandestine meeting at the library.

Why, oh why, had she not gone home and openly complained of how she had been maneuvered into accepting, of how she could not have refused without seeming discourteous, of how she intended to dance with him and make it very obvious to him that she wished for no further acquaintance with him? Why had she not done so? But it was too late now.

The opening set of country dances was a vigorous one. Jennifer felt hot and breathless when it came to an end and the viscount escorted her to where Aunt Agatha should have been waiting. She fanned herself in a vain attempt to cool her cheeks and calm her agitation. Aunt Agatha, someone told her, had gone to the withdrawing room with Samantha because Sam's hem was down. It was a small relief, but Lord Kersey lingered.

"Mama is not here either," he said. "I shall do myself the honor of remaining at your side, Miss Winwood."

She knew there would be no reprieve. The Earl of Thornhill was there and had been from the start. He had not danced the opening set but had stood on the sidelines, quizzing glass in hand. She knew, even though she had not once looked at him, that he had watched her through most of the dance. She had been aware of him with every nerve ending in her body and had resented the fact when she wanted to be free to feel awareness of no one but Lionel.

But it was her own fault. She must learn not to behave so rustically. She must learn not to allow others more accomplished in the social niceties to maneuver her.

The Earl of Thornhill came to claim his dance while the viscount was still at her side. The latter set a hand beneath her arm and closed it possessively about her elbow.

"Miss Winwood is otherwise engaged for this set," he said with chilly hauteur when the earl bowed.

"Really?" Lord Thornhill's eyebrows rose with a matching haughtiness. "I understood that this set had been promised to me." His eyes caught and held Jennifer's. "Following a pleasant but all too brief discussion of books at the library this morning."

She mentally kicked herself again for not mentioning it to anyone. Just as if there were something to hide. But he need not have mentioned it either. It was almost as if he was delighting in embarrassing her.

"Why, yes," she said, sounding surprised, as if she had just remembered something so insignificant that it had slipped her mind. "So it is, my lord. Thank you."

But she had concentrated so hard on the tone of surprise that she had forgotten also to sound chilly. She was not good at dissembling. And why should she dissemble? Why should she feel as if she had been caught out in some dreadful indiscretion? She resented deeply having been put in such a position. She would certainly see to it that such a thing never happened again.

Viscount Kersey released her elbow and bowed stiffly before moving away without another word.

"I do not blame him," the Earl of Thornhill said. "If you were mine, or soon to be mine, I too would be unwilling for any other man to pry you from my side. But he must be aware that it would not be at all the thing for him to remain with you all evening."

"Viscount Kersey is well aware of what is socially correct, my lord," she said, fanning herself again and hoping that the music would start and the set be in progress before Aunt Agatha returned.

"The dance has made you overwarm," he said. "And the ballroom was stuffy to begin with. Stroll on the balcony with me until the set begins. It is cooler out there." He held out his arm for hers, an arm that shimmered gold. He looked quite as striking in gold and brown and white as he had in black, she thought. It was perhaps his height and bearing and coloring that made him stand out in a crowd quite as much as Lionel did. He was taller than Lionel.

"Thank you." She laid her arm along his. The prospect of breathing in fresh air was too tempting to be resisted, as was the desire to be out of sight of her aunt until the dancing began. Though she would have to be faced afterward, of course. Doubtless there would be scolds. And what about Lionel? What would he say when he claimed the supper dance? Anything? There was nothing improper about her dancing with other gentlemen. It was quite the correct thing to do, in fact. But he had warned her particularly against the Earl of Thornhill. And he now knew that she had talked with the earl in the library this morning.

"Well," the earl said as they passed the French windows to the delicious coolness of the balcony, "do you like Mr. Pope?"

"Oh," she said with a laugh, "I have not had a chance even to open the book yet. I have been busy."

"Preparing for a ball," he said. "And the result has been worth every minute."

He looked down at her, warm appreciation in his eyes, and she was very aware of the low cut of her gown, a cut she had protested during her fittings. But even Aunt Agatha had approved the low décolletage and called it fashionable. She had, of course, worn something slightly more demure for her come-out ball. But not tonight. Jennifer was very well aware that she had more of a bosom than many other women. It was a physical attribute that made her uncomfortable.

"Thank you," she said.

"I suppose," he said, "that almost every moment of every day is taken up with busy frivolity. Are you enjoying your first Season?"

"It has hardly begun yet," she said. "But yes, of course. I have waited so long. Two years ago when Papa was planning to bring me out we had to change our plans because Lord Kersey was attending his sick uncle in the north of England.

We have been intended for each other for five years, you see. And then last year I was unable to come because my grandmother had died."

"I am sorry," he said. "Were you close to her?"

"Yes," she said. "My mother and her own mother died when I was very young. Grandmama was like a mother to me. She apologized to me when she was dying." The memory could still draw tears. "She knew that she was going to spoil my come-out, as she put it, and cause my official betrothal to be put off yet another year."

"You are positively ancient," the earl said with a smile.

"I am twenty," she said and then remembered that a lady never divulged her age.

"But at last," he said, "you have achieved your dream. You are enjoying a Season."

"Yes. And with Samantha. That at least has worked out well. She is almost two years younger than I." It was not so much the Season she was enjoying, though, as what it meant. Lionel. An official betrothal. Marriage. "Frivolity is good for a while. I do not believe I would like it as a way of life."

Most of the other couples who had been strolling had returned to the ballroom. The music was beginning for the second set. The Earl of Thornhill made no move to take her inside, and Jennifer was tempted by the coolness and the escape from the squash of guests inside the ballroom.

"Ah," he said. "You are not frivolous by nature, then. How have you spent your life until now? How do you envisage spending it after your marriage?"

"In the country, I hope," she said. "That is where real life is lived. I have managed Papa's home for a few years since Grandmama became too infirm to do it for herself. I like visiting my father's people and doing what I can to make life more comfortable for them. I like to feel useful. I was born to wealth and privilege—and to responsibility. I look forward to managing my husband's home. I am glad I have had some expereince."

They had strolled along the balcony and back. He drew her now to sit on a bench and she knew that he had no intention of joining the set. She did not really mind, though she did wonder if her absence would be noticed. They were not alone, though.

There were a few other couples still taking the air rather than dancing.

Jennifer took her arm from his when they sat down and rested her hands in her lap. He said nothing for a while. They listened to the music and the sounds of voices from beyond the French windows.

"What do you do?" she asked. "When you are not in London, that is. Or traveling on the Continent." She wished when it was too late that she had not asked. She did not want to have her ears regaled with shocking improprieties.

"I have led a rather useless life," he said. "For several years I gave myself up to every conceivable pleasure, imagining that I was really living, that everyone who led a more staid existence was to be pitied. The proverbial wild oats, one might say. That life was curtailed rather abruptly and thereby perhaps a few more years of my life were saved from uselessness. My father died a little over a year ago and precipitated me into my present title and all that goes with it. My estate is in the north of England. I have not been there since my return from Europe. But there are enough duties awaiting me there to keep my life staid and blameless for the rest of my days, I believe."

Wild oats. One of those oats was far worse than the typical indiscretion of young men, if Lionel was to be believed. But he had changed? The death of his father and the responsibilities it brought had caused him to turn over a new leaf. But the *ton* could be unforgiving, she knew. She wondered why he had come to London when he might have gone straight home to begin his new life—if indeed he was serious about doing so.

"Why have you come here instead of going home after such a long absence?" she asked. "And if there is so much to do there."

"I had something to prove," he said. "I would not have it said that I was afraid to show my face here."

Ah. Then there really was something beyond just the ordinary. She looked down at her hands.

"And under the circumstances," he said, "I am very glad that I am here."

His voice was softer. He did not explain his meaning. He did not need to. His meaning spoke loudly in the tone of his voice and in the silence that followed. But she was betrothed. He knew it. Perhaps he was merely speaking with meaningless gallantry. Perhaps he thought she liked to be flattered. And indeed there was treacherous pleasure to be gained from his unspoken words.

"The music is loud," she said—the first words she could think of with which to break the silence between them.

He stood up and offered his arm again. "So it is," he said.

She assumed, when she stood up and set her arm along his again, that he intended to stroll along the balcony with her once more. Instead he turned to the steps leading down into the garden and took her down them. She went without protest, knowing that she was allowing herself to be manipulated again, knowing that she should very firmly hold back and demand to be taken into the ballroom. Even her absence on the balcony might be construed as an indiscretion. Especially considering the identity of her partner and the heinous sin that everyone else except her seemed to know of.

But she went unprotestingly. It was so difficult to make a stand when one did not know exactly why one was supposed to do so. The garden was lit by lanterns. It was intended for use by guests during the evening. And it was not deserted. There was a couple seated on a wrought iron seat to one side of the garden. The earl turned her to stroll in the other direction.

"There is something about England and English gardens," he said, "that is quite distinctive and quite incomparable. One can see brighter, gayer, larger flowers in Italy and Switzerland. But there is nowhere like England."

"You did not stay away so long out of choice, then?" she asked. She was prying, she knew. And rather afraid that he would answer all her unasked questions.

"Oh, yes," he said, smiling at her, "entirely from choice. Sometimes there are more important things to be done than admiring flowers. And new places and new experiences are always to be welcomed. I came back as soon as there was no further reason to be away."

"I see," she said, watching the patterns of light and shade the lanterns made on the grass before her feet.

"Do you?" He laughed softly. "At a guess, I would say that they have not considered the lurid details fitting for a maiden's ears but have hinted at dark crimes and bitter exile. Am I correct?"

She wished the darkness could swallow her up. He was quite correct. But she felt foolish, young and gauche. She felt as if she had been caught searching his room or reading through his letters or doing something equally incriminating.

"Your life is none of my concern, my lord," she said.

He laughed again. "But you have been warned against me," he said. "Your aunt and your father will scold you for granting me this set. They will be even more annoyed that you have allowed me to take you from the ballroom. Kersey will be angry too, will he not? You must not allow this to be repeated, you know. You will be in serious trouble if you do."

He echoed her own thought—and gave her the opportunity she needed. She should agree with him, tell him that yes, this had been very pleasant, but she really must not dance with him or converse with him again. But his words made her feel as if she were a child instead of a woman of twenty. As if she could not be trusted to act for herself within the bounds of propriety. He had done something dreadful, but since then his father had died and he had been forced to grow up and change his ways. He could not go back and change whatever it was he had done wrong. But surely he should be allowed a chance to prove that he had changed. And surely she was old enough to make some decisions for herself instead of obeying blindly when no reason was given for restricting her freedom.

"I am twenty years old, my lord," she said. "There is nothing improper in my dancing with you or even strolling with you in a designated area." At least, she did not think it was improper. Though she had the uneasy feeling that others might not agree. Like Aunt Agatha and Lionel, for example.

"You are kind." He touched a hand lightly to hers as it rested on his arm. He had long, elegant fingers, she saw, looking down. It looked a capable and powerful hand. She resisted the instinct to pull her hand away. She would look like a frightened child after all. He spoke softly. "Is there anyone in this world whom you envy so much that it is almost a physical pain?"

She considered. "No," she said. "Sometimes there are aspects of appearance or behavior that I envy, but never seriously so. I am happy with my person and with my life as they are." It was true, she thought. For years, since she was fifteen, she had been happy, and now her happiness had reached its culmination. Or almost so. There were a few weeks during which to enjoy Lionel's company and to get to know him better. And then their wedding and the rest of their lives together. Happiness was soon going to turn to bliss. She felt an unexpected twinge of alarm. Life could not be that wonderful, could it? Or proceed quite so smoothly?

"Well," the Earl of Thornhill said softly, "I have felt such envy. I *feel* such envy. I envy Kersey more than I have ever envied any man."

"No." She looked up at him in some distress, her lips forming the word rather than expressing it out loud. "Oh, no, that is absurd."

"Is it?" His hand had closed about hers.

But in drawing her hand free at last and turning to make her way back across the garden and up the steps to the safety of the balcony, she made the mistake of turning in toward him. And of looking up into his eyes. And of pausing. And of noting that there was gentleness and something like pain in his eyes.

He kissed her.

Only his lips touched hers. His hands did not touch her at all. It would have been the easiest thing in the world to break away. But she stood transfixed by the wholly novel feeling of a man's lips against her own. Slightly parted. Warm. Even moist.

And then he stopped kissing her and she realized the full enormity of what had happened. She had been kissed. By a man. For the first time.

Not by Lionel.

By the Earl of Thornhill.

And she had not stopped him or pulled back her head.

And she did not now slap his face.

"Come," he said, his voice very quiet, "the set must be almost at an end. I will escort you back to the ballroom."

She set her arm on his and walked beside him just as if nothing had happened. She neither protested nor scolded. He neither justified himself nor apologized.

Just as if a kiss was a normal part of a stroll a man and woman took together instead of dancing.

Perhaps it was. Perhaps she was even more naive than she realized.

But of course it was not. A kiss was something a man and woman shared when they were going to marry. Perhaps even only when they were actually married.

She was going to marry Lord Kersey. She had looked forward so eagerly to his kissing her for the first time. To his being the first—and only—man ever to do so.

And now it was all spoiled.

The earl had timed their return very well. The music was just drawing to a close as he led her through the French windows to Aunt Agatha's side. He bowed and took his leave, and she stood beside her aunt feeling like a scarlet woman, feeling that everyone had but to look at her to know.

Everything was spoiled.

Viscount Kersey found the Earl of Thornhill outside the ballroom, at the head of the staircase. He was apparently leaving even though the ball had scarcely begun.

"Thornhill," the viscount called. "A moment, please." He smiled his dazzling white smile at Lady Coombes, who was passing on the arm of her brother, and joined the earl on the stairs.

"Yes?" The earl's hand closed about the handle of his quizzing glass.

Lord Kersey reined in his temper, conscious as he always was of his surroundings. "It was not wisely done," he said. "You must know that my betrothed, my soon-to-be wife, is not to be seen in your company, Thornhill. Certainly she is not to be seen stepping out of a ballroom with you."

"Indeed?" The earl's eyebrows rose. "Perhaps it is with Miss Winwood you should be having this conversation, Kersey. Perhaps you have some influence with her."

"She is an innocent." The viscount's nostrils flared, but he recalled the fact that they were in full view of anyone both abovestairs and below who cared to look. "I know what your game is, Thornhill. I am on to you. You would be wise to end it or it will be the worse for you."

"Interesting." The earl raised his glass to his eye and surveyed the other unhurriedly through it from head to toe. "You mean there will be a challenge, Kersey? The choice of weapons would be mine, would it not? I have a little skill with both swords and pistols. Or would you merely ruin my reputation? It cannot be done, my dear fellow. My reputation has sunk as low as it will go. I am reputed to have seduced my stepmother, got her with child, and run off with her, leaving my father to die of a broken heart. And if that was not quite devilish enough, I then abandoned her in a foreign land, leaving her among strangers. And yet here I stand as an invited guest at a *ton* event in London. No, Kersey, I do not believe there is a great deal you can do to my reputation that you have not already done."

"We will see." The viscount turned abruptly to go back upstairs. "Two can play at your game, Thornhill. It will be interesting to discover which of us plays it with the greater skill."

"Quite fascinating," the earl agreed. "I begin to enjoy this Season more and more." He bowed elegantly and continued on his way down the stairs.

Chapter 6

It was difficult to throw off the feeling that everything had been spoiled. Merely because the Earl of Thornhill had kissed her, Jennifer told herself, trying to minimize the importance of what had happened. All he had done was touch his lips to hers for a few seconds. It was really nothing at all.

But it was everything. Everything to spoil the pattern of life as it had been building for five years. Everything to upset her and everyone around her—not that everyone else knew the whole of it.

Aunt Agatha scolded in the ballroom. Very quietly and quite expressionlessly so that no one, not even anyone standing within a few feet of them, would have known that she was scolding. But she made it clear that if dancing with the Earl of Thornhill was not indiscreet enough to raise the eyebrows of society, leaving the ballroom with him, being absent with him for all of half an hour, was enough to ruin her reputation. She would be fortunate indeed if her absence had not been particularly noted and if she did not become the *on dit* in fashionable drawing rooms tomorrow.

It was in vain to protest that both the balcony and the garden were lit and that other couples were outside. The balcony and the garden were not for the use of a young unchaperoned girl who happened to be with a man who was neither her husband nor her betrothed, she was told. Especially when that man was a rake of the lowest order.

Jennifer now believed that he was indeed a rake. It was unpardonable of him to have stolen that kiss. And unpardonable of her to have allowed it, not to have protested her shock and outrage. She was unable to argue further with Aunt Agatha or to wrap herself about with righteousness. She felt horribly guilty.

Viscount Kersey danced the supper set with her and led her in to supper, but his manner was cold. Icy cold. He said nothing—that was the worst of it. And she was quite unable to bring up the topic herself. She was powerfully reminded of Samantha's opinion of him. But she could not blame him for his coldness this time, though she would have far preferred to be taken aside and scolded roundly. She felt very much as if she had been unfaithful to him. She felt unworthy of him. She had kissed another man when she was betrothed to Lord Kersey.

And yet Lionel was the only man she had ever wanted to kiss. She had so looked forward to the supper dance and to the supper half hour spent with him. But it had all been totally ruined—entirely through her own fault.

After supper Lord Kersey returned her to Aunt Agatha's side and engaged Samantha for the coming set. He took her out onto the balcony and kept her there the whole time—as punishment, Jennifer supposed. And it worked. It was agony knowing he was out there, even though it was only with Sam. She danced with Henry Chisley and smiled at him and chattered with him and was all the time aware of the absence of Lionel.

Yes, it was suitable punishment. If she had made him feel like this when she had gone outside, then she deserved to be punished. And it was the Earl of Thornhill with whom she had gone outside. And she had allowed him to kiss her.

She went home and to bed some time early in the morning, weary to the point of exhaustion, only to find that she could not sleep. She tried wrapping herself about with the warmth of the knowledge that in just a little over a week's time there was to be the dinner at the Earl of Rushford's and her betrothal was to be announced. After that all would be well. She would spend more time with Lionel and get to know him better. He would kiss her. There would be all the excitement of their approaching wedding. She pictured him as he had appeared this evening, handsome enough to bring an ache to her throat. He was hers—the man she loved, the man she was to marry.

And yet her mind kept straying to dark, compelling eyes and long, artistic fingers. She kept feeling his mouth on hers and reliving her surprise at the discovery that his lips had been slightly parted so that she had felt the soft moistness of the inside of his mouth. She kept remembering the physical sensations that had accompanied the kiss—the strange tightening in her breasts, the aching throb between her legs.

She kept remembering that she had talked to him and listened to him. She had revealed far more of herself than she had even done with Lionel, and had learned more of him than she knew of her own betrothed. He had convinced her that whatever had been in his past he had now reformed his ways and was prepared to live a responsible life. And then he had kissed her.

She felt sinful and spoiled. And unwillingly fascinated by the memories.

The morning brought with it no relief. Tired and dispirited, she wandered into Samantha's room only to find her cousin sitting quietly at the window, heavy-eyed.

"Have you been crying?" she asked, alarmed. Samantha never cried.

"No," Samantha said, smiling quickly. "I am just tired after last night. We were warned that the Season would be exhausting, Jenny, and it sounded marvelous, did it not? It has hardly started yet, and already it is simply—exhausting."

Jennifer sat down beside her. "Did you not enjoy last night's ball?" she asked. "You had a partner for each set. You danced twice with a few of them." Lionel, for example.

"I enjoyed it." Samantha got to her feet. "Let's go down to breakfast, shall we? And perhaps for a walk in the park afterward to blow away the cobwebs? I can feel them just clinging to me. Ugh!"

Samantha was not her usual exuberant self. Jennifer had counted on her being so. She had expected to find her cousin eager to talk about last night, to discuss her partners, to reveal her favorite. But she seemed unwilling to talk about last night. Jennifer felt her own spirits dip even lower.

"Sam," she said, "I thought you would cheer me up. You know that I was in disgrace last night, I suppose?"

"Yes." Samantha bit her lip. "I think he likes you, Jenny. He has never tried to dance with me. Yet he has danced with you twice. I think he really is the devil. He must know that you are betrothed. Lionel was upset."

"Lionel?" Jennifer frowned.

Samantha flushed. "Lord Kersey," she said. "You upset

him, Jenny. You ought not to have gone off with Lord Thorn-hill like that."

"You are scolding now too?" Jennifer asked quietly.

"Well, it was not right, you must admit," Samantha said. "You have a man, Jenny, and you have claimed forever that you love him. It was not right to step outside with the earl. Who is to know what you were up to, the two of you, out there?"

They were halfway down the stairs. But Samantha had stopped in order to stare accusingly at her cousin. And then, under Jennifer's dismayed gaze, she bit her upper lip, her eyes filled with tears, and she turned without another word to hurry upstairs again.

"Sam?" Jennifer called after her. But she was left alone in the middle of the staircase. Feeling wretchedly miserable and as much like eating breakfast as she felt like jumping into a den of lions.

It had really not seemed like such a dreadful indiscretion at the time. Had it been? Why had the French windows been open and lanterns lit both on the balcony and in the garden if guests had not been expected to stroll out there?

But guilt prevented her from feeling indignation against everyone who was condemning her—even Sam. For of course it had turned into an indiscretion. They were right and she was wrong. She had allowed a man who was not even her be-trothed to kiss her in the garden.

Samantha threw herself across her bed and sobbed into the pillow she held with both hands against her face. It had taken her a long while to erase all traces of last night's tears. Now she would have to begin all over again—after she had stopped crying again, that was.

She felt wretchedly guilty and wretchedly something else too. She would not put that something else into words.

She had a number of admirers already. She determinedly stopped sobbing and turned her head sideways so that she could breathe. She began to list them and picture them in her mind. There was Sir Albert Boyle. He was very ordinary, very kindly. There was Lord Graham, who was very young but quite dashing too. There were Mr. Maxwell, who made her laugh, and Sir Richard Parkes and Mr. Chisley, all quite worthy of her consideration. Perhaps a few of her new partners from last night would show further interest and become regular admirers too. Perhaps soon one or two of those admirers would turn into definite beaux. Perhaps soon she would be involved in a courtship. Perhaps Jenny would not be the only one married by the end of the summer.

But the thought of Jennifer distracted her.

He really had been very upset. Very angry. She had felt it as soon as supper was over and he had asked her for the next set. She had been annoyed, wondering why she should be expected to dance with him and smile at him and spend half an hour in his company when his eyes were so cold and his lips so compressed and his mind so obviously distracted. There were other gentlemen she could have been dancing with who would actually have looked at her and appreciated her.

She had been even more indignant when Lord Kersey had made it clear that he was not going to dance with her but expected her to step out onto the balcony with him.

"I am not sure, my lord," she had said to him, "that it is proper for me to leave the ballroom without a chaperone." She had suspected that he was doing it in order to punish Jenny. She did not want to be caught in the middle of a lovers' quarrel—if, indeed, that was what it was. If she was going to walk on the balcony instead of dancing, she would have preferred to do so with one of her admirers.

"It is quite proper," he had assured her. "You are the cousin of my betrothed."

And so she had allowed herself to be led outside—and straight down the steps to the garden below, where he took her to sit on a wrought iron seat that was out of sight of the balcony and the ballroom.

"What a mess," he had said. "What a bloody mess."

She would have felt more shock at the word he had used in her hearing if she had not been in the process of removing her hand from its resting place on his arm and if his own had not come shooting across his body to hold it where it was. She had felt remarkably uncomfortable—and still angry at being drawn into something that was none of her concern.

"Does she love me?" he had asked abruptly. "Do you know? Does she confide in you?"

"Of course she loves you," she had said, shocked. "She is your betrothed, is she not?"

"Yes," he had said. "Forced into it five years ago when she was no more than a child. When I was no more than a boy. She seems remarkably interested in Thornhill."

"She danced with him once at our ball and once at this," she had said, being drawn against her will into this quarrel or whatever it was between her cousin and her betrothed. She was still feeling angry that she was missing half an hour of the ball.

"Except that here they did not dance," he had said.

"They came out here," Samantha had said. "Or perhaps only out onto the balcony. There is no great indiscretion in that. We are out here. We are committing no indiscretion."

"No," he had said. "There is nothing even remotely indiscreet about a couple's being outdoors unchaperoned during a ball, is there?"

And as if to prove his point, which he had made obvious through the sarcasm of his tone, he had drawn his arm from beneath hers, circled her shoulders with it, raised her chin with his free hand, and kissed her.

Samantha had been so shocked that for a moment she had sat rooted to the spot. And then she had struggled to be free. She pushed at his shoulder, her palm itching to crack across his face. She was furiously angry.

But he had not let her go. He had used his superior strength to imprison her hands against his chest and had drawn her closer to him with both arms. His head had angled more comfortably against hers and he had kissed her again—with greater heat.

She had stopped struggling. And then she had stopped being passive. She had kissed him back. And somehow one of her arms had worked its way loose of its prison and was about his neck. For perhaps a minute she had mindlessly reveled in her first kiss.

He had looked down at her silently, his eyes glinting in the moonlight, when he finally lifted his head, and she had gazed back, only gradually realizing what had just happened, with whom she had shared her first kiss. Only gradually remembering that she had never greatly liked him, that she had always thought him cold.

"My lord," she had said uncertainly. She had wanted to be angry again, but anger had seemed inappropriate after her minute of undeniable surrender.

"Lionel," he had whispered.

"Lionel." She had spread one hand over his chest. She had not been able to think what to say to him.

"You see," he had said, "why chaperons are such a necessary evil?"

She had stared mutely back at him. Had he merely been demonstrating what might have happened between Jenny and the Earl of Thornhill? Was that what this was all about? But her mind refused to work quite clearly.

"Samantha." He had touched the backs of his knuckles lightly to her cheek. "I could wish that you had gone to live with your uncle a year or two sooner than you did. Perhaps he and my father would have chosen me a different bride. One more congenial to my tastes."

"I think you should take me inside," she had said, feeling a little sick suddenly.

"Yes," he had agreed. "Oh, yes, indeed I should."

But he had not immediately got to his feet. He had lowered his head and kissed her again. And to her everlasting shame, she had allowed it to happen even though this time she could not plead the shock of the totally unexpected.

They had climbed the steps to the balcony and strolled there in silence for the rest of the set. But his free hand had rested the whole time on her hand as it lay along her arm.

All night Samantha had not known what to make of the encounter. Except that he did not love Jenny and regretted the promise that had led him into the betrothal that was so soon to be announced. She did not know what his feelings were for her or even if he had any at all.

All night she had been tortured by guilt. She had allowed herself to be kissed—twice—by Jenny's betrothed. Worse than that—he was the man Jenny loved to distraction and had loved for five years. And Jenny, as well as being her cousin, was her very dearest friend.

Perhaps the kiss had meant nothing to him. Undoubtedly it had not.

Samantha wished the same could be said of her. If it had meant nothing, if she could shrug it off, perhaps she could feel simple anger and simple sorrow over the fact that Jenny's betrothed did not love her.

But the kisses had meant something. She had lain awake all night, and cried through much of it, fearing that she was in love with Lord Kersey—with Lionel. That perhaps she always had been and had protected herself from what had seemed so very undesirable and improper a passion by looking for faults in him.

But perhaps she was not, either. Perhaps she was merely reacting in a thoroughly silly and predictable way, falling in love with the first man to kiss her. As if kisses and love were synonymous terms. Yes, that was it, of course. She did not love him or even like him. She was angry with the way he had behaved to her last night. What he had done was unpardonable.

"Lionel," she whispered, closing her eyes and hugging the damp pillow to her bosom. "Lionel." Oh, dear Lord, how she hated him.

The Earl of Thornhill rather wished over the coming days that he had not conversed with Miss Jennifer Winwood at the Chisley ball. She was a beautiful and a very desirable woman. He wanted to know only those facts about her—the only sort of facts one needed to know about any woman. He had never felt in any way guilty about any of the women he had hired for casual sexual encounters or about any he had employed for longer periods of time as mistresses. When a woman was only a beautiful sexual object one did not have to have feelings for her beyond the physical.

He had no intention of even trying to make Miss Winwood his mistress, of course. He was not quite that base even if he had allowed the desire for revenge rather to obsess him. But he did intend to lead her astray, to compromise her, to cause her to break off her betrothal or, failing that, to cause Kersey to end it. Either way the resulting scandal and humiliation to Kersey would be marginally satisfying to himself.

It would have been far better to have seen to it that she remained to him just the luscious long-legged redhead whom he had dreamed of bedding from the first moment he had seen her—long before he had known of her connection to Kersey. And to have concentrated his mind on the numerous attractions of her person between that red hair and those long legs.

It had been foolish to allow her to become a person to him. She saw her life as one of privilege. She felt that she owed something in return. She felt that she had some responsibility to her father's dependents and would have to her husband's after she was married. She preferred the country to town. She felt that was where real life was lived. She did not often envy other people. She considered herself a happy person.

Damnation! He did not want to know any of those things.

Except that he could use them to soothe his conscience, he supposed. He could convince himself that he was about to do her a favor. She deserved better than Kersey. But perhaps after the scandal of a broken engagement she would be able to get no one else.

He had been surprised at her reaction to his kiss—though it could scarcely be called that when he had merely touched his lips to hers for a few seconds and had kept both his hands and the rest of his body deliberately away from hers. Even so he had been surprised that she had neither drawn away nor scolded afterward nor burst into tears. She had accepted the kiss, even pushing her lips back against his own for those brief seconds. And afterward she had behaved as if nothing untoward had happened between them at all.

It was gratifying. It had all been very easy so far.

He just wished that in order to soften her up, to make her comfortable with him and susceptible to his advances he had not had to converse with her. He just wished that he did not know she had taken that book of Pope's poetry to read just because she did not want to be narrow in her reading tastes.

He saw her the evening after the Chisley ball at the theater and bowed to her from his own box when he caught her eye. He had the impression that she had known for a long time that he was there but had deliberately kept her eyes averted. He did not make any attempt to call at Rushford's box, where she was seated with her party.

He saw her again the following afternoon in the park, where she was driving in a landau with Kersey, Miss Newman, and Henry Chisley, and touched his hat to her without either stopping to pay his respects or looking at any of the four of them except her. And he saw her the same evening at Mrs. Hobbs's concert. He sat on the opposite side of the room from her and Kersey and the Earl and Countess of Rushford and watched her for much of the evening though he did not approach her at any of the times when there was a break in the recitals and the other guests were generally milling about.

But at Richmond the next afternoon, at old Lady Bromley's garden party, he decided that he had left her alone for long enough. He was fortunate, he supposed, to have been invited to such a select gathering, but Lady Bromley was Catherine's grandmother and knew that he was not the father of Catherine's child—though clearly she did not know who was, or Kersey would doubtless not be among her guests.

Lady Bromley took his arm and strolled with him down by the river, which she was fortunate enough to have as one boundary of her garden. She walked very slowly, but he was quite content to match his pace to hers. The sun was shining, there was not a cloud in the sky, and somehow he intended before the afternoon was over to get Miss Jennifer Winwood alone again. To move one step closer to achieving his revenge—to winning the game, as Kersey termed it.

"I had a letter from Catherine just yesterday," Lady Bromley said. "The child is well and she is well. The climate seems to agree with her. And the company. She is doing well there, Thornhill?"

"She seemed remarkably contented when I left there two months ago, ma'am," he assured her quite truthfully. "Indeed, I would say she has found the place in this world where she best belongs."

"In a foreign country," she said with a click of the tongue. "It does not seem right somehow. But I am glad. She was never happy here. If you will pardon me for saying so, Thornhill, my son-in-law, the impecunious fool, should never have married her off so young to a man old enough to be her father."

Yes, the earl thought. Catherine was four months younger than himself. She had been his father's wife for more than six years before fleeing to the Continent with him. Yes, it had been criminal, especially given his father's ill health even at the time of his marriage and his consequent ill humor.

"Who is the German count?" Lady Bromley asked.

"German count?" The earl raised his eyebrows.

"With an unreadable and doubtless unpronounceable name," she said. "Mentioned twice in the course of the letter."

"I do not believe I met him," the earl said with a smile. "But it was only a matter of time before someone was taken into Catherine's favor, ma'am. She attracts a great deal of interest."

"Hm," she said. "Because Thornhill—your father, that is—left her a small fortune. And the child too."

"Because she is lovely and charming," he said.

Lady Bromley looked pleased, though she said no more. They were down by the river and three boats were out on the water, three gentlemen rowing them while their ladies sat at their ease looking picturesque. Jennifer Winwood, in a boat with Kersey, trailed one hand in the water and held a parasol in the other.

"A handsome couple," Lady Bromley said, seeing the direction of his gaze. "Recently betrothed, so I have heard, and to be married at St. George's before the Season is out."

"Yes," the earl said, "I had heard. And yes, a handsome couple indeed."

Kersey pulled the boat in to the bank a few minutes later and handed his lady out. She looked younger than her twenty years this afternoon, the earl thought, with her delicate sprigged muslin dress and straw bonnet trimmed with blue cornflowers and the frivolous confection of a blue parasol.

"Miss Newman?" The viscount smiled at his betrothed's cousin, the small blonde, who was standing close by in company with a few other young people. "Your turn. May I have the pleasure?"

It looked as if Miss Newman did not want the pleasure at all, the earl thought. Poor girl. But she stepped forward and set her hand in Kersey's. At almost the same moment Colonel and Mrs. Morris engaged Lady Bromley in conversation, and the Earl of Thornhill took advantage of the moment, perhaps the best the afternoon would provide.

"Miss Winwood," he said before she had had a chance to move from the bank to join the group with which her cousin had been conversing. He held out his arm to her. "May I escort you up to the terrace? There are cool drinks being served there, I believe."

The situation could not have been more perfect. There were several people observing them, including Kersey, who was powerless to do anything about it, short of making a scene.

And she was powerless to refuse without seeming quite ill-mannered. She really was looking incredibly lovely—a point that had no particular relevance to anything.

She hesitated for only a moment before taking his arm. But of course she was a gently bred young lady and quite inexperienced in the ways of the world. She really had no choice at all.

"Thank you," she said. "A glass of lemonade would be welcome, my lord."

The Earl of Thornhill, looking down appreciatively at her, wondered with some interest if he was playing the game alone this afternoon. Had Kersey not seen him on the bank with Lady Bromley? If so, why had he not kept Miss Winwood out longer? Or failing that, why had he not relinquished the boat to someone else and kept his betrothed on his arm?

It seemed almost as if Kersey had conceded this round of the game.

Unless somehow he was a more active participant in it.

Fascinating! It truly was fascinating.

But what, he wondered, *was* the game exactly?

Chapter 7

She had been aware of him standing on the bank of the river and had willed him either to move away by the time Viscount Kersey had brought in the boat or else to continue talking with Lady Bromley. But she saw Colonel and Mrs. Morris move up to join them and she remembered that when Lionel had taken her out he had kindly offered to take Samantha next, though Sam had protested strangely that she was not very happy on water. She was certainly happy swimming, something she did a great deal of at home during the summer.

Jennifer knew how matters were going to develop, almost as if all their actions were part of a play she had read or seen and all the people actors in that drama. She was quite powerless to change anything. She could only keep her eyes averted from Lord Thornhill and hope to lose herself among the group of acquaintances with whom Samantha had been conversing.

But of course the arrival of the colonel and his wife gave him the chance to extricate himself from the company of their hostess and he stepped forward as Lord Kersey was handing Samantha into the boat.

"Miss Winwood," he said, "may I escort you up to the terrace? There are cool drinks being served there, I believe."

She could hardly refuse without making an issue of it. His tone was civil and he was holding out an arm to her. But what alarmed her more than that fact was the realization that she did not really want to refuse. She had been very aware of him ever since the evening of the Chisley ball—and even before that—and always knew almost with a sixth sense when he was present at the same entertainment as she. She was always aware of him at every moment even though she rarely looked at him and even then did so unwillingly.

She did not want to be aware of him. She disliked him and even hated him. She wanted everything within her to concentrate on Lionel and these longed-for weeks with him before their wedding. It was not an easy time. Although they were spending more and more time in each other's company, they were not yet relaxed enough with each other to talk freely. It was because they were betrothed and everyone knew it but there had not yet been an official announcement, she told herself. After the Earl of Rushford's dinner next week all would change and everything would be as wonderful as she had imagined.

She did not need or want the distraction of the Earl of Thornhill. And she deeply, deeply resented the fact that he had kissed her while Lionel had not. And yet he was like a magnet to her eyes and her senses. Even when she could not see him, she thought about him almost constantly.

Now, forced into company with him again, she felt almost relief. Perhaps if she took his arm and walked up to the terrace with him and drank a glass of lemonade with him, the dreadful memory of the Chisley ball would be dispelled and the terrible unwilling . . . attraction would be over. There. She had never used that word before. But it was true, she thought with some dread. She was attracted to the Earl of Thornhill.

"Thank you," she said as coolly as she was able, taking his arm. "A glass of lemonade would be welcome, my lord."

Touching him again, standing close beside him again brought a vivid memory of that night and a rather frightening physical awareness with which she was so unfamiliar that she did not know quite what to do with it.

She would walk and converse, she decided. It was broad daylight. There were lawns and trees and flowers to be admired and a clear blue sky to gaze up at. It was only as she walked that she realized she had not looked back for one last sight of Lionel. He had looked so splendidly handsome and virile rowing her on the river. She concentrated her mind on her love for him.

"Do I owe you an apology?" the Earl of Thornhill asked.

"An apology?" She looked up at him, startled. His dark eyes were looking very directly back into hers.

"For kissing you," he said. "Don't tell me that it was a thing of such insignificance that you have forgotten about it." He smiled.

She could feel herself flushing. And could not for the life of her think of anything to say.

"I have not forgotten it," he said, "or forgiven myself for giving it. I could use the quietness of the garden and the moonlight for an excuse, but I had taken you down there and should have realized the danger and guarded against it. I am deeply sorry for the distress I must have caused you."

She had not been mistaken in him, then. Whatever he had been in the past, he was no longer a man without honor and conscience. He was a kind gentleman. She was glad. She had been saddened by her disillusionment. And yet she was disappointed too. She had the uncomfortable feeling that she would be altogether safer if he really were the unprincipled rake that kiss had made him appear to be. She could guard herself more easily against a rake.

"Thank you," she said. "It did cause me some distress. I am betrothed and only my intended husband has the right to—to—"

"Yes." He touched the fingers of his free hand lightly to the back of her hand. "If my apology has been accepted, let us change the subject, shall we? Tell me what you think of Pope's poetry."

"I admire it," she said. "It is written with great polish and elegance."

He chuckled. "If I were Pope listening to you now," he said, "I would go out and shoot myself."

She looked at him and laughed and twirled her parasol. "I meant precisely what I said," she told him. "I feel no great emotional response to his poetry as I do to Mr. Wordsworth's, for example. But I feel an intellectual response. That does not mean I like it less. Merely differently."

"Have you read 'The Rape of the Lock'?" he asked.

"I loved it," she said. "It was so amusing and clever and so . . . ridiculous."

"It makes one feel uncomfortable at every frivolity society has ever led one into, does it not?" he said. "Do you enjoy humor and satire in literature?"

"*She Stoops to Conquer* for humor and *Gulliver's Travels*

for satire," she said. "Yes, I enjoy both. And emotion and sentimentality too, I must confess, though gentlemen immediately
look very superior and politely scornful when a woman admits
as much."

The Earl of Thornhill threw back his head and laughed. "I
dare do no such thing now, then," he said. "Your tone made it
sound as if you were throwing down the gauntlet and daring
me to take up the challenge. Besides, I have been known to
shed a surreptitious tear or two over *Romeo and Juliet*. Not
that I would ever admit as much even if I were being stretched
on the rack."

"But you just did." She laughed.

They spoke about literature during the rest of the stroll up
the long lawns to the terrace and about dogs while they drank
blessedly cool lemonade. Jennifer did not know how they had
got onto the latter subject, but she found herself telling the earl
about her collie who loved to eat the cakes she smuggled to
him and who sensed when he was about to be taken for a walk
and tore around in circles and yipped and otherwise demonstrated wild and undignified enthusiasm until his expectations
were met.

"I miss him," she ended rather lamely. "But life in town
would not suit him. He is unaccustomed to being walked on a
leash."

"Come," he said, taking her empty glass from her hand and
offering his arm again after setting the glass on the table, "let
us stroll into the orchard. There will be no fruit to see at this
time of year and we are too late for the blossoms, but there
will be relief from the heat of the sun for a while until tea is
served."

Jennifer had no idea how much time had elapsed since they
had left the riverbank. It could have been ten minutes or it
could have been an hour. But for the first time in however
long it had been she looked about her with awareness and
noted that there were a few other people, in couples or small
groups, on the terrace and others in larger numbers strolling on
the lawns. One group was playing croquet while others
watched. Lionel and Samantha were nowhere in sight. They
had not yet come up from the river. They must be still out in
the boat or else standing on the bank as part of the group with
whom they had all gone down there.

She should be down there too, she thought, feeling disoriented for a moment, realizing how absorbed she had been in her conversation with the earl. She should be with Lionel. She wanted to be with him. She had looked forward to this afternoon, especially when she had woken up and seen how lovely the weather was. Perhaps there would be the chance to wander alone with him, she had thought, as she was wandering with the Earl of Thornhill now. It had seemed like a wonderful opportunity. Lionel was escorting both her and Samantha at the garden party. Aunt Agatha was otherwise engaged, as was the Countess of Rushford.

"Perhaps," she said, "you should escort me back to the river, my lord. I believe my cousin and Lord Kersey must still be there."

"If you wish." He smiled. "Though the thought of shade and quietness for a few minutes is definitely appealing, is it not?"

It was. And—treacherously—the lure of his company for a few minutes longer. Being with Lionel was not nearly as comfortable at present. There were too many tensions surrounding the facts of their betrothal and its announcement and their impending marriage. In time they would be this comfortable together. But not yet.

"Wonderfully so," she said, smiling conspiratorially at him. "Parasols are made to look pretty, my lord, but accomplish very little else."

"I had always suspected as much." He grinned at her. "But heaven forbid that women should ever admit it and become practical beings. How ghastly to think that the time may ever come."

She took his arm and allowed him to lead her toward the orchard. "Do you believe that women should be only ornaments to brighten a man's life, then?" she asked. "Nothing else?"

"I would have to take exception to the word *only*," he said. "All men—and women too—like to be surrounded by lovely ornaments. They make life more pleasant and more elegant. But life would be unbearably dull and lonely if there was nothing but the ornaments. They would soon lose their appeal and be fit for nothing else but to be hurled for the relief of frustration. A woman would quickly lose her appeal, no matter how lovely and ornamental she was, if she had nothing else to offer."

"Oh," she said. "Fit only to be hurled in a fit of temper."

He chuckled. "It is the reason for the failure of so many marriages," he said. "So many couples are trapped into a lifetime of boredom and even active misery. Had you noticed? And very often it is because they once thought that what pleased the eye would satisfy the emotions and the mind for the rest of their lives."

"You do not look for beauty in a prospective bride, then?" she asked.

He laughed again. "I do not yet know what I look for," he said. "I am not yet in search of a bride. But you are twisting my words. Lovely ornaments are important to life. There must be aesthetic pleasure to make it complete. But there has to be more too. Much more, I beleive."

The wife the Earl of Thornhill would choose eventually would be a fortunate woman, Jennifer thought. She would also have to be a special person.

It was indeed blessedly cool among the trees of the orchard. The branches overhead did not block the sun but muted its rays and gave a strange air of seclusion, though the lawns and the garden party guests were close by. It was almost like being back in the country, Jennifer thought and closed her eyes briefly against an unexpected stabbing of nostalgia.

"And what about you?" the Earl of Thornhill asked. "Your impending marriage is an arranged one. Did you have any hand in the choice?"

"No," she said. "Papa and the Earl of Rushford are friends and decided years ago that a match between their children was a desirable thing."

"And you did not fight against their decision tooth and nail?" he asked, smiling.

"No," she said. "Why should I? I trust Papa's wisdom and I approved his choice."

"And still do?" he asked.

"Yes."

"Because he is beautiful?" he asked. "He will certainly be a wonderful ornament for you to look at for the rest of your life."

She felt that she should be offended that he had somehow insulted Lionel. But there was a teasing gleam in his eye when she looked up at him. She thought of his belief that there had to be more than beauty to attract if a marriage was to have a hope of bringing a lifelong companionship and happiness. Yes, Lionel was beautiful and it was his beauty that had caused her to fall headlong in love with him. But there was more. There was his cool courtesy and sense of propriety. There was—oh, there was a whole character to be discovered over the next weeks and months. They were going to be wonderfully happy. She had waited five long years for the happiness they were soon to know.

"Do you love him?" he asked quietly.

But the conversation had become far too personal. She had not yet told Lionel that she loved him. He had not told her that he loved her. She was certainly not going to discuss her feelings with a stranger.

"I think," she said, "we should talk about poetry again."

He chuckled and patted her hand. "Yes," he said. "It was a dreadfully impertinent question. Forgive me. In a very short acquaintance I have come to think of you as a friend. Friends talk to each other on the most intimate of topics. But friends are usually of the same gender. When they are not, there must always be some barrier to total friendship, I suppose, unless they share a relationship that is intimate in all ways. I am unaccustomed to having a woman as a friend."

Were they friends? She scarcely knew him. And yet she found it remarkably easy to talk with him. But she ought not even to be with him. Lionel did not like it and Aunt Agatha had warned her quite severely against him. He was not quite respectable. And there was something about him that stopped her from being quite at her ease with him. Some . . . attraction. There was that word again.

"I have never had a gentleman as a friend," she said. "And I do not believe it is a possibility, my lord. I mean between you and me." She was surprised to feel a certain sadness. And surprised too and a little uncomfortable to find that they had stopped walking and that somehow she had come to be standing with her back against a tree while he stood before her, one hand resting against the trunk above and to one side of her head. "I am going to be married soon."

"Yes." He smiled down at her. "It was a foolish and impulsive notion, was it not, that we could be friends. But it is true for this afternoon, nevertheless. You feel it too, do you not? We are friends. Am I wrong?"

She shook her head. And then wondered if she should have nodded. And was not at all sure with which of his questions she had agreed.

"And so," he said, "I am forgiven for my indiscretion of the other night?"

She nodded. "It was as much my fault as yours," she said almost in a whisper.

She wondered, gazing at his smiling face and friendly eyes why she had ever agreed with Samantha's comparison of him to the devil. Or had she been the one to suggest it? She could no longer remember. But it was only his very dark coloring in comparison with Lionel's blondness that had made her think so. Now that she knew him a little, she found that he was a man she liked. She regretted that there could be no real friendship between them.

"No," he said. "I am more experienced in these matters than you. I should have known better, Jennifer."

It took her a moment to understand why she felt suddenly as if something intimate had passed between them—almost like the kiss they had shared in the Chisleys' garden. And then she realized that he had used her given name, as Lionel had still not done. She opened her mouth to reprimand him and then closed it again. He was her friend—for today anyway.

"Ah," he said. "Another indiscretion. Pardon me. Yes, I was quite right. It is impossible for two people of opposite gender to be true friends. There are other feelings that interfere with those of pure friendship. Alas, I could never be your friend, Jennifer Winwood. Not under present circumstances."

She saw her hand, as if it belonged to someone else, lift to his face and both saw and felt her fingers touch his cheek. And then she lowered it more hastily to lay it flat against the bark at her side, and bit her lip.

Tension rippled between them. But though her mind knew it and knew where it was likely to lead, the rest of her being seemed powerless to break free of it. Or perhaps did not really want to do so. She wanted—she needed—to feel his mouth against hers again. She wanted to feel his arms about her, his body against hers. Her head knew quite clearly that she wanted no such thing, but her body and her emotions were ignoring that knowledge.

"You have just forgiven me," he said softly, his mouth only a few inches from her own, "for a sin I am sorely tempted to repeat. And for one I knew would tempt me again if I had you alone and unobserved once more. No, there is not the smallest possibility of a friendship between you and me. And none of any other relationship. You are betrothed—to a man you love. I found you five years too late, Jennifer Winwood. Had I not, I would have fought him for you—every inch of the way. Perhaps I might even have won." He took a step back and removed his hand from the trunk of the tree.

"You could have anyone you want," she said, still gazing at him. At his darkly handsome features and tall, athletic physique. She did not care what he had done. Any woman would fall in love with him if she but got to know him a little. Any woman whose heart was not already given elsewhere, that was.

He chuckled and looked genuinely amused for a moment. "Oh, no, there you are wrong," he said. "There is at least someone I cannot have. Let me escort you back to the terrace. It must be teatime and it is probable that everyone has come up from the river."

"Yes." She felt depressed suddenly. She should be feeling relief and gratitude—relief at having escaped another dreadful infidelity and gratitude that he had had greater control and better sense than she had had. But she felt sad. Sad for him because he seemed to care for her but could do nothing to attach her interest because she was betrothed. And sad for herself because she had dreamed of just such encounters as she had had with the Earl of Thornhill—but with Lionel. How perfect—how utterly perfect—life would be if it was he who had kissed her at the ball and almost kissed her in the orchard and if it were with him that she had talked so comfortably and so freely on a variety of topics both important and trivial. If it were he with whom she was becoming friends.

She loved Lionel so very, very dearly. But she knew by now that it was no fairytale love that they had. It was a very real human relationship that did not come easily to either of them. They had both agreed that they wanted the marriage and she believed they both loved. But building companionship and friendship was something they would have to work on. Perhaps it would be easier once they had the more intimate relationship of marriage, once they lived together and shared responsibilities. But the dream of meeting in London and proceeding from that moment to living happily ever after had not become reality. She would admit it to herself now.

And yet it might have if they had had characters that were more compatible. She knew that it was possible to be comfortable with a man and to find it easy both to talk and to listen to him. But Lionel was not that man.

She loved hin but he was not yet her friend. Perhaps it was as well, she thought. Making him her friend would give her a goal to work toward after her marriage. One always needed goals in order to give purpose to life.

Viscount Kersey was on the terrace with Samantha and a group of other people. It seemed to Jennifer as if they all turned to watch her progress across the lawn from the orchard. And it seemed to her now, when it was too late, that after all it had been indiscreet to go just there.

The Earl of Thornhill did not linger when he had returned her to Lionel's side. But he took his leave in such a way as to embarrass her deeply, though she was sure that had not been his intention. He took her right hand in both his, gazed at her with intent eyes, as she remembered his doing that first afternoon in the park, and spoke quietly, but quite loudly enough for the whole group to hear since they had all fallen silent at their approach.

"Thank you, Miss Winwood," he said, "for the pleasure of your company."

The words were quite innocuous. They were meant to be. They were merely a courtesy, the type of words any gentleman could be expected to say to any lady after he had danced with her or walked with her. And yet somehow they came out sounding alarmingly intimate. Or perhaps it was just that she was feeling guilty at what had almost happened again, Jennifer thought, and was hearing his words with the ears of guilt. His words made it sound as if they had been very much alone together and very pleased with each other's company. She had to stop herself from turning to the gathered company to explain that he had not meant his words that way at all.

And then to make matters worse—though it was a gesture

as innocent as the words had been—he raised her hand to his lips. She wished he had not kept his eyes on hers as he did so. And she wished he had not kept her hand there for what seemed like several seconds. He meant nothing by it, of course, but—oh, but she was afraid that that would not be obvious to all those who watched. To Lionel in particular.

The earl walked away without a word to Lord Kersey or Samantha or any of the others. She felt the discourtesy and was surprised by it and disappointed in him. She did not watch to see where he went. She smiled at her betrothed and felt horribly uncomfortable.

"You were very brave to have gone walking with the Earl of Thornhill, Miss Winwood," Miss Simons said, wide-eyed. "My maid told me, and she had it on the most reliable authority, that he was forced to run away to the Continent with his stepmother when his father discovered them together in compromising circumstances."

"Claudia!" Her brother's voice cut across hers like a whip, so that she had the grace to blush even as she giggled.

"Well, it is true," she muttered.

"I see that tea is being served," Samantha said gaily. "I am starved. Shall we lead the way, Jenny? I am not shy." She laughed as she linked her arm through her cousin's and led her away to the tables, which a long line of footmen had just laden with platefuls of various appetizing looking foods.

Chapter 8

"What did Miss Simons mean," Jennifer asked, her voice low, her eyes directed at the grass before her feet, "when she said that he fled to the Continent after being caught in a compromising situation with his stepmother?" She blushed at her own words, but Lionel had started it, taking her off to walk alone when they had scarcely even started their tea. He had told her coldly that he was extremely displeased with her behavior.

"The question is an improper one," Viscount Kersey said, "coming from a young lady I have been led to expect to be well bred. But I believe Miss Simons's words spoke for themselves."

She was silent for a moment, digesting his words, anger warring in her with guilt. How dare he scold her as if she were a child, one part of her mind thought. And how dare he suggest in that cold voice that she was ill bred. And then the other part of her mind reminded her that she had once let the Earl of Thornhill kiss her and that perhaps she would have allowed it again this afternoon if he had cared to press the point. Yet another part of her felt like crying. The spring was not proceeding at all as she had expected.

"But he took her to the Continent with him?" She could not leave it alone. She had to know. Perhaps in knowing she would finally be able to shake herself free of the totally unwilling attraction she felt toward the earl. Not that it could really be called that. How could she feel an attraction to him when all her love was given to Lionel? "He took his stepmother? Without his father? Or was it after the death of his father?"

"It was before his father's death," Lord Kersey said, his words clipped. "It was the probable cause of his father's death.

He fled with the countess because she was in no fit condition to be seen by decent people in this country. There. Are you satisfied?"

There was a buzzing in her head and a coldness in her nostrils. No. She would not believe it. She must have misunderstood what Lionel had said. The earl had done . . . *that* with his own stepmother? He had caused her to be with child? And had taken her away for her confinement? And . . . and then what?

"Where is she now?" Her voice was a whisper.

He laughed. But when she looked at him, she saw that he was sneering, an expression that marred his good looks. She frowned and looked away again.

"Abandoned, of course," he said. "He grew tired of her and came home alone."

"Oh."

They had walked all the way to the bank of the river, she saw. There was one couple out in a boat, no doubt enjoying the luxury of being together while everyone was at tea. There was no one else on the bank.

"So you see," Viscount Kersey said, "why being seen in company with such a man can do irreparable harm to a lady's reputation. And why I must forbid you ever to speak with him again."

Jennifer turned her parasol slowly above her head while she watched the boat out on the river. "My lord," she said quietly, "I am twenty years old. And yet people persist in treating me like a child and telling what I must do and what I must not do."

"You are a young lady," he said, "and an innocent."

"I will no longer be an innocent in a little over a month's time," she said, turning to face him.

"You will be my wife." A muscle was twitching in his jaw.

Ah, yes. She would owe him obedience as she now owed obedience to her father—and to Aunt Agatha acting in her father's stead during her come-out. It was the lot of women. Only love could sweeten the pill. And she and Lionel loved each other. Did they not?

"Should I not at least be given a reason?" she asked. "If you must give me a command, my lord, should I not know why that command is given so that I may follow it as a rational choice of my own as much as from the need to obey? I have been warned several times to shun the Earl of Thornhill's company, but until now I have been given no reason to do so. I am a rational being even though I am a woman."

He gazed back at her, his handsome face tight with some emotion she could not read.

He does not understand, she thought. She felt a twinge of alarm, of uneasiness for her future, for the rest of her life. *He does not understand that I am a person, that women have minds just as men do.*

She loved him. She had loved him totally and passionately for five years. But for the first time—and she felt panic at the thought—she wondered if a blind, unreasoned love would be enough for her. She had thought that love would be everything. She had lived for this spring and for this betrothal and for her marriage. Was love everything?

"Of course you have a mind," he said. "If it is a good mind, it will recognize the wisdom of deferring to the greater experience and better judgment of the men who have the charge of you and of women considerably older than yourself. I hope you are not going to be difficult."

He might as well have slapped her face. She felt as dazed as if he had, and as humiliated.

"Difficult?" she said. "Do you wish for a placid, docile wife, then, my lord?"

"I certainly expect one who knows her own place and mine," he said. "I assumed from my knowledge of your upbringing and the fact that you have always lived in the country that you would suit me. So did my mother and my father."

And she did not? Because she had danced with the Earl of Thornhill and walked with him when no one had thought it necessary to explain to her why she should not? Perhaps, she thought—but the thought bewildered her because it was so new and so strange—perhaps Viscount Kersey would not suit her.

She gazed at him. At her beautiful Lionel. The man she had dreamed of daily and nightly for so long that it seemed she must have loved him and dreamed of him all her life. What had gone wrong with this Season?

"You seem rebellious," he said. "Perhaps you are regretting your acceptance of my offer three weeks ago. Perhaps you would like to change your answer now before the official announcement is made."

"No!" The answer and the sheer panic that provoked it were purely instinctive, but they came to her rescue and completely drowned out the strange doubts she had been having. "No, Lionel. I love you!"

And then she froze to the sound of her own words even as she gazed, horrified, into the very blue eyes that looked intently back. She had called him by his given name before she had been invited to do so. She had told him she loved him before he had said the words to her. She was deeply embarrassed. And yet she had spoken the truth, she thought. She bit her lip but did not lower her eyes.

"I see," he said. "Well, then, we have no quarrel, do we?"

Had they been quarreling? She supposed they had. There was a feeling of relief in the thought. It was natural for lovers to quarrel. Not that they were lovers exactly—not yet anyway. But they were betrothed. It was natural. He had been jealous and annoyed and she had been on the defensive. Now it was over. Now it was time to make up—as she supposed they would do dozens or hundreds of times during the course of the rest of their lives. This was real life as opposed to the life of perfection she lived in dreams. It was nothing to worry about.

"I do not even like him," she said. "He is bold and . . . a-and unmannerly. I danced with him at Papa's ball and at the Chisleys' only because I could not get out of doing so without seeming quite ill-mannered. And I walked with him this afternoon for the same reason. I would have far preferred to be with you, but you had promised to take Sam out in the boat. I do not like him, and now that I know what he has done, I shall certainly never speak with him again."

"I am glad to hear it," he said.

She twirled her parasol, feeling all the relief and lightheartedness that came at the end of a quarrel. She smiled. "Don't look as if you are still cross with me, then," she said. "Smile at me. These are such beautiful surroundings for a garden party, and I have so looked forward to being here—with you."

She blushed at her own boldness, but her heart was full of her love for him again. He had been jealous and she was touched—though she would never again give him even the whisper of a cause.

"And I with you," he said rather stiffly.

But then he smiled and Jennifer's heart performed its usual somersault. She held out her hand to him, realizing she had done so only when he took it and raised it to his lips. She wished—oh, she wished they were in some secluded spot, the orchard, perhaps, so that he could kiss her on the lips. It seemed such a perfect moment for their first kiss. The warmest, most relaxed moment they had yet shared.

"Almack's tomorrow evening," she said, "and the Velgards' costume ball the evening after. And then your father's dinner and ball two nights after that." She still smiled at him.

He squeezed her hand. "I can scarcely wait," he said. And he took her hand to his lips yet again.

She had heard it said, Jennifer thought, that it was good for couples to quarrel, that quarrels often cleared the air between them and made the relationship better than ever. It was so very true. She felt the warmth of his arm through his sleeve as they strolled up the lawn again, back in the direction of the house, and felt so happy that the old cliché of the heart being about to burst seemed almost to suit. It was all behind them, the rather slow, uncomfortable beginning to their betrothal. And any last-minute doubts—if they could be called that—had been put to rest.

She would determinedly avoid the Earl of Thornhill for the rest of the Season. She felt ashamed now of the ease she had felt in his company just this afternoon and the feeling she had had that there was indeed a certain friendship between them. She felt more discomfort than ever over the fact that she had allowed him that kiss at the Chisleys' ball. Knowing what she now knew of him, she would not find it at all difficult to snub him quite openly if necessary. His own stepmother! He had done *that* with his father's wife.

She closed her mind quite firmly to twinges of guilt over the fact that she was no longer making allowances for the possibility that he had finished sowing his wild oats and was now trying to make amends. Some things were unforgivable. Besides, he had abandoned his stepmother and their child and left them alone somewhere in a foreign land. He was not making amends at all. He was quite despicable. Quite loathsome.

"And so you see," Sir Albert Boyle said as he sat over an early afternoon dinner at White's with his friend, the Earl of

Thornhill, "I have been caught. Past tense, it seems, Gabe. Not even present tense, and certainly not future."

The earl looked at him keenly. "But you have made no declaration yet?" he asked.

"Good Lord, no." Sir Albert gazed gloomily into his port for a moment before taking a drink. "I said it would happen, Gabe. Appear one too many times in a ballroom and dance one too many sets, and someone will get it into her head that you are out shopping when in truth you are just browsing. Rosalie Ogden!"

"I thought that if you fell victim to anyone this year it would be to Miss Newman," the earl said.

"Ah." His friend said. "The delectable blonde. Every red-blooded man's dream." He looked down into his glass. "And the plain and ordinary and rather dull Miss Ogden, with whom I have danced and whom I have taken driving because Frank said she had not taken well, poor girl."

"And she is expecting a declaration? And her mother is expecting it?" The earl frowned. "You don't have to do it, Bertie. You have not compromised the girl, have you?"

"Lord, no," Sir Albert said. "She is not the type of girl one goes slinking off into grottoes with, Gabe. I thought about calling tomorrow actually. Before my nerve goes."

The Earl of Thornhill dabbed at his mouth with his napkin and set it down beside his empty plate. He wondered what he was missing. He and Bertie had been close friends for years—since their schoolboy days.

"Why?" he asked. "You are not in love with the girl by any chance, are you?" He could not imagine any man being in love with Miss Rosalie Ogden, though the thought was unkind. She seemed so totally without any quality that any man might find appealing. Bertie, on the other hand, was young and good looking and wealthy and intelligent and could surely attach the affections of almost any lady he cared to set his sights on.

Sir Albert puffed out his cheeks and blew air out through his mouth. "It's like this, Gabe," he said. "You dance with a girl because you feel sorry for her and imagine how sad and humiliated she would be going home and to bed knowing that she had been a wallflower all evening while the prettier girls had danced. And then you take her driving for the same reason, and walking and boating at a garden party and then dancing again at Almack's last evening. And then you start to realize that there is someone hiding behind the plainness and the quietness and the—the dullness. Someone sort of sweet in a way and someone who—well, who would bleed if she cut herself, if you know what I mean. Someone who loves kittens to distraction and cries over chimney sweeps' climbing boys and likes to slip up to her sister's nursery to play with her nieces and nephews instead of sitting in the drawing room listening to the adults converse. And then you realize that she is not quite as plain or as quiet or as dull as you had thought."

"You *are* in love with her," the earl said, intrigued.

"Well, I don't see stars whirling about my head," Sir Albert said. "So it can't be that, Gabe, can it? It is just that I am— well, a little bit fond of her, I suppose. It sort of creeps up on you. You don't notice it and you don't particularly want it or welcome it when you discover it. But it's there. And there seems to be only one thing to do about it. No, two, I suppose. I could leave London tomorrow—go visit my aunt in Brighton, or something like that. But I would always wait for word of her marrying some oaf and then I would always wonder if he was allowing climbing boys into their house and keeping kittens out. And if he was giving her children for her own nursery. Gabe, I think I must have been touched by the sun. Has it been hot lately? I have known her for less than a week. I cannot even realistically talk about anything creeping up on me, can I? Creeping is a slow process. Galloping, more like."

"You are in love with her," the earl said again.

"Well," Sir Albert said. "Whatever name you care to give it, Gabe. But I think I am off to call tomorrow. Brigham is her uncle and guardian. I'll have a word with him first. And with her mother too. I'll do the thing properly. I'll probably even go down on one knee when the moment comes." He winced. "Do you think I will do anything so unspeakably humiliating, Gabe?"

The earl chuckled.

"There is nothing for a dowry, by the way," Sir Albert said. "Or so Frank says, and he should know since his sister is a friend of her sister's. So I cannot be accused of acting in such haste out of any greed for her fortune, can I? Besides, it must be well known that my own pockets are well enough lined that I don't have to snatch at dowries."

"It will never be known for anything other than what it is," the earl said. "A love match, Bertie."

His friend grimaced and drained off his glass of port. "I have to be going," he said. "I am to drive her with her mother to the Tower this afternoon. I shall have to see how I feel afterward. Perhaps I will change my mind and be saved. Do you think, Gabe?"

The earl merely smiled.

"Are you coming?" Sir Albert got to his feet.

"No," the earl said. "I think I'll stay and drink another glass of port, Bertie. I shall drink to your health and happiness. Go and make yourself pretty for your lady love."

Sir Albert grimaced once more and took his leave. The Earl of Thornhill did not drink another glass of port, but he did sit alone at the table for a long while, turning his empty glass absently with the fingers of one hand, his pensive manner discouraging both acquaintances from joining him and waiters from clearing the table.

And then you start to realize that there is someone hiding . . . someone who would bleed if she cut herself . . . it sort of creeps up on you.

It was something entirely between him and Kersey, he thought. He had taken the fall for Kersey's evil, and he had watched Catherine suffer as a result of it. And now he saw a chance for a little revenge and had found himself consumed by the desire to accomplish it. Kersey knew it and had issued his own challenge. It was just between the two of them.

Except that Jennifer Winwood was caught in the middle. She was the pawn he would use to upset Kersey's life, to bring scandal and humiliation to his name. Very publicly. There was no better arena for this particular type of revenge than London during the Season.

Jennifer Winwood was unimportant. She would find someone else more worthy of her than Kersey. In fact, as he had told himself before, he was doing her a favor. If he could bring about an end to her betrothal, he would have done her a favor even if she did not realize it. Not that it really mattered. Having some measure of revenge on Kersey was all that was important.

Except that . . .

. . . someone who would bleed if she cut herself. When he

had apologized for having kissed her in the Chisleys' garden, she had admitted that it had disturbed her. *It did cause me some distress*, she had said.

. . . you start to realize that there is someone hiding . . . She enjoyed emotion and sentimentality in literature as well as humor and satire. She had a collie whom she missed, one that yipped and demonstrated wild and undignified enthusiasm when a walk was imminent. She had never had a gentleman friend. She had lifted her hand and touched his cheek when he had pretended sadness over the fact that her engagement made it impossible for them ever to be friends.

. . . someone who would bleed if she cut herself.

Damnation! He had no wish to hurt the girl. None whatsoever. And no wish to deceive her. And yet he had done nothing but deceive her, pretending to friendly and even tender feelings for her when he felt none.

Except that . . .

It sort of creeps up on you. You don't notice it and you don't particularly want it . . .

The Earl of Thornhill got abruptly to his feet and had to reach back a hasty hand to stop his chair from toppling backward. He needed air and exercise.

He needed to steel himself for the costume ball at Lady Velgard's this evening. He needed to remind himself how all-consuming the desire for revenge had become to him since seeing Kersey again.

"Do you suppose there will be any waltzes tonight?" Jennifer asked. Although it was a warm day outside, she was sitting on the floor of the sitting room she shared with her cousin, her back to a fire, drying her long hair. Her arms were clasped about her knees. She had the kind of beauty that Samantha had always envied. She could have been an Amazon warrior or a Greek goddess or a—or a Queen Elizabeth I. It was as Queen Elizabeth that she was going to the costume ball this evening. Samantha, on the other hand, saw only a milk and water miss when she looked in her own mirror, and she was to dress up tonight as—of all things—a fairy queen.

"I believe there almost certainly will be," she said. "There usually are, so I have heard, except sometimes if it is someone's come-out ball."

"I hope so." Jennifer rested one cheek on her knees. "Sam, was it not wonderful beyond belief to be granted permission to waltz at Almack's last evening? It was the happiest moment of my life—well, one of them, anyway."

"And I was stuck dancing it with Mr. Piper," Samantha said. "To say he has two left feet is unduly to insult left feet, Jenny."

Her cousin laughed. And looked wonderfully happy, as she had been looking for a few days now. Their roles seemed almost to have been reversed. Jenny was the sunny one, always on the verge of laughter. Samantha, on the other hand, was having to force her mood, to try to convince everyone else as well as herself that her first Season was all she had expected it to be.

"That was a pity," Jennifer admitted. "Whom would you have liked to dance it with, Sam? If you had your choice of any gentleman?"

Lionel, Samantha thought treacherously and quelled the thought instantly. Out on the river at Lady Bromley's garden party Lionel—Lord Kersey—had apologized for what had happened at the Chisley ball. He had been out of temper, he had claimed, and had forgotten that he was a gentleman. And then he had rowed her silently on the river, his eyes occasionally becoming locked with hers. When he had handed her out onto the bank, he had retained her hand in his for a second or two longer than was necessary and had squeezed it so hard that she had almost cried out in pain and had whispered hastily and fiercely to her.

"I wish," he had said, "I could forget again that I am a gentleman. Samantha, I wish . . . " But his voice had trailed off and his eyes had gazed into hers with dismay and remorse.

"Oh, I do not know," she said now with a shrug. "Sir Albert Boyle, maybe. Or Mr. Maxwell. Or Mr. Simons. Someone with both a left foot and a right foot and some feel for music." She laughed lightly.

Jennifer's eyes were steady on her. "Is there no one special yet, Sam?" she asked. "It is strange. Somehow I expected that you would fall wildly in love with some impossibly handsome gentleman with forty thousand a year after our first ball. You have a large court of admirers. Indeed, it seems to grow every day. But you seem to favor no one in particular."

"Give me time," Samantha said airily. "I intend to settle on no one less handsome than Li—than Lord Kersey."

"Or the Earl of Thornhill," Jennifer said, and then she flushed and turned her head to rest the other cheek on her knees. "I mean, someone as handsome as he."

If only the earl did not have that dreadful reputation, Samantha thought, her treacherous thoughts breaking free again. And if there was not the betrothal. He seemed to like Jenny and she . . . Well, she had been alone with him on two separate occasions. If only . . . If only Lionel were free. But she jerked her mind back to reality.

"He was not at Almack's last night," she said. "I wonder if he will be at the ball this evening."

"I hope not," Jennifer said. "Did you know that what that unspeakably stupid Claudia Simons said about him at the garden party was true? He did run off with his stepmother. She was increasing, Sam. And then he abandoned her and the child to come back here alone."

"His own father's wife?" Samantha felt genuine horror. "Oh, Jenny, we were right about him that very first time. Lucifer. The devil. He really is, is he not?"

"Except that he does not seem evil when one talks with him," Jennifer said. "He seems warm and friendly. But I suppose that is the nature of the devil, is it not? Oh, but I do not want to talk about him, Sam. I hope there are waltzes tonight. I want to waltz again with Lord Kersey and feel his hand at my waist. I want to dance just with him for half an hour." She had her eyes closed, Samantha saw. "I can hardly wait."

Samantha's spirits had sunk so low that she felt as if definite physical leaden weights were pressing down on her. Lionel, she thought. Oh, Lionel. How she too would love to be waltzing with him tonight. And . . . Oh, thought was pointless.

She hated her cousin suddenly. And then she turned her hatred against herself. And against Lionel. If he had tender feelings for her—and she was sure that he did—how could he be contemplating marriage with Jenny? But he was trapped into that by an unwritten agreement made five years before, when he had been only twenty.

Only Jenny could break the engagement. It would be horribly scandalous even for her to do it, but it would be impossible for him. An honorable gentleman just did not break such a promise. But Jenny had no reason to break off her betrothal. She would never do so, unless—unless she knew that he loved someone else.

Samantha tried to break the trend of her thoughts.

"Oh, Sam," Jennifer said, hugging her knees more tightly, her eyes still closed, "you really must find someone soon. You must find out for yourself what this happiness feels like."

Samantha rested her head against the back of the chair on which she sat and closed her own eyes. She felt suddenly both dizzy and nauseated.

Chapter 9

She wore a gold mask, but it did nothing to hide her identity. Nor was it meant to. It was a mere convention of a costume ball. She was all in gold and white and unmistakably dressed as Queen Elizabeth I. The rich, heavy gold and white brocade of her dress and the stiff ruff that fanned out behind her head were carried with a suitably regal bearing. Her dark red hair was set severely back from her face and curled all about her head.

She would have drawn eyes even if she had stood alone. But she stood with an Elizabethan courtier whose clothes matched her own in color and splendor. His own gold mask gleamed pale against his blond hair.

They were by far the most attractive couple in the ballroom.

The Earl of Thornhill, watching them after the courtier had joined his queen and her cousin and aunt after their arrival at Lady Velgard's costume ball, was not sorry about the fact that they drew such universal attention despite the presence of other clever and attractive costumes on other guests. And he was not sorry that they were so easily recognizable. It would all work to his advantage.

"Bertie is not coming tonight," Lord Francis Kneller said at the earl's elbow. "Do you know why, Gabe?" His tone suggested that he certainly did even if his friend did not.

She was glowing, Lord Thornhill thought, gazing across the room—as many other people seemed to be doing. Her mouth was curved into a smile. Something about the whole set of her body and head suggested that she was excited and happy. Happy with her partner. In love with him. Damnation. "Why?" he asked.

"Because Rosalie Ogden's mama thinks a costume ball too racy an event for her daughter to attend," Lord Francis said, emphasizing the girl's name. "Rosalie Ogden, Gabe. Bertie is not coming because she will not be here."

"He took her sightseeing to the Tower this afternoon, I believe," the earl said.

"Good Lord," Lord Francis said. "Good Lord, Gabe, is he touched in the upper works?"

"I believe," the earl said, looking at him at last and grinning, "it is called love, Frank."

"Well, good Lord." His friend seemed to have been rendered inarticulate.

"I suppose," the earl said, "it is only natural that we feel a twinge of alarm when one of our number turns his mind toward matrimony, Frank. It reminds us that we too are getting older and that responsibility and the need to be setting up nurseries are staring us in the eyeball."

"The devil!" Lord Francis said. "We are not even thirty yet, Gabe. Or even close to it. But Rosalie Ogden! He is seriously thinking of offering for her?"

"I have it on the best authority," the earl said, "that there is rather a sweet girl hiding behind the plainness and the quietness."

"There would have to be," Lord Francis said. "There is not even anything much for a dowry. Ah, a waltz. The opportunity to get my arm about some slender waist is not to be wasted, Gabe—I hope you noticed the pun. The fairy queen, do you think? No, she is swamped by her usual court. Cleopatra, then. I was presented to her at Almack's last evening so I can just stroll along and ask." He walked away without more ado, Roman toga notwithstanding, to claim the set with the lady of his choice.

The Earl of Thornhill stood where he was and watched. And assured a few fellow guests, who approached him in mock terror, that no, his pistols were not loaded. He was dressed as a highwayman of bygone years, all in black, including his mask. He wore a powdered wig, tied and bagged with black silk at the neck, and a tricorne hat.

Ah, he thought, so she had been granted permission to waltz. She was dancing it now with Kersey and smiling up at him, her attention wholly on him. And Lord, she was beautiful. Every time he saw her he seemed to be jolted anew by her beauty, as if he had forgotten it since his last sight of her. He was glad she was able to waltz. And if one was being danced this early in the evening, there must be several more planned for the rest of the night.

He intended to dance one of those waltzes with Miss Jennifer Winwood. It might not be easy to get past the defenses of Lady Brill and Kersey. And even the Countess of Rushford, Kersey's mother, was present tonight and keeping a proprietary eye on her son and his affianced bride. But somehow he would do it. He had no real fear of failure.

If Lionel was irresistibly handsome as a gentleman of the present age, Jennifer thought, as a gentleman of Queen Elizabeth's court he was—well, there were not words. He was irresistibly handsome. She waltzed with him and felt that her feet scarcely touched the floor. It was surely the most divine and the most intimate dance ever invented. He was drawing all eyes just like a magnet, of course, as he always did. She basked in the fact that it was with her he danced and to her that he was betrothed. She felt that she was somehow picking up some of his reflected splendor.

He was there—the Earl of Thornhill. At first she had thought he was not. Most of the guests were recognizable despite ingenious costumes and masks. But he was not easy to recognize, except for his height, which first drew her eyes his way. His hair was white and long and tied back beneath his hat. He made an alarmingly attractive highwayman, she thought. She was sure it was he when he stood beside a pillar instead of dancing the first set—and when he watched her the whole while. He was, of course, wearing a wig, she realized. A powdered wig, old-fashioned like the tricorne and the skirted coat and the long topboots.

She wished he had not come. Although she did not look directly at him, she saw him constantly nevertheless and was aware of him at every moment, as she always was. And yet now there was a certain horror in the fascination she felt for him, knowing what she now knew of him. His stepmother! He was a father. He had a child, abandoned somewhere on the Continent with the child's mother. She wondered if he had left them quite destitute or if at the very least he had taken some measures to support them.

And she tried not to think about him at all.

It was easy to avoid him. Lionel, although he danced with her only once, hovered close between sets, and Aunt Agatha kept careful watch over her choice of partners and Samantha's. She did not, as so many of the chaperones did, find a cozy seat in a corner and while away the time gossiping with other ladies. And Lionel's mother engaged her in conversation between each set. It was like having a small army of bodyguards, Jennifer thought in some relief. She was not going to have to face the embarrassment of refusing to dance with him.

But then he made no move toward her, either.

It was unalloyed relief she felt, she told herself, refusing to recognize a certain feeling of inexplicable depression.

And then, well into the evening, events became so strange that Jennifer was left feeling bewildered and exposed and not a little frightened. The Earl of Thornhill had moved closer. She sensed it without having to look to be sure. But Lionel looked long and consideringly in the direction where she knew the earl stood, though he said nothing. He would redouble his watch over her, she thought in some relief. But instead, he turned to his mother and to Aunt Agatha with a smile, commented on the heat in the ballroom, and suggested that they go to the dining room in search of a drink. He would do himself the honor of watching over their charges until their return.

They went.

Samantha, close by, was surrounded by her usual court of admirers. Some of them were talking with Jennifer too, though Lord Kersey continued to stay close beside her. But then he was gone, without a word or a sign, and he was smiling warmly at Samantha and taking her by the hand and leading her onto the floor for the waltz that was about to begin.

No one had yet asked Jennifer to dance, and it seemed that every gentleman turned to watch in chagrin as Sam was taken from beneath their very noses. In a moment, Jennifer thought afterward, one of them would have turned back and solicited her hand. Lionel must have thought that one of them already had. He must have thought that it was safe to leave her side, even though his mother and Aunt Agatha had left the ballroom.

But there was that moment when she stood alone, bewildered and exposed and a little frightened.

And in that moment a gentleman did indeed step forward and bow and reach out a hand for hers. A tall, black-masked highwayman in the fashion of the previous century, his long, powdered hair and tricorne hat making him look quite devastatingly attractive.

"Your majesty," the Earl of Thornhill said, "will you do me the honor?"

It was so much easier to tell oneself that one was going to issue a cold snub than actually to do it, Jennifer found. That, of course, was why she had been content to be hovered over all evening. She found it almost impossible to look into his eyes and refuse him.

"I-I—" she said.

He smiled at her. His hand was still extended. She felt as if eyes were on them but could not look about her to see. She felt doubly exposed and bewildered. She had promised Lionel. But it was merely a dance. A waltz. If she refused the Earl of Thornhill, she would not be able to dance it with any other gentleman.

She set her hand in his. "Thank you," she said.

But she would not leave the ballroom with him. The French windows were open, as they had been at the Chisley ball, and the ballroom was warm. But she would not set one toe out onto the balcony.

She had thought the waltz intimate when she had danced it with Lionel. It seemed even more so with the earl. It was his superior height, she decided. And his hand, warm and strong against the back of her waist, was holding her a little closer than Lionel had done—and a little closer than her dancing master had done. He was holding her just a little too close. If she swayed toward him even slightly in the course of the dance, she would touch him—with her breasts.

She should have said no, she thought, now that it was too late. A very firm, chilly no. She darted a look up into his eyes. They were looking steadily back, as she had expected they would. They looked even darker than usual and more compelling through the slits of his mask. She looked down sharply.

"I thought we were almost friends," he said quietly.

"No." She drew breath to say more, but left the one word to stand alone.

"They have been warning you against me again," he said. "I should not have taken you into the cool seclusion of the orchard, should I? Was he very angry with you? Would it help if I explained to him that nothing improper happened?"

"Is it true," she asked, and she blushed, knowing what she was about to say, "that you fled to the Continent with your stepmother?"

"Ah," he said, "they really have been busy. I would not use the word *fled*. It gives the impression of running in panic or guilt. But yes, I accompanied the Countess of Thornhill, my father's second wife, to the Continent." He was watching her keenly, she saw when she looked up briefly again. His head had bent slightly toward hers. People were watching. She could feel them watching.

"She had your child," she said. She did not know how she got the words past her lips. She did not even know why she would want to say them.

"She gave birth to a daughter in Switzerland," he said.

"And you abandoned them there." She was breathless. Her voice was accusing. She wished—oh, she wished she had said no. Why had Lionel been so careless after protecting her all evening and after telling his mother and Aunt Agatha that he would look after her?

"I left them in their new home there," he said, "while I came back to mine."

Another couple twirled close to them and his arm tightened about her, drawing her even closer. He did not relax it after the couple were safely past.

"Do you have any other questions?" he asked.

"No." She was being almost overpowered by that same feeling she had had when he kissed her in the Chisleys' garden. At a totally inappropriate time. When he had just admitted . . . "Please do not hold me so close. It is unseemly."

She raised her eyes unwillingly to his as his hold relaxed just a little. And then found that she could not look away again.

"You should not have asked me to dance," she said. "Not that first time or any time since. It is not right. You should have stayed away."

"Why?" His voice was very quiet. It sounded like a hand would feel slowly caressing its way up her back. "Because I am not respectable? Or because you find it impossible to say no?"

She bit her lip. "You just admitted—"

"No," he said. "That is a poor choice of word. I just gave you a few facts. Gossipmongers love to take facts and twist them and squeeze them and sensationalize them until they are almost unrecognizable as truth."

"But you cannot deny the facts," she said.

"No," he said, and he smiled.

"Are you saying, then," she said, "that the facts do not mean what they appear to mean?"

"I am saying no such thing," he said. "I will leave the facts with you and the interpretation of those facts that Kersey and others of your family or acquaintances have put upon them in your hearing. But you have liked me, have you not? We were almost friends at the garden party, were we not?"

His eyes held hers, and his voice beguiled her. She wanted to believe in his innocence. When she was with him, she could not believe him the villain everyone else thought him and that even she had concurred with. When she was with him, he was . . . her friend. And something else—something more. But she was afraid of the direction her thoughts were taking and brought them to a stop.

"Tell me," she said, gazing earnestly at him, "that you are innocent of those things people say about you."

"My father's wife was never my mistress," he said. "Her child is not mine. I left her in comfort and security in Switzerland because there was no further need for me to stay with her. Do you believe me, Jennifer?"

She drew in a sharp breath at the sound of her name on his lips—again. And she swayed toward him until the tips of her breasts touching his coat brought her jolting back to a realization of where she was. But they were very close to one set of opened French windows, and he waltzed her through them before she could look about her to see if she had been observed. She felt dazed, almost as if she had been in some sort of trance. She had forgotten for perhaps seconds, perhaps minutes, that she was dancing with him in a crowded ballroom and that in the nature of things their every look and gesture were being observed.

She was thankful after all for the comparative privacy of the balcony. And for its coolness.

"Yes, I believe you," she said. "Yes, I do."

"Gabriel," he said, his head close to hers. "It is my name."

"Gabriel." She looked at him, startled. Gabriel? He was the angel Gabriel, she thought foolishly. Not Lionel, but this man whom she and Sam had called Lucifer.

"On your lips," he said, "my name sounds like an endearment." He closed the gap of inches between their mouths and touched hers with his own for a few brief moments.

It was hardly a kiss. It was even less a kiss than the other one had been. But he had continued dancing on the balcony and now they were at the next set of French windows and reentering the ballroom. But whereas he had probably intended the light touching of mouths to happen out of sight on the balcony, it actually happened a fraction of a second too late—they were fully in the doorway and fully in view of any of a few hundred people who happened to be looking their way.

Jennifer froze, terrified to turn her head to the right or the left, terrified to look away from his eyes.

He did not look away from hers. "If you dare to look into your heart," he said, "and find that it has changed since last you looked, pay heed to it. It is not too late—yet. But soon it will be."

Her eyes widened as the meaning of his words hit her. "Nothing has changed," she said. "Nothing at all. I am going to be married in a month's time. It is all arranged. I love him."

His eyes smiled a little sadly. "You would not admit to that the last time we spoke," he said. "It is true, then? What I have felt since meeting you, what I feel, is entirely one-sided?"

She bit her lip again. "You must not say such things," she said. "Please. You say that we are almost friends and yet you try to upset me. You try to make me feel doubts when I feel none. You try to make me admit that I—"

"No," he said softly. "Not if it will upset you to do so, Jennifer. Not if it will hurt you, my love."

There was such an aching stab of . . . longing? deep in her womb that for a moment she closed her eyes. But the music was drawing to a close. Blessedly the set was coming to an end.

Oh, blessedly.

My love. My love.

He bowed over her hand when he had returned her to the edge of the floor and they were flanked by Aunt Agatha on the one side and the Countess of Rushford on the other, and raised it to his lips.

Aunt Agatha was tight-lipped and smiling all at the same time. Lionel had not yet returned from the floor with Samantha. The countess was smiling and linked her arm through Jennifer's.

"It is hot in here, my dear," she said. "Come, stroll with me about the ballroom and onto the balcony. Let us be seen smiling and conversing together. Sometimes, I know, these things happen, and it is almost invariably not the young lady's fault. Smile, dear. We have a great deal of smoothing over to do."

Her arm was not as relaxed as her person appeared to be, Jennifer noticed. She also noticed that her smiling future mother-in-law was angry.

Jennifer smiled. And looked about her as the two of them strolled around the perimeter of the room in the direction of the French windows to find that everyone seemed to be looking at them. At her. It seemed hardly an exaggeration.

"Some cool air would be pleasant," she said, holding onto her smile with a conscious effort.

My love. My love. The words, spoken in the voice of the Earl of Thornhill, echoed and reechoed in her head.

"Well, my ethereal fairy queen." His blue eyes smiled at her through the slits of his golden mask. "Are you able to grant wishes?"

Samantha looked at him warily. Although she had been chatting brightly with several gentlemen since the last set ended, because she loved Lionel she was always aware of him when they were in a room together. She had seen him send his mother and Aunt Aggy away and had heard what he had said to them. He had sent them away so that he could ask her to dance, she thought a few minutes later. But he did not need to send them out of the way in order to do that. It was quite unexceptionable for him to dance with her. In doing so now, though, he had left Jenny alone for the moment. But only for a moment. Then she was dancing with the Earl of Thornhill.

Had Lionel not seen the danger? Was it not his duty to protect Jenny from the attentions of that man?

"Jenny is dancing with the Earl of Thornhill," she said. "She could not help it. She could hardly have said no without appearing rude."

"Yes." He glanced over his shoulder. "So she is."

He was neither surprised nor annoyed. Almost, Samantha thought, as if he had planned it. But that made no sense. He had warned Jenny to stay away from the earl. He had made her promise never to speak with him again.

"You must be looking forward to the evening after tomorrow," she said brightly.

"Must I?" His eyes were back on her. He was smiling in a perfectly sociable manner. He was dancing at the perfect distance from her. No one looking at him would realize that there was that special light in his eye, the one that had been there during their outing in the boat.

"Don't," Samantha said. "Don't look at me like that."

"How can I help it?" he asked. "But I am sorry."

Samantha felt intensely unhappy. She was deeply and quite unwillingly in love with him. And he seemed to share her feelings. But it was not right. He had made his offer to Jenny and had been accepted. Perhaps he had been more or less forced into it, but he had done it nevertheless, and now he was honorbound to live by it. It was not right that he look at her in this way and speak in this way. It was not fair—either to Jenny or to her.

In the last couple of days she had come to see Lionel as a weak, perhaps even dishonorable man, and the knowledge hurt and confused her. She loved him. But she would love him in the secret of her heart for the rest of her life, she had decided. She would not share sighs and lovelorn looks with him behind Jenny's back.

She could not.

"I have made you unhappy," he said.

"Yes." She looked into his eyes. "Jenny is my cousin and my closest friend. She is like a sister to me. I want to see her happy."

"So do I," he said. "I care for her. Sometimes—" He looked away from her and they waltzed in silence for a while. "Sometimes we have to be cruel in order to be kind. Sometimes trying to protect other people from hurt only succeeds in bringing them greater and longer-lasting pain in the end."

She did not know what he was trying to say. But despite herself she felt the stirrings of hope, the beginnings of a response that she had been quite determined to keep at bay tonight and forever in the future.

He looked directly into her eyes, still smiling, still waltzing with studied elegance. "If you and I protect her from pain now," he said, "do you believe that we can hide the truth from her for the rest of our lifetimes? Do you believe she will not be more hurt by it in the future, when it is too late for anything to be done about it?"

Samantha felt as if she was about to faint. "The truth?" she said. "What is the truth?"

He looked at her and twirled her about the corner of the ballroom, saying nothing. But looking everything.

"But we cannot tell her," she said.

"I cannot." His smile faded for a few moments while he gazed deeply into her eyes. "I am a gentleman, Samantha. A gentleman cannot do such a thing even to prevent a lifetime of unhappiness for three people."

"You want *me* . . . ?" He wanted her to tell Jenny that she loved Lionel and that he loved her. That only Jenny and the betrothal that had not yet been officially announced stood between them and happiness. Oh, no. No. "No," she said. "No, I could not possibly. This is not right. It is not right at all."

A part of her—a base part that horrified her—was tempted. Another part was repelled, repelled by him and repelled by her reaction to him. She could not love him, surely. He was no gentleman. Not really. A gentleman could not suggest such a thing. Not even when the alternative was to marry the woman he did not love.

Jenny. Oh, poor Jenny. She loved Lionel to distraction. And she deserved happiness. She did not deserve this sort of deceit and trickery.

"I will not do it," she said firmly. "I could not. But for Jenny's sake, if you feel that you cannot give her your full loyalty even if not your heart, you must tell her yourself. An honorable man would do that. An honorable man would not expect me to do it for him."

"For us," he said. "But it does not matter. I see that I have asked too much of you. And you are right. It was a dishonorable and ungentlemanly suggestion. I am ashamed that my heart tempted me into making it on the spur of the moment."

Samantha was suddenly very aware of her youth. She was only eighteen years old. She resented it when people sometimes called her young and innocent and naive. And yet she felt all three at this moment. She had the feeling she had been caught up in something beyond her experience and beyond her ability to handle. She had fallen in love with Lionel because he was handsome and because he had kissed her—was there any other basis for her feelings if she was strictly honest with herself? And he had fallen in love with her because . . . *Was* he in love with her? Why? Why so suddenly? Could his feelings be so deep that he was willing to upset the plans of five years and cause scandal in doing so?

She felt bewildered and frightened.

"I would rather," she said quietly and unhappily, "that we changed the subject, my lord."

"Ah," he said. "Yes. Of course."

They began to exchange opinions on the various costumes about them.

Chapter 10

Sir Albert Boyle found his friend, the Earl of Thornhill, at home late in the afternoon of the following day. He was in the sitting room of his own apartments abovestairs, drunk.

It was neither the place nor the time of day in which to be inebriated. And Lord Thornhill was not the type of man to let himself get thoroughly foxed. Especially at home alone during the daytime. Not that he was very obviously drunk. Apart from the slight dishevelment of his clothes and hair and his slouching posture and the fact that there were two empty decanters in the room, one on a desk and the other on the hearth at his feet, and an almost empty glass dangling from one hand, he looked quiet enough. He was not dancing on tables or roaring out bawdy ballads.

But Sir Albert, waved to a chair by a careless hand—the one that held the glass—knew his friend well. He was drunk.

"Well," the earl said. There was no slurring in his speech. "Is the deed done, Bertie? You have come here to celebrate? Ring for another decanter, my dear chap. These two seem to be empty."

"She accepted me," Sir Albert said. He did not approach the bell pull. He eyed his friend warily.

"Of course." The earl refrained from adding that the girl would have had to be a blithering idiot to refuse. "My felicitations, Bertie. You are floating on clouds of bliss?"

"She had tears in her eyes the whole time I talked with her," Sir Albert said, ruining his fashionably rumpled hair by running the fingers of one hand through it. "And she put her mouth up to be kissed when I was only intending to kiss her hand. She kisses prettily." He flushed.

The earl regarded his friend through the inch of brandy left in the bottom of his glass. "Ah, the innocence of true love," he said. "So you have a slave for life, Bertie. That will be comfortable for you."

Sir Albert got to his feet and crossed to the window, where he stood, gazing out. "I am terrified, Gabe," he said. "The tears. The look of surprise followed by hope followed by happiness and adoration. It was enough to turn any fellow's head. It is enough to make me conceited for life."

"But you are terrified." The earl chuckled.

"It is such an enormous responsibility," Sir Albert said. "What if I cannot make her happy? What if I come to take her for granted just because she was so easily won? What if she accepted me only because she cannot expect many such chances? What if—"

The earl swore, using language so profane that there could be no further doubt that he was severely inebriated.

"Bertie," he said, reverting to decent English, "if you cannot see the stars clustered about your head, old chap, you have to be blind in both eyes."

"It is just the responsibility," Sir Albert said again. "The power we have over other people's lives sometimes, Gabe!"

"Well." The earl laughed. "Am I to wish you happy, Bertie, or am I to commiserate with you?"

"Wish me happy, if you will," his friend said, turning from the window to look at him. "What is the occasion for the private party, Gabe?"

The earl laughed again and raised his glass. "You have been busy today," he said. "You have not heard?"

Sir Albert frowned. "I called in at White's," he said, "and came on here when you were not there. Yes, I heard. You have to expect that people will grasp at any straw to break your back, Gabe, when your reputation is on such shaky footing. Was there a quite ghastly mixing of images there? No matter. Take no notice of it. Of the malice, I mean."

"One wonders—" The earl paused to drain off the brandy that remained in his glass. "One wonders if Miss Winwood is able to take no notice of it."

"Well, there is that." His friend resumed the seat he had been waved to at the start of his visit. "And it is unfortunate with her betrothal to Kersey about to be officially announced—not that there is a member of the *ton* or a footman or a groom who does not know of it. Gabe, you did not actually kiss her in the Velgard's ballroom last evening, did you? The truth can get vastly distorted in the retelling."

"Yes, I did." The earl chuckled. "In the doorway to the balcony, actually. I imagine we were far more easily seen there and by far more people than if I had done it in the middle of the dancing floor."

"Then you owe her an apology, do you not?" Sir Albert looked troubled. He had defended his friend against a large group at White's, all of whose members had insisted that it really had happened and that before it had, the two had had eyes only for each other and had waltzed indecorously close and had disappeared onto the balcony with the obvious intention of getting closer. It had been the joke of White's, the day's story in which everyone delighted. The Lord only knew what was being done to the poor girl's reputation in the drawing rooms of London, where the ladies would delight in the story in an entirely more vicious manner.

"Do I?" The earl narrowed his eyes on his glass before hurling it onto the hearth and watching in apparent satisfaction as it shattered. "I think not, Bertie. She did not exactly fight me off. Besides, it was merely a kiss. Hardly even that. A momentary meeting of lips."

"In full sight of the gathered *ton*," Sir Albert said.

"Life becomes dull when the Season is a few weeks old," Lord Thornhill said, his voice cold and cynical. "The *ton* needs some sensation to gossip about. Miss Winwood and I have obliged them."

"But it will be far worse for her than for you, Gabe." Sir Albert was indignant at his friend's apparent unconcern at what had happened—and what was happening. But he knew the impossibility of talking sensibly with a man who was very far from sober despite his quiet manner and articulate speech. "I know you fancied her from the first, but she is spoken for. There must be some other beauty you can flirt with if you feel that way inclined. The blonde, for example. Miss Newman."

"No one but the delicious redhead will do," the earl said, "Today she and I are being gossiped about. Today her betrothal is on shaky ground. Today Kersey will be feeling foolish at the very least. I am well content." His tone was almost vicious.

"Good Lord, Gabe." Sir Albert leapt to his feet again. "You

are not trying to end the girl's betrothal, are you? Are you that desperate for her? You will ruin her, that's what you will do. Will you be proud of yourself then?"

"Sit down, Bertie, do," the earl said. "It hurts my eyes to look up at you. But ring for another decanter before you do. I am thirsty if you are not."

"You are foxed," his friend said, glaring at him.

"And so I am," the earl agreed. "But not nearly foxed enough, Bertie. I am still conscious. Send for more, there's a good chap."

"If you weren't drunk," Sir Albert said, "I would draw your cork, Gabe. I swear I would. But if you weren't drunk you would not be saying such insane things. So you fancy her but can't have her. So you were a little indiscreet last night—no, more than a little. It can be patched up provided Kersey or Rushford don't lose their heads. Apologize to the lot of them, Gabe, or at the very least stay away from them. Leave London. It is the only decent thing to do."

"But . . . " The Earl of Thornhill narrowed his eyes and spoke so quietly that he sounded almost menacing. "I am not expected to be decent, Bertie. If I can debauch my own step-mother, I am capable of any outrage."

Sir Albert stared down at him. "There is no talking to you in your present state," he said. "If I were you, Gabe, I would get your man to bring up a very large pot of very strong coffee. And a large bowl of very cold water for you to plunge your head into a few times. I shall leave instructions to that effect on my way out. Good day." He turned to leave the room.

The earl, still sprawled in his chair, chuckled once more. "She is a fortunate woman, Miss Rosalie Ogden, Bertie," he said. "She will be acquiring a mother hen to care for her for the rest of her days."

Sir Albert Boyle, his back bristling with indignation, left the room.

The Earl of Thornhill rested his head against the back of his chair and stared upward. Closing his eyes was not a comfortable experience. He could not summon up enough energy to get to his feet to pull on the bell rope and order up more brandy. Besides, he had the feeling that he had had altogether too much already. Oceans too much, if the truth were known.

He had made a curious discovery in the course of the afternoon. Self-loathing was the perfect antidote to the effects of liquor on one's system. Even if he drank another ocean or two of brandy, he would not be able to drink himself into insensibility, he suspected. His body might become more and more foxed. His mind would remain coldly, coldly sober.

He could not possibly have slapped a glove in Kersey's face and been content to put a bullet between his eyes or the tip of a sword through his heart. Oh, no, that would have been altogether too easy and too unsubtle. And it would have renewed the scandal against Catherine and brought her further dishonor.

No, no, he had taken the far cleverer and more devious course of tampering with the man's life, making him look like a fool before the *ton*. Showing the world that Kersey, despite his title and his prospects and his wealth and good looks, could not keep a beautiful woman. Causing him the embarrassing scandal of a broken engagement.

And like the upright, honest, honorable man he was, he had tackled the task indirectly, working on Kersey's betrothed so that at the very least she would so compromise herself that Kersey would feel obliged to turn her off, or at the best she would feel so compromised that she would break with Kersey. Either way, Kersey would be embarrassed and humiliated.

Fine revenge indeed. Oh, very fine and admirable.

Yes, I believe you, she had said last night. *Yes, I do.* He could see her eyes now, gazing at him with earnest trust through the slits of her golden mask as he had waltzed her through the French windows, toward which he had carefully maneuvered her. And then at his prompting, she had spoken his name.

He wished he could drown out the echo of her voice and the words she had spoken. He wished he could close his eyes and no longer see hers. But the room spun about him when he tried—and he could still see her eyes.

I love him, she had said. *I love him. I love him. I love him.*

Today she was doubtless in deep trouble with her family and with Kersey and the Rushfords. Today she was doubtless the subject of eager and malicious gossip the length and breadth of fashionable London. Today she was doubtless in deep distress.

Yes, I believe you.
Gabriel.
I love him.

The earl turned his head from side to side against the back of his chair, but he succeeded only in making himself feel dizzy and nauseated. The sound of her voice, soft and earnest, would not go away.

He wondered if she would be able to weather the storm, if he had gone just too far last night and forced her to go too far . . .

The power we have over other people's lives, Bertie had just said. It was a relief to hear Bertie's voice in his mind instead of hers for a while. Until he really heard the words, that was, repeating themselves over and over again, just as her words had been doing all afternoon. *The power we have over other people's lives.*

His plan was proceeding perfectly. Even better than he could have hoped. It was poised for completion tomorrow night. The Earl and Countess of Rushford's ball was surely the event at which the betrothal of their son was to be announced. And though he had not been invited to the dinner that was to precede the ball, he had unexpectedly had an invitation to the ball.

It was there he had planned his most outrageous assault on Jennifer Winwood. It would be quite perfect. He would ruin the ball—except for the gossipmongers—wreck Kersey's betrothal, and humiliate him in the most public manner possible. The fact that he would also ruin his own reputation once and for all had seemed immaterial to him. He really did not care.

But there was Jennifer Winwood, caught in the middle. The one who would probably suffer the most. No, the one who *would* suffer the most. The innocent one. The one it was so easy to mislead because she was so ready to believe the best of other people. Because she wanted to believe the best of him. Because she wanted to be his friend.

Yes, I believe you. Yes, I do. If he had not been drunk, the Earl of Thornhill would doubtless not have put his hands to his ears to stop the sound of her voice. But he was drunk.

Gabriel.

She made his name sound like an endearment, he had told her. The one spontaneous truth he had spoken to her. It did not sound like an endearment now. It sounded like a curse straight from hell.

No, he could not proceed. It was perhaps too late now to give in to a crisis of conscience, but better now than not at all. Perhaps last night's indiscretion could be smoothed over. Apparently Lady Rushford had walked about with the girl during the set following the one she had danced with him, and had smiled and looked unconcerned. Wise woman! It was far better to have done that than to have whisked her home in disgrace.

Perhaps, with Kersey's mother behind her and the grand dinner and ball before her with its public announcement of her betrothal, today's scandal would become tomorrow's stale and forgotten gossip.

If he stayed out of the way.

If he left town and remained away for the rest of the Season. If he kept himself out of her life and out of sight of the *ton*.

He would set his servants about packing his things and send word ahead to Chalcote and arrange for the journey, he decided. He should be able to leave within three or four days, perhaps sooner. In the meanwhile, he would stay at home.

The Earl of Thornhill got to his feet, relieved now that his decision was made, now that he had pulled himself back from committing a great evil before it was quite too late. But the combination of a change in position and a releasing of his self-loathing was too much for him. He staggered and fell to his hands and knees while the room spun about him at dizzying and unrelenting speed.

Lord, how much had he drunk, anyway?

The door of his sitting room opened quietly to admit his valet, who was carrying a large pot of coffee on a tray.

Bless Bertie, mother hen par excellence.

Jennifer was riding in the park, seated in an open barouche beside Viscount Kersey, the Countess of Rushford opposite her, Aunt Agatha beside the countess. Jennifer was wearing a white muslin day dress of fashionable but modest design, chosen carefully for her by Aunt Agatha, and her straw bonnet. She was smiling brightly and looking steadily into the eyes of anyone who cared to look into hers and conversing with all who drew near and with all to whom they drew near. Her left hand rested on Lionel's sleeve. His left hand covered it.

It was what must be done, the countess had said briskly and quite firmly when she had called earlier at Berkeley Square with her son. It would be nonsense to behave as if there were something to be ashamed of merely because the Earl of Thornhill, who was a disgrace to his name and his rank, had chosen to behave with such outrageous vulgarity. Rushford, she had explained, was to make it quite clear to Lord Thornhill that despite his invitation to tomorrow evening's ball, he would be unwelcome there.

Lionel had stood quietly behind his mother's chair while she had said all this, and Jennifer had studiously not looked at him. But she had got together her courage finally to ask the countess and Aunt Agatha, who had also been present, if she might have a private word with Lord Kersey.

It was necessary, she had felt. Her father had summoned her during the morning and scolded her roundly—which was a mild way to describe his blazing anger—and told her to be prepared to return to the country for a very long stay if the Earl of Rushford decided that she was no longer worthy of his son's hand. He and Rushford had quite a quarrel over this business, he had explained, and he would be damned before he would be put even more in the wrong by a chit of a daughter. She had better be very careful. Aunt Agatha had been tight-lipped and curiously quiet all day. Sam had not emerged from her room.

Last evening's incident—the kiss at the French windows—had burst into scandal this morning, Jennifer gathered. She was the *on dit* of fashionable drawing rooms. She was in disgrace. Everything was in ruins. Lionel would no longer want her. Nor would any other respectable gentleman. Not that she wanted any other gentleman. If she lost Lionel, she would want to die. It would be as simple as that.

Curiously, she did not really blame the Earl of Thornhill. Not really. He had protested his innocence and she had believed him. His kiss—if it could be called that—had been meant for the privacy of the darkness out on the balcony. It had been a kiss of friendship. Except that he had called her—Jennifer had tried all through a sleepless night not to remember what he had called her. But the words had spoken themselves over and over to her weary mind.

My love, he had called her.

Yes, she needed to talk with Lionel. There was enormous relief in the discovery that the countess had not had a change of heart since last evening but was still willing to face down the scandal and make light of what had happened. But it was not quite enough.

"Very well," Lady Rushford said, getting to her feet. "For five minutes, dear. Kersey and I must leave soon so that we can all get ready to be seen in the park when everyone else is there. Lady Brill?" She left the room with Aunt Agatha.

Viscount Kersey stayed where he was and said nothing.

Jennifer forced herself to look at him. He was very pale. Very handsome. "There was nothing in it," she said. "He explained to me that he did not do those dreadful things that everyone believes he did, and I believed him. That was all."

His eyes met hers finally and she was reminded again of what Sam had always said of him. She shivered involuntarily. "What did he tell you?" he asked.

"That his stepmother was never his mistress," she said, her cheeks hot. "That the child she had was not his."

He gazed at her in silence for a few moments. "And you believed him," he said. "You are incredibly naive."

"My lord," she said, moving steadily ahead into her greatest nightmare, "do you wish to continue with our betrothal? Would you prefer that I changed my answer now, before any announcement has been made?"

Again the brief silence, while Jennifer died a little inside. "It is too late for that," he said. "The announcement is a mere formality. Everyone knows."

"But if it were not too late," she persisted, "you would prefer that I cried off?"

She thought he would never answer. Silence stretched between them. "The question is academic," he said. "We are betrothed. If you cry off, I will not have you say that you did so at my request. My mother has her heart set on the match—as do my father and yours."

"And you?" She was whispering.

"And I," he said.

She searched his eyes. But they were blank. Cold. He did

not love her. He would be quite happy if their betrothal came to an end. Except that he felt they had proceeded too far with it. And his parents and her father had their hearts set on it, as they had for five years.

And his heart was set on the match. So he said. But did he mean it? Could she bear it if he did not? Could she bear to be married to him, fearing as she now did that he was marrying for appearance's sake and for his parents' sake? Fearing as she now did that he did not love her?

But could she bear to lose him? To give him up entirely of her own will—against the will of everyone else concerned? She could teach him to love her. She could love him into loving her. She could show him that despite what had happened in the last days and weeks with the Earl of Thornhill, she was capable of loyalty and fidelity and devotion. It would not even take any effort on her part. It was what she wanted more than anything else in the world.

Before either of them could say anything else, Aunt Agatha and the Countess of Rushford were back in the room and the countess was taking charge of the situation again with great energy and calm good sense. Her general air of placidity was quite deceptive, Jennifer was discovering. They were to drive in the park, the four of them, and show the fashionable world how ridiculous was any gossip that had been making the rounds during the course of the day.

"We will confound and disappoint all the tabbies," she said with a laugh. "Oh, my dears, you look so very handsome together. Tomorrow night's ball will be the greatest squeeze of the Season. The greatest success. And I am going to be the happiest mother in town."

And so at the fashionable hour they were driving in the park. It was not so very difficult after all, Jennifer found. No one was so ill-bred as to cause any scene either by look or by word or by gesture. And playing a part gradually developed into living the part. She really was feeling happy. A crisis in her life was passing, thanks to the good advice of her future mother-in-law. And Lionel, sitting beside her, was smiling at others and smiling at her. And touching her hand. And once or twice raising it to his lips. There was warmth in his eyes again.

She had been very foolish. It had been all her fault. She was, as Lionel himself had said, incredibly naive. But finally

she had learned her lesson. From now on there was only Lionel and what she owed him. If he was disappointed in her
now, she would teach him to be proud of her. If he did not
love her now, he would in future.

She turned her head and smiled at him, her heart in her
eyes. He smiled back, his eyes roaming her face and fixing
themselves on her lips. He leaned a little toward her and then
straightened up for good manners' sake, his smile more rueful.

His mother, watching closely from the seat opposite, nodded her approval and turned her smile on the occupants of a
landau that was passing.

Chapter 11

There was an atmosphere of gaiety and and an air of expectancy among the forty guests who sat down to dinner at the Earl of Rushford's table. Everyone knew what announcement was to be made at the end of it, but the knowing did not dampen enthusiasm. Neither did the near scandal of a few days before, which had blossomed gloriously for a few hours only to die down again, as so many would-be scandals did. Not that the dying was to be much lamented. There was always a new one eagerly waiting to take its place.

Samantha smiled, as everyone about her did, and conversed with Mr. Averleigh on her left, and even flirted with him a little. One quickly learned how to flirt in fashionable society, how to hide behind smiles and blushes and sparkling eyes and witty responses. How to draw compliments and admiration and then hold the gentleman concerned at arm's length. Not that that always worked. She had had to refuse a marriage offer that very morning from Mr. Maxwell and was very much afraid that she might have hurt him. And Aunt Aggy had been puzzled and her uncle had been annoyed with her—both had approved his suit.

Samantha continued to smile—indeed, she redoubled her efforts—when the dreaded moment came and the Earl of Rushford got to his feet to make the announcement they had all been waiting for. She did not hear his actual words. But there was a swell of sound as many pretended surprise, and applause and laughter—and Lionel was on his feet and drawing Jenny to hers and kissing her hand. And the two of them were smiling radiantly into each other's eyes and looking as if happily-ever-after were not a strong enough term to describe what their future was to be.

And yet, Samantha thought, withdrawing her eyes from

them under the pretense of lifting her wine glass, Lionel did
not love Jenny. And Jenny—well, Jenny did love him. But
also she had been unduly upset over the incident with the Earl
of Thornhill. And Samantha? Well, her feelings were immaterial. Except that she constantly felt wretched and could not at
all concentrate on becoming especially fond of one gentleman
from her flatteringly large group of admirers. And she was not
even sure that Jenny was going to be happy. She herself could
have borne it, she felt, if only she knew that the two of them
loved each other. She would know then that her own feelings
were quite wrong and must be put firmly behind her.

Well, she thought when Lady Rushford got to her feet finally to signal the ladies to leave the dining room, it was done
now. Finally done. Now it was quite official and unalterable.
Any faint and absurd hope that might have lingered somewhere far back in her brain was now firmly dashed.

It was a relief. Yes, it really was.

She drew close to her cousin in the drawing room, no easy
matter when it seemed that all the ladies, without exception,
were trying to do the same thing. Jennifer saw her and turned
with shining eyes to hug her tightly.

"Oh, Sam," she said, "wish me happy." She laughed. "Wish
me what I already have in such abundance that I believe I may
well burst with it."

Samantha could not afterward remember what she said in
reply. But she did wish it. Oh, she did. She wished Jenny all
the happiness in the world. Her own feelings did not matter in
the slightest.

It was much later in the evening. Jennifer was hot and
flushed and footsore. But happier than she could remember
being. Now, tonight, at last, the dreams she had had for five
long years of what this Season would be like were coming
true.

She was the focus of attention and admiration—not that
these things were important in themselves, she knew. But
every woman has some hidden vanity and enjoys attention,
even when there is one single gentleman who holds her heart.
The Earl of Rushford had danced with her and made it clear
that he was pleased with her. Even Papa—wonder of wonders—had led her into a set.

And Lionel—oh, Lionel had danced with her twice, both waltzes, and had declared his intention of dancing the final set with her. A man was to be excused the minor impropriety of dancing with his betrothed three times in one evening, he had said, his head bent close to hers, his eyes smiling warmly. And if the *ton* did not agree, well, then, the *ton* might go hang.

She had laughed with delight at his outrageous words.

And everyone was watching them. It was no vanity to believe that. It was true. Everyone could see that Lionel was looking at her as if he would devour her. And she did not care that they would see too that she adored him.

All doubts—if there had been any doubts—had been put to rest tonight. He had been angry and hurt yesterday. Understandably so. It had all been her fault. But now, tonight, he had put that anger aside and his true feelings for her were there for all to see—on his face and in his eyes.

He had not come to the ball. It was no surprise—she was sure that Lionel and his father would have made sure that he did not come. But it was an enormous relief. She dreaded seeing him again. It was certainly wonderful that she did not have to do so tonight of all nights. Tonight she could no longer even hear his voice in her head. Tonight she was finally free of him.

The Earl of Rushford had been called from the ballroom a short while ago. Not that Jennifer particularly noticed, but then a footman came to ask Viscount Kersey to join his father in the library, and Lionel left her side after smiling regretfully at her and squeezing her hand.

He was gone through most of the next set, which Jennifer danced with Sir Albert Boyle. She found his company interesting since he told her with a smile that she must wish him happy as he wished her. He had recently become betrothed to Miss Rosalie Ogden. She always felt a special interest in Sir Albert because he was the first gentleman she and Sam had met in London. She hastily closed her mind to the other gentleman who had been with him in the park that day.

But despite her interest in Sir Albert, she was disappointed in the long absence of her betrothed. Even if they could not dance together all evening, she could at least gaze at him much of the time. He was dressed tonight in varying shades of light green to match the color of her own gown. Aunt Agatha had thought a pale color suitable for a young lady who was now officially betrothed. Jennifer smiled secretly to herself. She wondered if five years from now or ten she would still be restless when Lionel was out of her sight for longer than a few minutes.

And then he was there again, in the doorway with his father, his face as pale as his shirt, his smile completely gone, his expression severe. What had happened? Something clearly had. Bad news? Was that why first the earl and then he had been summoned from the ballroom? His father, she saw when she shifted her glance to him, was looking decidedly grim. The set was coming to an end, but she could not hurry toward them to ask what it was. It would not be seemly. She was forced to allow Sir Albert Boyle to escort her back to Aunt Agatha's side and to wait for Lionel to come to her. What was wrong? Oh, poor Lionel.

Whatever it was, he would be glad that the evening was almost at an end. There could be no more than one or two sets remaining.

Jennifer watched in some concern, fanning her hot face, as the Earl of Rushford, followed closely by his son, made his way toward the raised dais on which the orchestra sat, climbed onto it, and stood there, his arms raised for silence. He was holding a single sheet of paper in one hand. Lionel stood beside him, his expression stony, his eyes downcast.

A hush descended on the ballroom as the guests gradually became aware that their host was waiting to address them. Jennifer took one step forward but stopped again.

"It distresses me to make any announcement to destroy the mood of the evening and put an abrupt and early end to the festivities," the earl said, his voice stern and clear. "But something disturbing has been brought to my attention this evening, and after consultation with my son and careful deliberation, I have decided that I have no choice but to speak out publicly and without delay."

The hush in the ballroom became almost loud. Jennifer, for no reason she could fathom, felt her heart beat faster. She could hear it beating in her ears.

"This letter was delivered to the house an hour ago," the earl said, holding the sheet of paper he held a little higher. "And one of my servants was bribed to deliver it into the hands of one of my . . . guests. Fortunately, my servants are loyal. Both the letter and the bribe were put into my butler's hands and then into mine."

Whatever could it be, Jennifer thought in the murmuring that followed, that it had necessitated this public display? She started to fan herself, but she stopped when she realized that everyone about her was still.

"I will read this letter," the earl said, "if you will indulge me for a few moments." He held the sheet of paper up before him and read. " 'My love, Your ordeal is almost at an end, this farce of an evening that you felt obliged to suffer through. To-morrow I will contrive to see you privately, as I have done many times before. I will hold you again and kiss you again and make love to you again. And we will make plans to steal away together so that we may kiss and love whenever we wish. Forgive my incaution in sending you this tonight, but I know you will be disappointed at not seeing me there. I have been advised to stay away after our almost open indiscretion of a few evenings ago. I will be sure that my messenger gives a large enough bribe that this will be placed in your own hands—and next to your heart after you have read it. Would that I could be there too. Until tomorrow, my love. Thorn-hill.' "

Jennifer stood very still. She was beyond thought.

"My servant was bribed," the Earl of Rushford said, "to deliver this into the hands of Miss Jennifer Winwood."

She had become a block of stone. Or a block of ice. Sound—sounds of shock and of outrage—swelled about her. It was something that was happening at a great distance from her.

"In the last week or so," the earl said, having somehow imposed silence on his gathered guests again, "my son has more than once overlooked what was apparently the unfortunate but harmless indiscretion of youth and innocence. As a man of honor and sensibility, he has stood by his commitment to Miss Winwood and shielded her name from scandal and dishonor. It appears that he had been much deceived. And that the countess and I have been much deceived. We have been deceived in a friendship of many years' standing. I will make it clear here and now that there will be no further connection between my family and Miss Winwood's, that the betrothal announced earlier this evening is no longer in existence. Good night, ladies and gentlemen. You will excuse me, I am sure, if I feel that there is no longer anything to celebrate tonight."

Lionel was standing beside his father, looking stern and dignified and very handsome. It was as if the part of Jennifer that was not her body had detached itself from that body and was observing almost dispassionately. It was as if what had been said and what was happening had nothing to do with her.

The Earl of Rushford stood, feet apart, on the dais, watching his guests depart. None of them approached him. They were perhaps too embarrassed to do so. Or perhaps they were in too much of a rush to get ouside so that they could glory in the retelling of what had just happened. Lionel continued to stand there too, straight-backed and pale, his gaze directed downward. Everyone was leaving. Most people did not look at her. Again, it seemed as if they were in the grip of a massive embarrassment.

Then someone grabbed her wrist with painful tightness—Aunt Agatha—and someone else grasped her other elbow in a grip that felt as if it might grind her bones—Papa. And together they turned her and propelled her from the room faster than her feet would move, or so it seemed. Somehow, although everyone was leaving, nothing impeded their progress. Everyone fell back to either side of them, almost as if they had the plague.

And then—she did not know how it could have been brought up so fast—she was inside her father's carriage, Papa beside her, Aunt Agatha across from her, Samantha next to Aunt Agatha, and the carriage was in motion.

"I have a horse whip in the stables," her father was saying, his voice so quiet that Jennifer knew he was more than angry. "Prepare yourself, Miss. I will be using it when we arrive home."

"Oh, no, Uncle," Samantha wailed.

"Gerald—" Aunt Agatha said.

"Silence!" he said.

They all stayed silent during the remainder of the journey home.

"I am sorry, my lord."

His valet's voice somehow got all mixed up with his dream. He was trying to leave London, but no matter which street his carriage turned along, there was always a press of traffic ahead of them and tangled vehicles and angry, excited people arguing and gesticulating. And no way past. And then his valet was standing at the door of the carriage, addressing him in his most formal manner. "I am sorry, my lord."

"Sorry, dammit. Out of my way. Get up, Gabe. Get up before I throw a pitcher of cold water over you."

For a moment Bertie was there too, adding confusion to the melee by trying to force a high-spirited horse past his carriage. And then the Earl of Thornhill woke up.

"I am sorry, my lord," his valet said again. "I tried to—"

"Get up, Gabe."

Bertie, resplendent in ball clothes, pushed the valet unceremoniously aside, grasped the bedclothes, and flung them back. He was quite furiously angry, the earl realized, shaking off the remnants of sleep and waving off his man.

"Go back to bed," he told him. "Good Lord, Bertie, what the devil are you doing here at this time? What time is it, by the way?" He swung his legs over the side of the bed, sat up, and ran his fingers through his hair.

"Get up!" Sir Albert ordered. "I am going to give you the thrashing of your life, Gabe."

The earl looked up at him in some surprise. "Here, Bertie?" he said. "Is the space not rather confined? And you do not have a whip, my dear chap. Will you at least allow me to put on some clothes? I have an aversion to being thrashed, or even to holding a conversation, while I am naked." He got to his feet.

"You are slime," Sir Albert said, his voice cold with contempt. "I have always defended you from all who have defamed you, Gabe. But they have been right and I have been wrong. You were probably giving it to your stepmother after all. You are slime!"

The earl turned, having not quite reached his dressing room door. "Have a care, Bertie," he said quietly. "You are talking about a lady. About a member of my family."

"You disgust me!" his erstwhile friend said. "You are slime."

"Yes." The earl disappeared into his dressing room and came back a moment later tying the sash of a brocaded dressing gown about his waist. "So you said before, Bertie. Would it be too much to ask that you explain the reason for the violence of your feelings—at this time of the night, whatever time it is?"

"Your bribe was not high enough," Sir Albert said very distinctly. "Your letter fell into the wrong hands."

The earl waited, but clearly Bertie had finished. "Next time I try to bribe someone," he said, "I must remember to double the sum. Corruption is more expensive than it used to be, it seems. My letter, Bertie? Which one is that? I have written four or five in the last few days."

"Don't play stupid," Sir Albert said. "She has doubtless been at fault too, Gabe, meeting you in private, allowing intimacies. But she is basically an innocent, I believe, just as Miss Ogden is and all the other young girls who have just made their come-out. They are no match for experienced rakes bent on seducing and ruining them. It was Rushford himself who intercepted that letter, you may be interested to know. He read it aloud to the whole gathering. She is ruined. I hope you are satisfied."

The Earl of Thornhill looked at him silently for a while. "I think we had better go into my sitting room, Bertie," he said at last, turning to lead the way, and lighting a branch of candles when he got there. "You had better tell me exactly what happened tonight."

"How could you!" Sir Albert said. "If you had to be seducing a lady of virtue when there are all sorts of women of another class who would be only too pleased to earn the extra income, did you also have to be so mad as to risk exposing her to the whole *ton*? Did you have no fear that the letter would fall into the wrong hands?"

"Bertie." The earl's tone had become crisp. "Assume for a few minutes, if you will, that I do not know what you are talking about. Or pretend you are recounting the story to a stranger. Tell me what happened. In what way have I ruined Miss Winwood? I assume it is she I have ruined?"

Sir Albert would not sit, but he did calm down enough to give a terse account of what had happened in the Rushford ballroom less than an hour before.

"Did you see the letter?" the earl asked when the story had been completed.

"Of course not," Sir Albert said. "Rushford was holding it. He read it in its entirety. Why would I want to see it?"

"For a rather important reason actually," the earl said. "You know my handwriting, Bertie. That letter would not have been in it."

"Are you trying to tell me that you did not write the letter?" his friend asked, incredulous.

"Not trying," Lord Thornhill said curtly. "I am telling you, Bertie. Good Lord. You believe I am capable of that?"

"You are capable of kissing the girl in sight of the whole *ton*," Sir Albert reminded him.

Ah, yes. Righteous indignation was denied him. Yes, this was something he might well have done. It was rather clever actually. And had obviously worked like a dream.

"Gabe," his friend said, frowning, "if you did not write it, who did? It makes no sense."

"Someone who wanted to embarrass me," the earl said. "Or someone who wanted to ruin Miss Winwood."

"It makes no sense," Sir Albert said again.

"Actually," the earl said, smiling rather grimly, "it makes a great deal of sense, Bertie. I believe I have just been outplayed in a game over which I thought I had complete control."

Sir Albert looked his incomprehension.

"It is time you were in your bed," Lord Thornhill said. "Staying up all night and tripping the light fantastic through much of it can be ruinous on the complexion and the constitution, you know, Bertie."

"I may be a fool and a dupe, but I beleive your denials," Sir Albert said. "However, it does not change the fact that she is totally ruined, Gabe. She will never be sent another invitation. She will never be able to show her face in town again. I doubt that her father will be able to find her a husband even in the country. It is a shame, I rather like her. And if you are to be believed, she has done nothing to bring on her own ruin."

"Sometimes," the earl said, indicating the door with one hand, "these things happen, Bertie. I need the rest of my beauty sleep."

"And you will not be able to show your face here either," Sir Albert said, moving toward the door.

"Now that," the earl said as his friend was finally leaving, "I would not count upon, Bertie."

Very cleverly done, he thought grimly, alone again at last. He did not bother to move back into his bedchamber. He knew that there would be no more sleep for him tonight.

Very cleverly done indeed.

When Viscount Nordal's butler opened the library door the next morning to announce the arrival of the Earl of Thornhill, the viscount at first refused to see him and instructed his servant to throw him out. However, when that nervous individual reappeared less than a minute later with the news that the earl intended to stay in the hall until he was admitted, the viscount directed that he be shown in.

He was standing behind his desk when the earl strode in.

"I have not a word to say to you, Thornhill," he said. "Perhaps I should have sent you a challenge this morning. You have brought ruin on me and my whole family. But fighting a duel with you would suggest that I was defending my daughter's honor. As I understand it, there is no honor to be fought for."

"I will buy a special license today," the earl said curtly, wasting no time on preliminaries, "and marry her tomorrow. You need not concern yourself with a dowry for her. I have fortune enough with which to support her."

The viscount sneered. "Not quite what you anticipated being forced into," he said, "when you have been enjoying the pleasures of the marriage bed without benefit of clergy and expected to go on doing so. Is it possible that you care enough for the opinion of your peers to do the decent thing, Thornhill?"

The Earl of Thornhill strode across the room and rested both hands flat on the desk before leaning across it to address himself to his prospective father-in- law. "I will make one thing clear," he said. "To my knowledge Miss Winwood is as pure as she was on the day her mother bore her. And if I am to marry her, I will meet anyone who wishes to assume otherwise. Yourself included."

The viscount bristled. "Get out!" he said.

"Your daughter's name and honor seem to mean nothing to you," the earl said, "except as they reflect upon your own. Very well, then. The only thing that can happen today—the *only* thing—is for her to affiance herself to me, for us to marry without delay. With your daughter safely and honorably married, you will be able to hold your head high again, Nordal. And eventually so will she."

Viscount Nordal looked back at him with silent loathing.

The earl removed his hands from the desk and took a step back. "It is early for a lady to be up and dressed the morning after a ball," he said, "but I do not imagine Miss Winwood has been troubled by too much sleep. I will see her now, Nordal, before I leave about other business. Alone, if you please."

Viscount Nordal's hand went to the bell rope behind his left shoulder.

"Have my daughter sent alone to the rose salon," he told the butler, who appeared almost immediately. "While we wait, Thornhill, I believe we have a little business to discuss. Have a seat."

The Earl of Thornhill sat, both his expression and his mood grim.

Chapter 12

Jennifer awoke feeling some amazement that she had slept at all. In fact, she seemed to have slept quite deeply and dreamlessly. But she awoke quite early without any of the illusions one so often has that the unpleasant events of the day before were merely dreams. Perhaps it was the soreness of her back and derrière when she moved. Sam's tears and pleadings and Aunt Agatha's admonitions had had their effect on Papa. He had not sent to the stables for a whip. He had used a cane instead and bent her over the desk in the library just like a naughty child while he did so.

It was all over. Everything that made her life worth living. Over when she was still only twenty years old. There was nothing left to make the rest of it worth living and never would be. Curiously, this morning her mind still had that strange detachment of the night before. She knew what had happened and she knew what the consequences were and what they would be for the rest of her days. But only her mind knew. No other part of her had begun to react to them yet.

She sat up gingerly, moving her legs over the edge of the bed. He had done it one more time and this time had ruined her completely. She had trusted him despite all the evidence and all the warnings from older, more experienced people than she. And he had done this to her. Lionel was lost to her. There was to be no more betrothal, no marriage. No more Season.

She realized suddenly what had woken her this early. Through the half open door into her dressing room she could hear her maid and someone else moving about, opening and shutting doors and drawers. They were packing her trunks. She was to leave some time today for the country. But she was to go home only temporarily. Only until Papa could make arrangements for her to take up residence in some suitably remote location with a lady companion. The lady companion, she had understood, was in reality to be her jailer.

Wherever it was he banished her to, she was to spend the rest of her life there.

Her maid had set a plain morning dress over a chair in her room and a bowl and jug of water on the dresser. Jennifer got to her feet and washed and dressed herself. She brushed her hair and twisted it into a simple knot at her neck. And then she sat down on the edge of the bed again. She could not go down to breakfast, she had just remembered. She was confined to her room until the carriage was ready for her.

She had not been given any chance to defend herself, she realized. But it did not matter. The truth mattered little in such circumstances. The fact was that for reasons of his own the Earl of Thornhill had written that letter and Lionel's father had read it and then exposed her and turned her off publicly. The fact was that she was ruined beyond redemption. Nothing could change that. There was no point in exerting herself to try to get someone to listen to her.

There was a tap on the dressing room door, the murmuring of her maid's voice and a footman's. Perhaps it was her breakfast tray, she thought, wondering if it would hold nothing but dry bread and water. Or perhaps they were ready for her. Papa doubtless wanted to get her on her way as soon as possible.

"You are wanted downstairs, Miss," her maid said, appearing in the doorway, looking nervous. The servants doubtless knew the whole story. Servants always did. "In the rose salon without delay."

It was not the carriage, then. And the summons was not to the library. Of course, that did not necessarily mean that she was not to be caned again. Perhaps Papa had sent for the whip after all this morning. Perhaps she should weep as soon as she saw it and every time he used it. He had been incensed last night when she had remained quiet during her beating. It was not that she had not felt every stroke. It was just that her mind had been too numb to react.

The rose salon was empty. She walked across to the window and gazed out onto the square beyond the railings. She had loved London. There was a sense of energy and excitement here that she never felt in the country, though the country was where she thought she would prefer to do her day-by-day living. She supposed now it was as well she felt that way.

She wondered what Lionel was doing at this precise minute. Viscount Kersey. She no longer had the right even to think of him as Lionel.

And then the door opened and closed behind her. She did not turn. She was not sure she would not grovel when she actually saw the whip. She was still very sore from the cane.

"Miss Winwood?" The voice came from close behind her.

She spun around, eyes wide, all the numbness and passivity of the past hours gone without trace. "You!" she said. "Get out. *Get out*!"

He looked cool and elegant, booted feet set slightly apart, hands clasped behind his back. She hated him with such intensity that she would have killed him if she had had a weapon.

"I have come to save you from disgrace," he said. "We will marry tomorrow."

Her eyes widened further and her hands clenched into fists at her sides. "You have come to gloat," she said. "You have come to mock me. Well, gaze your fill, my lord. I have not looked in a glass this morning, but I would guess that I am not a pretty sight. This is what you have done to me. Enjoy the sight and then get out."

"You are unnaturally pale," he said, "and have shadows beneath your eyes. Your eyes are wild and unhappy. Apart from that, I see the same beauty I have admired since I first saw you. I will procure a special license today. We will marry tomorrow."

She laughed. "Yes, you mean it," she said. "Of course. It is the only explanation. For some reason you decided that you wanted me. I was unavailable because I was betrothed. But that was not going to stop you. You stalked me and preyed upon my innocence and gullibility and gradually compromised me more and more until last night that lying letter, which you fully intended would fall into the wrong hands, completed your scheme. You are diabolical. We were right to call you

Lucifer, the devil. It is an irony beyond humor that you have the name of an angel."

He watched her steadily. She had not even shaken his calm. She itched to take her fingernails to his face.

"I did not write or send that letter," he said.

She looked at him incredulously and laughed. "Oh, did you not?" she said. "It wrote itself and sent itself, I suppose. And I suppose you did not lie with your stepmother or father her child or abandon her in a foreign country in order to return here for fresh prey."

"No," he said.

His calm infuriated her. "And I suppose you did not deliberately set out to free me from my betrothal," she said.

He opened his mouth to speak and then closed it again.

"So that I would marry you." She glared at him scornfully. "Did it not matter to you that I was to marry the man of my choice? Did you imagine that I would gladly give him up for you? Or that I would happily accept the replacement once it was made? Did you imagine that I could ever do anything but despise and loathe you?"

"No," he said.

"But it did not matter," she said. "The state of my heart does not matter to you. My happiness does not matter to you. Possessing me is all. You must very much like what you see, my lord Gabriel."

His eyes moved down her body and up again. She was very much aware of her large breasts and generous curves.

"Yes," he said.

"I suppose it did not occur to you," she said. "that with Lord Kersey lost and my reputation in shreds I would refuse you."

"We will marry in the morning," he said, "and attend the theater in the evening. We will drive in the park the following afternoon and attend Lady Truscott's ball in the evening. We will face down this scandal before I take you to my estate in the North."

"You must be mad." She was whispering. "All this smacks of insanity. I will not marry you. You must be insane to think that I would."

"Consider the alternative," he said.

The alternative was imprisonment in some remote part of

the country for the rest of her life. Her earlier numbness gone, the prospect was suddenly terrifying. Her father would do it, too. She had no illusions about him. No sentiment would persuade him to relax the sentence after a year or so and bring her home to the country.

He was going to cut her hair before she left. She had a sudden memory of that detail. He had said it after the caning. And he had meant it. For some reason it became in that moment the most terrifying detail of all that was facing her.

"He is going to have my hair cropped close to my head." She had said the words aloud. She could almost hear the echo of them. And his eyes had lifted to her hair.

"There will be no company," he said, "no pretty clothes. No marriage. No running of a home and attending to those less fortunate than yourself. There will be no one less fortunate than you. There will be no children."

She fought panic and clenched her fists, trying to convert it into fury against him again.

"We will marry tomorrow morning," he said.

It would be worse. A thousand times worse. She looked at him in some horror, at his tall figure, at the breadth of his shoulders, at his dark hair and eyes and aristocratic features. She reminded herself of the villainies of which he was guilty, of the fiendish way he had stalked her and brought her to ruin just so that he would have her for himself. And yet all she could see and feel and hear was the scissors, cold against her head, chopping through the thickness of her hair.

She bit her lip hard.

Her hand was in both of his suddenly, cold and limp in his warm, strong ones. And he was on one knee in front of her. She watched him in shock, her feelings numb again.

"Miss Winwood," he said, "will you do me the great honor of being my wife?"

He gazed up at her, his expression quite unfathomable. Looking handsome and romantic and quite as if he could not possibly be guilty of any of the fiendishness she knew him guilty of beyond a doubt.

The alternative was the scissors. It had all boiled down to that almost farcical triviality. The scissors and the sight of her hair falling in heavy locks to the floor to be swept up and burned. She fought a wave of nausea.

"Yes." She closed her eyes. She was not quite sure she had spoken the word aloud.

But she must have. He was on his feet again and squeezing both her hands very tightly. "I will make it my life's work," he said, "to see to it that you will in time be glad of your answer."

"It would be a waste of your energy," she said, looking deliberately into his eyes. "After tomorrow morning you will possess my body, my lord. It seems to be important to you. You will never possess my heart or my respect or my esteem. I will hate you every day for the rest of my life."

"Well." He kissed the back of each hand in turn, squeezed them again, and released them. His manner was brisk. "There is much I must do today. You will remain at home. I am sure you would not wish otherwise. You will—" He paused suddenly and looked into her eyes. "Were you harshly treated after your return home last night?"

She smiled. "My father is a stern man, my lord," she said. "You brought great humiliation on him."

He frowned. "Did he touch you?" he asked.

"With his hands? No." She was still smiling. "He used a cane."

He closed his eyes briefly. "I will leave instructions," he said, "that you are to be gently treated for the rest of today and tomorrow morning. After that you will be under my protection."

"Do you have a cane too?" she asked. "It is a very effective weapon for imposing discipline, my lord. I am still sore this morning."

"It is the last you will ever feel," he said. "My word of honor on it."

She laughed. "I am enormously comforted," she said. "Your honor, my lord?"

He looked at her steadily for a few moments and then made her a formal bow. "Until tomorrow morning," he said. He turned and left the room, closing the door behind him.

Well, Jennifer thought. Well. But she could not—or would not—force her mind past the single word. She stood where she was until the door opened again several minutes later to admit both Aunt Agatha and her father.

"Well, Miss," her father said. "It seems that total disgrace is to be avoided after all. Though how I am to hold up my head today when I leave this house I do not know."

"Well, Jennifer." Her aunt was smiling rather stiffly. "We have a busy day ahead of us. We have a wedding to prepare for."

A wedding. She was to be married. Not in a month's time in St. George's with half the *ton* in attendance. Tomorrow in some obscure church—she did not know where. And not to Lionel, to whom she had been promised for five years, whom she had loved and longed for for five years. To the Earl of Thornhill.

She was to be the Countess of Thornhill.

His wife.

"Yes." She moved across the room toward her aunt.

The Earl of Thornhill received much the same reception at the Rushford mansion as he had at Nordal's. Except that this time, when he sent the message that he would remain in the hall until he was admitted, he immediately broke his own vow by following the butler up the stairs, despite that servant's protest, and was at his shoulder and able to walk past him when the door to the earl's private apartments was opened by a valet.

"No," he said for the benefit of the servants and both astonished men in the earl's dressing room—Kersey was with him there—"I will not be turned off."

The Earl of Rushford, thin-lipped and furious, nodded his dismissal to the servants, ignoring the apologies of his butler. Viscount Kersey stood where he was and sneered.

"I have come," the Earl of Thornhill said, "for Miss Winwood's property."

"For . . . ? I will have you tossed out for this, Thornhill." Lord Rushford's voice vibrated with fury.

"I believe," Lord Kersey said, raising a quizzing glass to his eye, "he is asking for the letter, Father. By what right do you claim that slut's, ah, property, Thornhill?"

"I have the honor of being the lady's betrothed," Lord Thornhill said coldly and distinctly. "I am reluctant to slap a glove in your face, Kersey, as I am sure you are well aware. The lady has suffered enough at our hands. But if you utter one whisper of an insult about her from this moment on, you will leave me with no choice. Now, the letter." He held out an imperious hand to Rushford.

The earl drew in a sharp breath. "The letter," he said, "has been burned. My house is sullied by even the ashes of such filth."

"So you are going to marry her." Lord Kersey chuckled until he caught his father's stern eye on him.

"Ah." Lord Thornhill's hand returned to his side. "I feared it. And since it is you who tell me, Rushford, I believe you. It was wisely done, too, though I will pay you the courtesy of believing that perhaps you did not realize it. If the letter still existed, there would be more men than just me who could have vouched for the fact that it was not in my hand."

"You would have been foolish not to have had some lackey pen it for you," Lord Kersey said. "But denial would be pointless. Who else would have had a motive to write it—and sign your name to it? You have destroyed my happiness, Thornhill, and made a good pass to destroy my name. Only the bold action of my father averted that chance and brought me the sympathy of the *ton* instead. My father's name too might have been brought to humiliation. For that fact more than any other I find your behavior unforgivable."

"The bold action of your father destroyed the name of an innocent young lady instead," Lord Thornhill said, "and in the cruelest manner imaginable. For a man newly affianced and apparently deep in love, you have recovered from her apparent defection with remarkable speed, Kersey. If I were you, I would put on a longer face when you go out. You would not wish it said, I am sure, that you were glad to be set free, that perhaps you had maneuvered to be free."

The viscount's eyes flashed. "It would be like you to spread such slander, Thornhill," he said. "I merely ask you to consider whose word is more likely to be trusted among the *ton*. The answer is rather obvious, is it not?"

"I must ask you to leave, Thornhill," Lord Rushford said. "My son has suffered a severe shock at your hands and at the hands of the woman I cannot bring myself to name. And the countess and I have suffered a painful disappointment in her. If you dare to come back, I will have you thrown out bodily. I trust I make myself understood?"

"Assuming that the question is rhetorical," Lord Thornhill said with a bow, "I will leave it unanswered. Good day to you."

It had been a slim hope, he thought as he made his way from the house on foot. If he could have proved that the letter was not in his hand, perhaps he could have set up enough doubt in fashionable drawing rooms that her way back into society would be made a little easier. Though, of course, there was no denying the fact that he was the one who had kissed her openly at the Velgard's costume ball and that she had been the one he had kissed.

No, it had been a slim chance. And he had not really expected that the letter would still exist. If he had been Rushford, he would have burned it. If he had been Kersey, he would have burned the house down too as an extra precaution.

He had paid the call for another reason. He had wanted them to know that Jennifer Winwood was to be his wife, that they would carry on any sort of a campaign against her at their peril. And he had wanted Kersey to know that he understood fully and that the game was not yet at an end.

Kersey had won the first round. There was no doubt about that. Far from suffering humiliation at the loss of his betrothed, he had deliberately arranged matters so that he could be free of her. He had wanted to be free of her. And he had done it in such a way that his adversary was stuck with her instead—though the earl winced away somewhat from the word he had used in his mind. She deserved better than that attitude. She was a total innocent, a victim of the plotting and cruelty of both Kersey and himself.

When he had told her earlier that he would devote his life to making sure that she would one day be glad of her decision, he had meant it. He would see to it that her reputation was restored and that for the rest of her days she would have whatever her heart desired. He would salve his conscience perhaps a little by doing that.

But the game with Kersey was not over. Somehow he would have his revenge. A more satisfactory revenge than a mere humiliation. Somehow he was going to find a way to kill Kersey.

In the meantime there was a special license to be obtained and all sorts of arrangements to be made.

Good Lord, he thought, stopping suddenly on the pavement, this time tomorrow he was going to be a married man.

But there was panic in the thought. He pushed it from him.

Samantha tapped hesitantly on Jennifer's door after luncheon. Although Jennifer had not come down for that meal, Samantha had learned that she was no longer in disgrace or in solitary confinement. She had learned to her utter astonishment that Jenny was to marry the Earl of Thornhill tomorrow.

"May I come in?" she asked, peering around the door. "Or would you rather I went away?"

Jennifer was sitting curled up on a chair, a cushion hugged to her bosom. "Come in, Sam." She smiled wanly.

Samantha came into the sitting room and glanced toward the half open door into the dressing room. There was a great bustling going on in there. "Your things are still being packed?" she asked. Could she have possibly mistaken?

"To be removed to Grosvenor Square tomorrow," Jennifer explained. "I am to be married, Sam. It is a great triumph, is it not? I must be the first of those presented at Court this spring to be married. And I will be a countess, no less." She bent her head to rest her forehead against the top of the cushion.

"Oh, Jenny." Samantha gazed at her in some distress. "It is better than the alternative, at least."

"That is exactly what he pointed out," Jennifer said with a little laugh. "Do you know why I eventually said yes, Sam? For an enormously important reason. Papa was going to have my hair cropped short before sending me away today. I said yes so that I would not have to have my hair cut."

She buried her face against the cushion. Samantha could not tell whether she was laughing or crying. Not that it really mattered. The emotion was the same.

She could think of nothing to say to her cousin. Nothing that would console her. She seated herself on a sofa and gazed at Jennifer's bowed head and thought back with horrified guilt to the unwilling elation she had felt last night—and still felt today. She did not really feel happy. Oh, no, she did not. It hurt dreadfully to watch Jenny suffering and to know the cruel circumstances that had brought about that suffering. Though Jenny had been so indiscreet . . . perhaps. Something worried her.

"Jenny," she said and then bit her lip. It must be the last thing her cousin wanted to talk about. "When did you have those clandestine meetings with him? We have always been together or with Aunt Aggy."

Jennifer's head shot up. "What?" She was frowning.

"The letter—" Samantha, facing those hostile eyes, said no more.

"That letter was a cruel hoax," Jennifer said. "He is deranged, Sam. He is obsessed with me. It was all lies. He did it to make sure that my betrothal would end and in such a way that I would be ruined and would have no alternative but to marry him instead. He is having his way. I will be marrying him tomorrow. But I have told him that I will hate him for the rest of my life. To such a man that probably does not even matter. I think my b-body must be all he wants."

Samantha stared at her. "I cannot believe that he could be capable of such dreadful cruelty," she said.

"Well, believe it." Jennifer buried her face again. "He denied having written the letter. Can you imagine that, Sam? If he did not, who did, I would like to know? Who else could possibly have wanted to ruin me and to end my engagement?"

"No one." Samantha continued to stare at her bowed head. "No one, Jenny." Except herself. Not that she had ever wished even one moment of suffering on Jenny, of course. Never that. But she had dreamed of the engagement's somehow coming to an end. Lionel had said that if only he had met her, Samantha, before Jenny . . .

And Lionel had wished his betrothal at an end. He had felt trapped by it. He had wished he was free to pay court to Samantha. But Lionel did not wish any harm to Jenny either. Lionel was a man of honor. Samantha frowned.

Jennifer was looking at her and smiling rather bleakly. "I am not very good company today, am I?" she said. "Don't you envy me, Sam? The Countess of Thornhill this time tomorrow?"

"Jenny." Samantha leaned forward. "Perhaps it will not be so very bad. He is very handsome and he has wealth and property. At least you will be able to console yourself with the knowledge that he was willing to go to great lengths to win you. I believe he must love you deeply."

"If you love someone," Jennifer said, "you do not deliberately cause that person deep misery, Sam."

"I did not say he was perfect." Samantha smiled. "I am just trying to help you to see the bright side. I know that at this moment there must seem nothing bright in life to you at all. But think about it. Lionel—Lord Kersey—promised himself to you a long time ago, when he was a very young man. Did he make great efforts to see you in the years following? To press forward your marriage? Has he professed deep love for you this Season or tried to make an earlier wedding date than that arranged by his parents and Uncle Gerald?"

"What are you trying to say?" Jennifer was angry, Samantha saw.

"Only that perhaps in a way the Earl of Thornhill loves you more than Lord Kersey does," Samantha said. "Only that perhaps life might not have turned into the idyll you expected if you had married the viscount and that perhaps it will not turn into quite the nightmare you expect now."

The anger died from Jennifer's eyes and she smiled. "Sam," she said, hurling the cushion, but not with any great force. "You could sell a hat to a milliner. I swear you could. It really does not matter when all is said and done, does it? I'll never know what life would have been like with Lord Kersey. And I dare not think of it now or I will become a watering pot. Aunt Agatha has instructed me to be in my very best looks for tomorrow. For my wedding day."

She smiled again and then spread her hands over her face and broke into wrenching sobs.

"Oh, Jenny." Samantha in her turn clutched the cushion to her bosom and found herself wondering treacherously how long Lionel would deem it proper to leave it before he called on her.

And then she hated herself for thinking of her own hopes when her dearest friend was in such misery.

Growing up was not nearly the pleasant, uncomplicated business she had expected it to be. Sometimes it was downright frightening.

Chapter 13

It was the first of several weddings to unite members of the *ton* that were the primary purpose and inevitable result of the Season. It should therefore have been a singular triumph for the bride and her family, something to gloat over with well-bred condescension for the rest of the spring.

But this particular wedding, though it united a peer of the realm with the daughter of a viscount, was not a large, fashionable affair. It did not take place in St. George's or any other fashionable place of worship. It took place in a small church, where the rector was willing to perform the service at such short notice. And it was not attended by a large number of fashionable guests—merely by the groom's two friends, Sir Albert Boyle and Lord Francis Kneller, and by the bride's father, aunt, and cousin.

Jennifer, walking down the cold aisle of an empty, echoing church with her father and coming to a halt beside her bridegroom, tried to hold her mind blank. She tried not to think of the wedding in one month's time that she had been expecting.

She had not looked at her bridegroom, though she saw now in some surprise that he wore buckled shoes and white stockings. He was dressed as if for an evening social event. As was she. Aunt Agatha had insisted on white silk and lace, the finest of her evening gowns. Just as if it were a special occasion.

She supposed it was.

His hand, when it took her own, felt warm. And large and strong. She looked at it, at the long, well-manicured fingers. There was fine lace at his wrist and a blue satin sleeve. His hand squeezed her own slightly.

It was, she realized, a significant moment. A significant symbol. She had placed her hand in his and thereby surrendered all of herself to him for the rest of her life. To a man who had seduced his stepmother and then abandoned her and her child. To a man who was ruthless enough to do anything in order to win the object of his obsession. She was surrendering to him because she did not want to have her hair cut off.

He was speaking, repeating what the rector said to him. He was promising to worship her with his body and to endow her with all his worldly goods. She felt the hysterical urge to giggle and involuntarily gripped his hand more tightly in order to stop herself.

And she promised—she could hear herself as if it were another person—to love, honor, and obey him. To obey him. Yes, it was total surrender. Something he had forced her into. Something for which she would hate him for the rest of her life. Yet she was promising to love him. Solemnly promising before witnesses and before God.

She looked up into his face for the first time. He was the handsome stranger of Hyde Park, the gentleman whom she had come to like and believe despite herself. The first—and only—man to have kissed her. Dark hair, dark eyes—focused steadily on hers—finely chiseled features. Devil with an angel's name. Her husband. That was what the rector was saying. He was her husband.

He bent his head and kissed her lips. Briefly and lightly as he had done twice before. As on both those occasions, she felt his kiss right down to her toes. His eyes smiled at her—a kindly, reassuring expression that hid the triumph he must be feeling. He had won. In no time at all. He had seen her and desired her and taken her away from Lionel and married her himself.

She wondered suddenly what he would do when he tired of her, as he surely would. He would put her away with as much callousness and as much ruthlessness as he had used to get her, she did not doubt. She felt an inward shiver.

Aunt Agatha was dabbing at her eyes with a confection of a lace handkerchief. Samantha was weeping openly. Her father was looking relieved. They all hugged her and shook the earl by the hand. His friends, smiling and overhearty, shook his hand more firmly and kissed Jennifer's. Lord Francis called her the Countess of Thornhill.

She was. Yes, she was. His countess, his wife, his possession.

He handed her into his carriage—she had a general impression of dark blue velvet and luxury—and a footman closed the door. She had hoped that Sam or perhaps his friends would ride with them. But no, they were to come on to Papa's for the wedding breakfast by other carriages.

She had been alone with him before. There was nothing so very strange about it. She must accustom herself to being alone with him. She was his possession.

At first he drew her arm through his and covered her hand with his own. They sat in silence until the horses had been set in motion. His arm and his hand were warm, but her own hand, sandwiched between the two, could draw no warmth or comfort to herself.

And then he released her arm in order to set his about her shoulders and draw her close to him. "You are like a block of ice," he said. "The church was cold and your gown is thin. Though I do not suppose either of those two facts is the real cause." He lifted her chin with his free hand, his palm warm beneath it, his fingers cupping her jaw. He set his mouth to hers again. "It is not going to be the nightmare you expect. I promise you it will not."

The side of her head was brushing his shoulder. She let it rest fully against the warm satin there and closed her eyes. She must not try to fight her way free. She was his wife. Besides, she was so very weary. She had slept last night in mere fits and starts. She would be inclined to believe that she had not slept at all, except that she could remember bizarre dreams.

"Jennifer." His voice was low against her ear. It was always so hard when she listened to his voice or when she was within the aura of his physical presence to believe that in reality he was the very devil. "We are man and wife, my dear. We must make the best of it. If either of us is to find any happiness in what remains of our lives, we must find it in each other. If we try very hard, perhaps we will not find the task altogether impossible."

Almost, she thought, as if he had been forced into this marriage as much as she had. She felt a flash of anger, but she quelled it. Any strong emotion might precipitate her out of the welcome lethargy that had taken her through the morning. She did not want to wake to full reality yet.

"You look very beautiful today," he said. "I am more proud than I can say that you are my wife."

And then his mouth was on hers again, warm, not at all demanding. His lips were parted. She wondered idly if all men kissed like this—if it was the way to kiss. But she would never know. She felt warmth seep into her flesh and into her bones. She pushed her lips back against his, reaching for greater comfort.

She was half asleep by the time the carriage drew to a halt outside her father's house. Half asleep and half dreaming. But when she opened her eyes and he drew back his head, it was Gabriel, Earl of Thornhill, at whom she gazed, not Lionel, Viscount Kersey.

With a sharp jabbing of pain, which seemed almost physical, she understood that she was married to this man. That there would never again be Lionel. Never again the dream, except perhaps during the kindest—or cruelest—sleep.

The wedding breakfast proceeded with surprising ease. Perhaps it was because everyone—except Jennifer—tried very hard. Almost too hard, the Earl of Thornhill thought. The topics of conversation were too trivial and were clung to for too long. There was too much animation over trivialities and far too much laughter, especially from Frank and Bertie, and from Miss Newman. But he was grateful even so. Awkward silences and inappropriate solemnity would have been unbearable.

He was married. Without any chance to make his own choice, without any time to consider and digest what it was he had been forced into, he was married—to a woman who hated him with very good reason. She believed his perfidies far worse than they really were, and perhaps in time he could clear himself of some charges to her satisfaction. But he could not clear himself of everything.

He was horribly guilty. And if she knew the full truth, it would be worse for her than what she now believed. At least now she believed that he had wanted her and had deliberately set about getting her. How would she feel if she ever learned that he had not wanted her at all?

No, that was not strictly true. He had been moved by her beauty and by her innocent charm from the first. And powerfully attracted sexually. Perhaps if he had met her under different circumstances, he would indeed have set about wooing her. But he had not.

Bertie had been coldly satisfied at his news and had held out a hand as a signal that their quarrel was at an end. He had even agreed to attend the wedding. Frank had been incredulous and then inclined to find the whole matter a great lark. He too had agreed to come.

It felt somehow reassuring to have his closest friends at his wedding. He had relatives scattered about the north of England—and of course there were Catherine and the child who was officially his half-sister in Switzerland. But there had been no time to summon any of them, even if it had seemed appropriate to do so.

He took his bride home in the middle of the afternoon. It was perhaps only then that reality began to hit him. He was taking her to his home, now hers too. Her belongings had been delivered there in the morning. Maids had been bustling in the dressing room adjoining his own before he had left for church, unpacking her clothes. His servants, well aware that this was his wedding day and that his bride was coming home with him, were dressed in their best uniforms and had been lined up for inspection in the hall. There was a general buzz of excitement, hastily quelled by one frown from his housekeeper, as he stepped over the doorstep with his countess on his arm.

His servants applauded with an enthusiasm that went a little beyond politeness.

He smiled down at Jennifer and was relieved to see that she too was smiling. Whatever her personal feelings for him—he had not had one smile from her all day—she was prepared to play her part for his servants and hers, it seemed. He walked with her along the row of servants while his housekeeper introduced each to his wife. She smiled at all of them and stopped to talk to a few.

And then his housekeeper was preceding them up the stairs at his direction.

"You will show her ladyship to her rooms, if you please, Mrs. Harris," he said, when they reached the first landing.

She nodded politely and went on ahead to stand a few stairs up the next flight of stairs, out of earshot.

He kissed his wife's hand. "You are exhausted," he said. "You will rest for a few hours, my dear. Alone. I will not disturb you."

She flushed, her eyes on their hands.

"We will leave that for tonight," he said, "after the theater."

It had been arranged during the breakfast that her aunt and her cousin and Frank would share his box at the theater with them this evening.

But she raised her eyes to his. "You cannot really be serious," she said. "I cannot be seen at the theater. Not after what happened just the evening before last. It would be far better if we left for the country."

"No," he said, "it would not, Jennifer. Frank and Bertie will be putting it about this afternoon that we have been wed this morning. By this evening it will be general knowledge. News of you and me will travel faster even than usual under present circumstances. Tonight we must appear in public. And we must smile and look happy, my dear. We will dare anyone to cut our acquaintance. If we creep away now, we may find it impossible ever to come back."

"I do not want ever to come back," she said.

"You will." He released her hand. "If only to bring out our own daughters when the time comes."

She bit her lip.

"Go now," he said, "and rest. We will face the *ton* together this evening, and you will find that it is not impossible after all. Very few things are."

She turned without a word and left him. He watched her climb the stairs behind Mrs. Harris, tall and elegant and shapely, her dark red hair arranged in intricate curls at the back of her head and down over her neck.

Perhaps he would not have chosen a bride quite so precipitately if he had been given the choice, he thought, and perhaps he would not have chosen her. But one thing was sure. His loins ached for her. It was no easy thing to watch her go to her bed in the apartments adjoining his own and to know her his wife, their marriage as yet unconsummated, and yet not go to join her there.

He wished at least as strongly as she did that there was not this infernal compulsion to appear before the *ton* tonight as man and wife. He would give a chunk of his fortune to be able to go to bed with her instead and seek out an evening's entertainment of a different nature.

She was powerfully reminded during dinner of the one vow she had made to him just that morning. She had promised to obey him for the rest of her life.

Somehow, seated adjacent to him at the long table in the dining room, she responded to his efforts to keep a conversation going. A little social training was a marvelous thing, she thought. One was able to talk politely on a variety of topics even when there was nothing to say and even when talking was the last thing in the world one felt like doing.

But one topic was difficult to introduce. She left it until she could not delay any longer without leaving it altogether.

"My lord," she said, looking up into his face for one of the few times since the meal had begun, "will you please excuse me from attending the theater this evening? It has been such a busy day. And I did not sleep very well either last night or this afternoon. I have a h-headache. I do not feel very well." Her voice trailed off. She sounded feebly abject even to her own ears.

"Gabriel," he said, reaching across the table to touch his fingers lightly to the back of her hand. "I will not be 'my lorded' all through life by my own wife. Say it."

"Gabriel," she said obediently. The most unsuitable name there ever was.

"I do not believe you, my dear," he said. "And if I did I would require you to attend the theater anyway. And I will ask you to smile and hold your head high. You have done nothing to be ashamed of. Nothing whatsoever."

"Except," she said softly, "being naive enough to fall into your trap."

He removed his hand from hers. "Tomorrow evening," he said, "we will be attending Lady Truscott's ball. You will find it a great deal easier to do if you keep your courage this evening."

"If?" she said. "I do not believe I have a choice, do I?"

"No," he said, "you have no choice, Jennifer."

She could scarcely move her mind beyond the terrifying ordeal of appearing before the *ton* less than forty-eight hours after being stranded in the Earl of Rushford's ballroom while he read that letter aloud. But if she did try to edge her mind forward to assure herself, as she would normally do, that it would eventually be over and she could creep home to the comfort and privacy of her bed, she realized that there was no comfort to be had there.

Today was her wedding day. Tonight was her wedding night. Before she could expect any privacy or comfort tonight, there was that to be lived through. She looked involuntarily at her husband and shivered. What would it feel like? she wondered. Would the pain be more powerful than the humiliation? She knew what was to happen. She had known for some time, but if she had been in any doubt, Aunt Agatha had put it to rest early this morning by describing the process with brisk and surprisingly graphic frankness.

She owed him obedience. She must let it happen. And she must hope that she could keep her mind as mercifully blank as she had kept it this morning.

"It is time to leave," he said, setting down his napkin on the table, getting to his feet, and reaching out a hand to assist her. "The carriage will be here soon. You certainly do not want the added embarrassment of making a late entrance, I am sure."

Jennifer scrambled to her feet with almost ungainly haste.

It seemed that the very doormen at the theater stared at them askance. It seemed that everyone else who was within the doors or on the stairs or otherwise not yet within the theater moved aside to give them room and fell into an incredulous silence. It seemed that all eyes in the theater, many of them assisted by quizzing glasses or lorgnettes, turned their way as they stepped into the earl's box, and as if all conversations were instantly terminated and others begun after but a moment's pause. Excited, buzzing, shocked conversations.

It seemed—no, it *was*, Jennifer thought. She clung to her husband's arm and looked frequently up into his smiling face, her own mirroring his expression. She responded to what he said to her with words of her own. She had no idea what he said or what she said in reply. She kept her chin high.

Lord Francis Kneller was there already with Aunt Agatha and Samantha. He got to his feet, took Jennifer's hand and kissed it, smiling at her and leading her to the chair which her husband held for her. She seated herself.

"Bravo, ma'am," Lord Francis said and winked at her before resuming his seat beside Samantha.

Her husband sat down beside her and lifted her arm to rest along his. He bent his head close to her as she directed her eyes on the empty stage.

"You look lovely and wonderful and regal," he said. "Look about you and smile even more if you meet the eye of someone you know."

It was the hardest thing she had yet done. Except that she found when she did it that eyes were not directed at her at all. No one had even as much courage as she, she thought, raising her chin a notch higher. They could not meet her eye to eye and so pretended hastily to be looking elsewhere. She saw Sir Albert Boyle in a box opposite with Rosalie Ogden and her mama and another older gentleman, and smiled warmly at him. He smiled and bowed his head in her direction.

It was working, she thought several minutes later, just as the play was about to begin. Their entrance had obviously caused something of a sensation. Most people would not look directly at them when they thought themselves observed. But there had not been a great booing or hissing. No one had jumped up onto the stage to demand that they leave and not dare to contaminate decent people with their presence ever again. A few people had inclined their heads to her. One or two had even smiled.

Everyone, her husband had said, would know that they were married. Sir Albert and Lord Francis had made it easier for them by making sure that word spread this afternoon. Doubtless they had ridden in the park and made the wedding the sole topic of their conversation.

Two evenings ago, she thought suddenly, perhaps at about

this exact time, her betrothal to Lord Kersey was announced. This evening she was another man's wife.

Before she could shake off the distressing thought and before the play could begin, she was aware of another of those almost imperceptible pauses in the general conversation, followed by a renewed buzz of talk. And she saw instantly why. The box close to theirs in which she had sat one evening last week, had been mercifully empty thus far, but now it was filling—with the Earl and Countess of Rushford, another older couple whom Jennifer did not know, and Viscount Kersey escorting Horatia Chisley.

It was perhaps the most intensely painful moment of her life, Jennifer thought. A hand clamped down hard on hers as she was about to get to her feet to flee she knew not where.

"Smile!" her husband commanded. "Look at me while I talk to you."

She smiled and looked. And had no idea what he said to her, his eyes warm on hers.

"Brave girl." She heard his words at last. "It will become easier, my love. You do not think so now, but it will. I promise." He raised her hand and held it to his lips.

She felt intense hatred for him. He had caused this. She should be there in the other box with her betrothed, radiant with the expectation of her coming nuptials. This man had seen to it that that dream was shattered. To be replaced by this.

Samantha leaned close to say something to her. She was flushed and bright-eyed and looked very unhappy, Jennifer thought. Poor Sam. All this must be ruining her Season too.

And then, as the play began and she turned her attention at last and gratefully to the stage, she heard the echo of Lionel's laugh. Was he too masking heartache with laughter? she wondered.

Oh, Lionel. Lionel.

"There. You see?" her husband said hours later when they were in the carriage on the way home—Lord Francis had escorted Aunt Agatha and Samantha—"it is all safely in the past. You carried it off wonderfully well."

She set her head back against the cushions of the carriage and closed her eyes. "Gabriel," she asked quietly, "why did you do it? Could you not have simply asked me and if I had said no accepted defeat? Why the letter? I was in the ballroom when it was read, surrounded by half the *ton*. You cannot imagine the horror and humiliation. How could you have done that to me?"

He did not touch her. There was a short silence.

"I know nothing of the letter," he said. "I did not write it or have it written or send it. Someone else did so, knowing that it would be easily believed in light of other things that had happened between us."

"I suppose," she said wearily, "that it was not you who kissed me in full view of everyone at the Velgards' costume ball either? And that you did not deliberately kiss me there instead of out on the balcony or not at all?"

He did not answer.

"It does not matter anyway, does it?" she said. "We are married and I am halfway to being respectable again and there is no point in hankering after what is gone forever."

"Kersey?" he said. "The time may come when you will realize you had a narrow escape from him, Jennifer."

She could not speak for a while. Her teeth were clamped together. "I cannot command anything, can I?" she said. "I would ask you, Gabriel, I would beg you please never to mention his name to me again. If there is one shred of decency in you, do that for me."

They traveled the rest of the way to Grosvenor Square in silence. And entered the house and ascended the stairs together in silence. He stopped outside her dressing room door. The door was ajar and there was light within. Her maid was in there, waiting for her.

"I will join you shortly," he said, bowing over her hand.

"Oh, yes, I have no doubt of that," she said, her voice bitter, knowing that she would be wiser to keep her mouth shut. "It is what you have waited for, is it not? But not really for very long at all. You have arranged all with admirable speed."

She wondered as he set his hands behind him and regarded her quietly if he would break the promise he had made to her yesterday morning. She wondered if he would cuff her. Or if he would set about a more ordered chastisement. She would have no recourse. She was his property. And she had provoked him.

"Yes," he said quietly, "it is what I have wanted. I will be with you shortly, Jennifer, to make love to you."

And there. As she stepped inside her dressing room as he pushed the door open for her, her stomach churned quite as painfully as her face would have done if he had given her the back of his hand. He had put it into words and terrified her.

She heartily despised herself.

Her maid, she saw, had set out her best nightgown and was smiling knowingly at her.

Chapter 14

It had not by any means been an easy day. He still could not quite digest the fact that he was married. The evening had been a dreadful ordeal. He had had to force himself through this twice now, facing the *ton*, refusing to hide from them, daring them to cut him. Except that this time it had been worse because this time an innocent was involved with him, and loss of reputation was always worse for a woman than for a man.

Kersey had basked in the situation at the theater. He had looked tragic and brave and had been gravely attentive to Miss Chisley. He had laughed once early in the evening, seemed to realize that gaity was not appropriate to the image he wished to project, and had not laughed again. Far from being embarrassed at the ending of his betrothal, he was cleverly enlisting the sympathy of the *ton*.

It would be the greatest pleasure in the world to kill him.

But it was his wedding night, the Earl of Thornhill reminded himself after he had dismissed his valet. And it was difficult to face, much as he wanted her. She hated him. She had not made any secret of that. It was going to feel like violation, like rape. And yet it was something that had to happen. The only chance either of them had for a measure of contentment in their future was somehow to make something normal out of their marriage.

Her dressing room was empty and in darkness. He passed through it, tapped on the door into her bedchamber, and opened it. His wife's room. It felt strange to know that this empty room in his house was now his wife's.

She was not in bed. She was standing facing the fireplace, looking down into it though there was no fire. She wore a white, lace-trimmed nightgown. Her hair was loose and hung heavy and shining to her waist. He had hoped she would not braid it or try to stuff it beneath a nightcap. She did not turn, though she must have heard his tap and the opening of the door. Her shoulders hunched slightly.

Oh, Lord, he thought, he wanted her. But the knowledge made him feel guilty, though she was his wife and though he fully intended to have her. It should not be so easy for him. He was the guilty one. For her this would be the culmination of all the horrors that had happened to her in the past two days. Except that he knew one small fact about her that might give him a thread of hope. She responded to his physical presence. Slightly and unwillingly, perhaps, but quite unmistakably. She had kissed him in the carriage this morning just as he had kissed her.

"Jennifer." He had stepped up close behind her but found it difficult to touch her.

She turned and looked at him with a pale, set, defiant face. "Yes," she said. "I am here. I am yours. You will find, I believe, that I know my duty and will perform it without protest."

Lord!

"And without enjoyment," he said.

"Enjoyment?" Color flooded her face, but he saw immediately that it had been brought there more by anger than by embarrassment. She spoke the next words slowly and distinctly. "You are the wrong man to bring me that, my lord Gabriel."

He set his hands on her shoulders, felt the tension there, and massaged them with his hands. "This will not do," he said. "This anger and this bitterness. They are understandable though I am not as guilty as you believe me to be. But they will only bring you intense unhappiness, Jennifer, and perhaps even destroy you."

"You have done that already," she said.

"Perhaps." He moved his hands in and worked at the taut muscles of her neck. "But I have married you and I am seeing to it that you are not cut off permanently from the people of your own class. And I intend to be gentle with you. Meet me halfway. I am not the man of your choice. You believe that I have trapped you into marriage and you are partly right. But like it or not, you are in the marriage. For life. I cannot give you happiness unless you are prepared to receive it. Don't close your life to it merely in order to punish me."

"I know what is going to happen on that bed," she said, her face pale and set again. She had not given an inch. His massaging hands had met nothing but resistance. "I know just how it is done though it has never been done to me before. Do it, please. Get it over with and leave me to sleep. I am tired."

Deliberately defiant and rather vulgar words, which she could not possibly have spoken just two days ago.

He lowered his head and opened his mouth over hers.

He could feel her lips trembling. They were quite unresponsive, but she did not pull away. He slid one of his arms about her shoulders and the other about her waist and drew her against him. And felt for the first time the slimness of her long legs against his own and her curves against his body. Her full breasts pressed to his chest. *Do it, please. Get it over with* . . . His body clamored to be allowed to give it to her just as she wanted it. His mind ruthlessly imposed control.

He kissed her gently, moving his mouth in a soft, warm caress over her closed lips until the tautness started to go and she leaned into him and her lips relaxed. He licked them lightly with the tip of his tongue, tested the seam of her lips and found it relaxed, prodded through, and licked at the soft moist flesh inside.

Her hands, he realized, had moved up and were gripping the satin collar of his brocaded dressing gown almost at the neck.

He ran his tongue along her teeth until they parted, and then eased it inward. She made a sound in her throat. He took his mouth from hers and kissed her eyes, her temples, her jaw, her chin, her throat. He found fine lace trimming in his way. He kissed her mouth again and found her lips parted.

Her hands, he noticed, were flat on his shoulders, gripping tightly.

He kissed her and opened the buttons of her nightgown. He slipped his hands inside to the warm silky skin of her shoulders and found the tightness gone from her muscles. He moved his hands down over the sides of her breasts and beneath them. He felt suddenly weak at the knees.

But she drew a sharp breath, jerked her head back away from his, and stared at him with wide eyes.

"Beautiful," he murmured to her, gazing back at her through half-closed eyes. "Beautiful, my wife." He stilled his hands. "Kiss me."

She was breathing in jerky gasps, but she brought her mouth obediently back to his. He rather thought that he might have bruises on his shoulders with the imprints of her fingers in the morning.

He stroked her breasts lightly as his tongue circled about hers. He touched his thumbs to her nipples and found them hard and peaked. She gasped, drawing cool air in about his tongue. Lord, he thought, he could not wait. He wanted to be inside her now. He wanted to be thrusting mindlessly toward release. But he needed his mind. Quite desperately. Take her now like a heedless, dominant male and he might forever kill any faint chance they had for some sort of amiable marriage.

"Come." He withdrew his hands from inside her night-gown and set one arm about her waist. "I think we had better lie down on the bed."

"Yes," she said, looking at it as if it were the executioner's block.

He kept his arm about her waist while he blew out the three candles that stood on the nightstand beside her bed. Then he turned her in the darkness, slid his hands beneath the shoulders of her nightgown again, and lifted away the fabric—off her shoulders, down her arms. It slid to the floor. She made a sound rather like a moan and was silent again.

"Lie down," he told her, edging her back onto the bed. He removed his dressing gown and dropped it to the floor before joining her there.

She was rigid again.

"I am going to love you, Jennifer," he told her, sliding an arm beneath her shoulders and turning her onto her side against him, "not punish or humiliate you. Love in its physical form can be very beautiful." He took her mouth with his again. Could it? He had only ever performed this act to relieve a physical craving. It had only ever been intensely satisfying.

She was incredibly beautiful. He explored her body lightly with his free hand, learning the shape and feel of her naked. And this was not for one night only or for as long as he cared to employ her. This was forever. She was his wife. He would plant his seed in her. She would bear his children. They would grow old together. Strangely, there was nothing frightening in the thought.

"My love," he found himself whispering against her mouth. "My love."

He would not touch her where he most wanted to touch her. Not with his hand. Not yet. She was only just beginning to relax again and accept the fact that the marriage act—for him, at least—involved nakedness and the touching and caressing of every part that modesty had kept hidden through her life. He sensed that he must wait for the more intimate and ultimately more pleasurable touches of full foreplay.

He turned her onto her back and lifted himself over her. He nudged his knees between her thighs and she opened them without further bidding. She was relaxed, acquiescent, heated. He slid his hands beneath her, positioned himself carefully, and mounted her slowly but steadily, moving without pausing beyond the unfamiliar barrier of virginity, though he felt her sudden tension and gasp of pain and panic, until his full length was embedded in her. He held still there, waiting for her body to master the shock of being penetrated for the first time.

God! Dear God in heaven, the urge to let go and to drive on with the act was almost overpowering. He clenched his teeth hard and pressed his face into her hair. She had raised her knees and slid her feet up the bed. He could feel the slim length of her legs against his own. Her body beneath his was soft and warm and intensely feminine.

He drew a few steadying breaths and lifted his weight onto his elbows. His eyes had become accustomed to the darkness and he could see that she lay with her eyes closed, her head thrown back on the pillow, her mouth slightly open.

Lord, he thought, watching her face as he withdrew slowly and as slowly he sheathed himself in her again, she was enjoying it. He watched her as he loved her with steady, rhythmic strokes. He would continue the rhythm, he decided, feeling her inner muscles begin to clench involuntarily about him, until she had come to full pleasure. Even if it took another half hour.

And then she opened her eyes. For one moment, so brief that he thought afterward he might have imagined it, they were heavy with passion. Then they were fully open and even in the darkness he could see them fill with tears and he could see the tears spill over. With his body he could feel her first sob even before it became sound. He knew that she was fighting to control both tears and sobs. But she failed miserably.

He closed his own eyes and did what he had been fighting not to do for what had seemed like an eternity. He abandoned control and drove into her swiftly and deeply until he felt the blessed spasms of release and his seed sprang in her.

He lowered his weight onto her body and his face into her hair again. Her sobs sounded as if they were tearing her apart.

He moved to her side, disengaging himself from her body, and brought her with him, his arms locked about her. The very best thing he could do for her at the moment, one part of his mind told him, was to leave her alone. That was what she must want more than anything else in the world. But the instinct to comfort was stronger in him. He cradled her in his arms while she wept, murmuring some nonsense into her ear, stroking his fingers through her hair with light fingertips.

When she quieted eventually, he took a corner of the sheet and dried her eyes and his chest with it. Her eyes were closed, he saw. She made no move to pull away from him. When he drew the bedclothes up about her, she seemed even to cuddle closer to him.

He held her, his mind and his heart numb. He should leave. He should give her privacy for the rest of the night. God, how was he going to be able to come back tomorrow night to do this to her all over again? And yet how could he not? What sort of a nightmare of a marriage were they facing?

Tomorrow morning he would tell her everything, he decided. And yet everything would not exonerate him. Far from it. If she knew everything, she would know she had been only a helpless pawn in a game. That she had been of no importance to either of the players—to either Kersey or himself. How would he convince her then that he would make her the figure of primary importance in the rest of his life?

And would it be enough even if he could convince her?

Numbness did not last nearly long enough sometimes, he thought. He must leave. He must not indulge himself like this with the physical pleasure of holding her warm and naked body while his own relaxed into the physical satiety that followed a vigorous sexual encounter. He must leave.

But even as he made the decision he realized that incredibly she was asleep. The physical and emotional exhaustion of two days had caught up with her and she slept snuggled up to his body like a trusting child.

He felt a tickling in his throat and swallowed. He had not cried for so long that he was not sure he would know how to do it. He swallowed again and tried to blink the moisture from his eyes.

She was warm and relaxed and comfortable. And for a moment—just for the merest moment—she did not know where she was. But then she did, and her very first thought was a treacherous one. She was glad he was still holding her. She was glad he had not gone back to his own room, as Aunt Agatha had assured her he would after he had done that to her. He was warm and solid and she could hear his quiet breathing. Strangely and quite unreasonably she felt safe. She would have gone all to pieces if he had left her.

She kept her eyes closed and grief washed over her again. Grief because this was her wedding night yet he was not Lionel. When she had opened her eyes earlier as he was . . . doing that to her, she had . . . what? Expected to see Lionel? Had she kept her eyes closed imagining that it was he making love to her? No, not really. Not even at all. She had firmly shut her mind to Lionel, not invited his image into her marriage bed. But even so . . .

Oh, the reality of it all had hit her at that moment. She was naked on the bed, spread wide, and her body was being used by someone who was not herself. It belonged to him, to be used for the rest of their lives whenever and however he chose to use it. She was no longer in possession of her own body or of her own person. She had felt in that moment all the total and permanent loss of privacy. Even the inside of her body—there—no longer belonged to her.

And yet she had been enjoying it. The amazing and totally

unexpected intimacy of his kiss, the touch of his hands on every part of her body, especially on her breasts, about which she had been self-conscious for several years because they were larger than anyone else's she knew, the feel and smell of his naked body—she had relaxed into the enjoyment of it all. And when he had—well, when he had come inside her, hurting her and then frightening her because she had not thought there would be enough room, and when he had started to move, she had thought she would swoon with the wonder of it.

It was not that she had imagined he was Lionel. It was just that when she had opened her eyes and seen in the darkness that he was not Lionel, but Gabriel, she had felt deep grief. For if she could lose Lionel so cruelly one night and enjoy this just two nights later with the man who had torn her away from him, how could she convince herself that she really loved Lionel? And yet if she did not, then everything she had lived for in the past five years had been an illusion. And if she could be enjoying this with this man, how could she feel moral outrage against him?

She had wept for the weakness of her body and the fickleness of her heart. She had felt all the humiliation and horror of weeping openly while he was still doing that to her, but she had been quite unable to stop herself. She had been at the point of exhaustion.

She had wept because he was not worthy of her liking or her respect. Because he was totally without honor. Because he had cruelly destroyed her and severed her relations with the man she had loved deeply—or perhaps not loved at all—for five years. And because she had enjoyed his two kisses while she was still betrothed to Lionel and was enjoying the deep intimacy of the marriage act with him.

She had wept because her body wanted to love him while her mind and her heart never could. Never.

And yet she was married to him for the rest of her life. She would live with him in the intimacy of daily life unless he chose to give them separate establishments. She would get to know his habits and his preferences and his tastes and perhaps his thoughts just as she now knew Papa's and Samantha's. And she would bear his children. His seed was in her now. He would continue to put more there until she conceived—and she would continue to enjoy the process.

She was a married lady. No longer a virgin. And this was the man who owned her. Not Lionel. Gabriel. He smelled musky, she thought, inhaling slowly and deeply. And sweaty. He smelled wonderfully masculine. She tipped her head back suddenly, alerted perhaps by a change in his breathing. His dark eyes were looking back into hers.

He lifted one hand and stroked the backs of his fingers over her temple. "I am so very sorry, my dear," he said softly. "I know the words are woefully inadequate, but they are the best I can do. It is a damnable mess I have got you into, but there is only one way out. We can only go forward and try to make something workable out of what seems impossible tonight."

She stared at him, remembering the Chisleys' garden and the library and Lady Bromley's orchard. Remembering that she had liked him.

"Can you try?" he asked. "Will you try?"

She really had no choice. She really did not. "I cannot." She closed her eyes. "Gabriel, I cannot bear the thought of you touching your father's wife as you have touched me tonight. I cannot bear the thought that somewhere in Europe you have a child who is both your daughter and your half-sister. It is horrible and obscene. I cannot bear it."

She tried to pull away from him, but his arms tightened. She felt horrified suddenly, and dirty, remembering that she had enjoyed what he did to her.

"Listen to me," he said, his voice stern. "That I am guilty of one offense does not mean that I am therefore guilty of every offense of which I have been accused. You believed me once, Jennifer. I have never touched my stepmother unlawfully. I am not the father of her child. I did not abandon her. I took her away because she was miserable and afraid and desperate. I took her because my father might have done her harm and because the blackguard who had impregn— well, who had impregnated her had taken himself off as soon as it appeared that his fun might bear consequences and then denied all association with her. I took her away to a place where she could bear her child in peace and comfort, and I left her there because she had discovered that it was a place where she could start again and perhaps find respectability and even happiness."

She pressed her face against his chest. She was so naive. She had always believed everything he had told her, despite warnings, despite all the evidence against him. She was believing him now.

"Tomorrow," he said, "we will write to her, Jennifer. Both of us. You will ask for the truth and I will beg her to tell it. You may read my letter before I send it. If that will not satisfy you, I will take you to Switzerland after I have reestablished you here with the *ton*. You will believe it when you see her—and when you see her blond, blue-eyed daughter. Catherine is as dark as I am."

"You do not need to take me or to write," she said. "If you say it is so, I will believe you." Her voice was toneless, but she knew she spoke the truth. If he said it, God help her, she would believe him. She wanted so very, very badly to believe him. The realization startled and rather frightened her.

"No," he said quietly. "We will write so that you will feel not a shadow of a doubt. Of that at least I am not guilty. Just as I am not guilty of writing that letter. The other things, yes, to my shame. I wanted to end your betrothal. I wanted to charm or force you into it. I even went as far as compromising you with that kiss. But I could not have been so wantonly cruel as to write that letter and ensure that it fell into the wrong hands on just that occasion. I could not have done that to you."

The temptation to believe him was strong. But if not he, then who? There was no one else. It would make no sense.

"I think you are right," she said, drawing her head back and looking at him in the darkness again. "I think we have to go on and just hope that time will bring some healing, some—well, something. I think you are right. I am so tired of hating."

His fingers, feathering through her hair, felt soothing. "After a week or two of appearances here," he said, "I will take you to Chalcote, my dear. You will like it there, I believe. There we can learn to be comfortable together."

"Chalcote," she said. "Is that not near Highmoor House?"

"Yes." His hand stilled for a moment. "Just a few miles away."

"That is where—" she said, and broke off. That was where

Lionel's uncle lived. That was where Lionel had spent the spring two years ago when she should have been making her come-out and when they should have become officially engaged.

"Yes," he said, seeming to read her thoughts. "Two years ago. Just before I went north to spend the summer with my father. I did not spend the summer as it happened. I left within the month with my stepmother."

She closed her eyes. "Chalcote," she said. "I want to go there. Perhaps there I can forget. Perhaps there we can make something of this marriage after all, Gabriel."

She was giving in to the enemy again. She had no moral fiber at all, she believed. But he had not done that horrible thing with his stepmother. She believed him on that. And he said he had not written that letter. It made no sense, but he was adamant about it while admitting everything else.

Something was nagging at her consciousness. Something that was almost there but not quite. Something that maddeningly refused to present itself to her conscious mind for consideration.

"Jennifer," her husband was saying, "whether you wish it or not, I will be claiming my marital rights each night. I believe it is essential to any hope we have for the future. But only once each night. If I desire you more than once, you will have the right to refuse the second and any succeeding time."

She swallowed and rested her forehead against his chest.

"I desire you now," he said.

She could say no. He was giving her that freedom. That power. She had no idea how long they had slept. But it was still dark. If she wished, she could spend the rest of the night alone. She could have herself back to herself at least until tomorrow night.

She tipped up her face once more. "Then have me," she said. "I am your wife."

She could feel as soon as he drew her close against his length and kissed her that he was very ready for her again. She felt a deep throbbing where she was already sore and wanted him there once more.

She closed her mind to the knowledge that he was the wrong man and that if she had any firm moral convictions at all, she would be fighting with everything she had against this powerful physical attraction she had always felt for him.

"My love," he whispered against her mouth.

She wondered if he meant it.

Chapter 15

He sat down alone to breakfast. He was considerably later than usual. Although his servants held to their usual impassive expressions, he could almost imagine the smirks and knowing looks they exchanged behind his back. He felt almost embarrassed.

Jennifer had been deeply asleep when he woke up, disoriented, her body pressed to his and entwined with his. It had taken him several minutes to free himself and remove himself from her bed without waking her. Indeed, she must have been deeply asleep not to have woken.

He had covered her to the chin before picking up his dressing gown and going through her dressing room to his. He had been afraid that the chill of the morning and the removal of his body heat would waken her. Or perhaps that strange embarrassment he felt had caused him to cover her so that her maid would not realize that she slept naked. Her maid was going to discover that fact of her mistress's marriage sooner or later anyway.

The post had been delivered already. A small pile of letters was stacked neatly beside his place a the breakfast table, and even a few invitations, he could see, if he was not mistaken. That at least was surprising. He had thought the best he could do was to take Jennifer to those entertainments for which he had already received invitations before the scandal, and to places, like the park and the theater, for which he needed no invitation at all.

He shuffled through the pile and stopped abruptly at one letter. Good Lord, what a strange, strange coincidence. It was a letter from Catherine, the first he had received since his return. He picked it up eagerly, wondering if there was anything in it that might set Jennifer's mind at rest while they waited several weeks, perhaps a few months, for a reply to the letters they would write this morning—or perhaps this afternoon. She had said last night that she believed him, but he could feel the confusion of her mind. He knew that there was a large element of doubt mixed in with the belief, and the fear that he was making her into his dupe.

He read carefully and smiled to himself as he set the letter down and ate his breakfast before tackling the rest of the pile or reading his newspaper.

An hour later he wandered back upstairs, even though this was the time of day he usually spent at White's and there was nothing stopping him from going there today. Indeed, he would probably have to endure merciless teasing and some ribaldry from a few friends and acquaintances if he did not go.

He went into his dressing room, opened the door quietly into his wife's to find it empty, opened the door even more quietly into her bedchamber, and went in.

She was still sleeping, the covers pushed down to her waist. Her face was half buried in the pillow he had used, one hand pushed beneath it. Her hair, tangled and gloriously rich in color, acted as a kind of blanket but it could not totally hide the creaminess of her skin and the full shapeliness of the breast that was not hidden against the mattress.

Her maid, he noted ruefully, had been in already. There was a cup of chocolate on the nightstand, looking as if it was probably cold. Well, his servants could at least be thoroughly satisfied now that the marriage of their earl and countess had been consummated.

He was glad that she was sleeping so long and so deeply. She must have been totally exhausted in every way. He felt cautiously hopeful this morning. Hopeful that something might be made of the marriage that neither of them had either wanted or expected. She was tired of hating, she had said, though two days ago she had sworn to hate him for the rest of her life. And though she had wept while he was consummating their marriage, doubtless because he was not Kersey, she had allowed him to have her a second time. He had given her the freedom to refuse and she had used that freedom to say yes.

He had loved her with slow thoroughness, and her body had responded, first with relaxation, and then with pleasure. She had said nothing and had kept her eyes closed and her body still. She had kept her arms on the bed at her sides. But he had read the signs of increased body heat and deeper breathing and tautened muscles giving place again to relaxation and a sighing of expelled breath just before he released into her.

There was pleasure to be found together in bed. It was not everything. It was not even perhaps very much when they must live together out of bed all day. But it was something. Perhaps a physical tenderness would in time translate into emotional contentment.

She stirred, stretching in a manner that caused an immediate tightening in his groin. He wondered if he should turn and tiptoe from the room before she awoke fully, but he stayed where he was, watching her. He had called her his love more than once last night while in the process of making love to her. He had not done so deliberately. It had not been part of his plan to show her some tenderness. The words had been spontaneous. Had he meant them? He had never used them to any mistress or casual amour.

Was she his love?

And then she rolled over onto her back, stretched again, her palms pushing against the headboard of the bed, and opened her eyes. Her head turned sharply as she became aware of him standing there.

God, but she was magnificent. His eyes confirmed what his body had felt during the night. He had an unexpected flashing image of his child suckling at one of those breasts. "Good morning, my dear," he said.

He could almost see her mind registering the fact that he was fully dressed while she was naked—and exposed to the waist with her arms raised above her head. She lowered them hastily and jerked the bedcovers up to her chin. She colored rosily. He found the gesture of exaggerated modesty curiously endearing. He had been beneath those covers with her all night and they had twice been as intimate together as man and woman can be.

"Good morning, my l-lor—Gabriel," she said. "What time is it?"

"I believe it lacks a little of noon," he said. He smiled. "But only a very little."

Her eyes widened. "I never sleep late," she said.

"You have never before had a wedding night," he said, and

watched her flush deepen. "I have something to show you," he said. "Will you do me the honor of joining me at the breakfast table in half an hour?"

"Do I have a choice?" she asked.

Ah, the night and the physical union and sexual pleasure it had brought them both had not healed many breaches after all. Perhaps none.

"Yes," he said. "You may eat alone if you wish, my dear. Your days may be almost entirely your own, if you so choose, and your nights too except for the one use of my rights I have told you I will insist upon. You are not my prisoner, Jennifer. Only my wife."

He could hear her drawing breath. "Half an hour?" she said.

"I will ring for your maid as I go back through your dressing room," he said. He took a step forward and leaned over her to kiss her fully and somewhat lingeringly on the mouth. "Thank you for the free gift of yourself you made me last night. It was more precious to me than jewels." He had a hand on either side of her head on the pillow.

"I am your wife," she said.

"Yes." He gazed into her eyes. "Are you sore this morning? It was perhaps selfish of me, even with your permission, to use you a second time when your body was newly opened."

He did not believe he was trying to shock her. He did not know what his motive was. To establish some intimacy between them, perhaps, that was not just physical. He felt the strange need to be able to talk with her on even the most intimate of topics. He felt the need for—for a marriage.

"Gabriel." She touched her fingertips to his cheek as he remembered her doing in Lady Bromley's orchard, and then closed her eyes and bit her lip. "Nothing. It does not matter. No, I am not sore." She laughed a little but did not open her eyes. "I suppose I could have used it as an excuse to be free of you tonight and perhaps tomorrow night, could I not? I do not want to be free of you. I cannot be, and I do not want the illusion of freedom. I want to know that this is my life forever after. I want to accustom myself to the knowledge and to the fact. I can only go forward. You were quite right about that. Make me feel married to you, then. Take me as often as you wish, night or day. I want to forget how and why we came together and what I left behind. Make me forget. You can, you know. I believe you must have realized that I find you attractive and always have."

There was enough in her words to chill him for an eternity and to warm him for as long a time. He stood up and she opened her eyes.

"Yes." He nodded. "We are going to fall in love, Jennifer. We are going to be happy together despite the seemingly insuperable odds. I promise you." He turned and made his way through her dressing room, pulling on the bell rope as he did so, and back to his own. His heart was heavy—and soaring with hope.

Although she pulled her nightgown back on before going through into her dressing room, she knew that her maid must have seen her naked in bed. She felt intensely embarrassed and could feel herself flush hotly when her maid came bustling into the dressing room carrying a pitcher of steaming water.

Jennifer made her way down the stairs half an hour later, her hair neatly dressed, her morning gown covering her modestly. In some ways it was hard to believe that what had happened during the night had really happened at all, except that even with her previous knowledge and what Aunt Agatha had told her, she could not possibly have dreamed such intimacy and such sensations. And she could feel that it had happened. She was sore, despite what she had told him, but it was not a totally unpleasant feeling.

She was a married lady. She was married to Gabriel, Earl of Thornhill. She drew a deep breath as the footman at whom she had smiled warmly opened the door into what she assumed must be the breakfast room. What must he think, he and all the other servants, of the fact that she was coming down to breakfast well after noon? They would think that she had been kept busy by her bridegroom through much of the night and had caught up with her sleep during the morning, that was what. And they would not be far wrong.

She braced herself for her sight of him again. He really must be the devil or a wizard of some sort. When she could not see him, she could keep her mind partly sane and know him for who and what he was. And yet when she saw him, and especially when he was close to her . . . Well, she had understated the case when she had told him that she found him at-

tractive. She was very much afraid that her body was beginning to crave his and that her mind was being dragged along
with it.

And yet these feelings were not wholly unwelcome, she
thought, as she entered the room and he hurried toward her
from where he had been standing before a window to take her
hand and raise it to his lips. Something deep inside her—close
to where twice last night he had shared her body—somer-
saulted and she yearned to forget everything and let herself
fall in love with him, mind and soul as well as body. With her
body she already loved him, she realized, but she refused to
allow her mind to ask her how it could be so when for five
years she had loved another.

No, these half unwilling feelings for him were not unwelcome. She must make the best of the life she had been forced
into—by him. The rest of her life, long or short, was all she
would ever have, after all.

"Come and sit down," he said, leading her to the place next
to the head of the table, and seating her. He signaled to the
butler to bring her the hot dishes and to fill her coffee cup.
"Will you be pleased to know that we have received invitations this morning to a ball, a concert, and a rout? Addressed
to the Earl and Countess of Thornhill, by the way. News travels faster than light in London during the Season."

Each morning usually brought a dizzying number of invitations. Three was a very paltry number. But it was certainly
three more than she had expected—or wanted.

"I would prefer to go home to Chalcote," she said, deliberately calling it home, accustoming her mind to the fact that it
really was home now because it was his and she was his wife.

"Soon." He covered her hand on the table with his. "We
will be seen in all the right places for a week first. As much as
anything, I have a mind to show you off and to throw every
other male in London into the doldrums because you are mine
and beyond anyone else's reach."

He smiled and looked almost boyish in his lightheartedness.
But he had made a mistake to remind her of the obsession to
have her to himself that was responsible for her being here
now with him. Could there be any kinship between obsession
and love? Could he ever love her? He had promised earlier in
her bedchamber that they would fall in love. Not she, but they.

Did he not love her yet, then? It was so hard to understand why he had acted as he had.

"No," he said very quietly after signaling the butler to leave, "don't look haunted again. I said the wrong thing, did I not? I have a letter to show you when you have finished eating. I think you will be a little happier after you have read it."

She was not hungry. She made to push her plate away from her but his voice stopped her.

"Eat every mouthful," he said. "We will sit here until you have done so. You might have eaten—or not eaten—alone, Jennifer, but you agreed to allow me to join you here. Now you must endure my playing tyrant. You are not going to make yourself ill from lack of food."

She picked up her knife and fork and ate her way doggedly through the food she had allowed the butler to put on her plate. No, she was not going to let it happen either. She was not going to present a wan, skeletal aspect to the world. And if her womb was to house his child for nine months, as it probably would soon, she would make it a warm and welcoming and well-fed place. It would be her child too.

"There," she said, looking up at him with some defiance when she was finished. "Are you satisfied?"

He was smiling at her with what looked to be affection as well as amusement. He chuckled. "Are you planning always to be so obedient?" he asked. "Life with you might just be paradise, my love. I want you to read this letter, if you will. Aloud. It arrived just this morning." He handed her a sheet of paper.

It was covered with closely spaced writing in an elegant hand. *My dearest Gabriel,* she read. Her eyes flew down the page to the signature. *Catherine.* His stepmother!

"Aloud, please," he said again.

" 'My dearest Gabriel,' " she read in a monotone after drawing a deep breath, " 'Time flies along so fast. I fully intended to send a letter speeding after you within a few days of your departure. Forgive the delay. I wanted—and want—to thank you in a more permanent fashion than the words I have already spoken to you for all you have done for me when you might with perfect justification have turned your back on me. I want to thank you for giving me and Eliza more than a year of your life. I will not forget your sacrifice, my dear.' "

Jennifer looked up at him. He was watching her with eyes that seemed to burn.

" 'I dread to think what would have happened to me without your kindness and protection,' " she continued. " 'I know I do not deserve the happiness I feel in this lovely home you found for me, in this beautiful country, in my daughter, and—oh, yes, Gabriel—in the new love I have found, which quite puts into the shade the old love. You said it would happen to me and it has. He is Count Ernst Moritz. I do not believe you met him, though I was acquainted with him before you left. He is very close to a declaration. My woman's intuition assures me of it! But more of that in another letter. This is to be a letter of thanks.

" 'Gabriel, I was so very foolish. I owed your father loyalty, for he was never harsh with me. I was seduced by youth and beauty and a charm that proved selfish and heartless. But no matter, I have Eliza and so I would not change the past. She is so very fair and so wonderfully blue-eyed. It is, perhaps, a pity that she so resembles her father, but I can console myself with the certain knowledge that she will be a great beauty.

" 'I ramble. Has Society accepted you back, Gabriel? I should have insisted, perhaps, that you allow me to announce the truth so that your name would be cleared. I hope at least that HE is not in town this Season. Do not seek revenge if he is. He has given me Eliza and so I was the winner of that encounter. Seek love for yourself, my dear. I cannot think of anyone who more deserves it—though I do not believe the woman exists who deserves you.

" 'I grow sentimental. And I run out of paper! Write to me. I miss your good sense and your cheerfulness. I remain your affectionate Catherine.' "

Jennifer folded the letter carefully back into its original folds and slid it across the table to her husband. She did not look at him.

"Well?" he said. It seemed almost as if there was anxiety in his voice. Perhaps there was.

She looked up at him. "I told you last night that I believed you," she said.

"But you had doubts." His thumb played with the corner of the letter. "Do you have any now?"

She shook her head. "Is he in town?" she asked. "The child's father?"

His hand stilled. She wondered if she imagined that his whole body tensed. He shook his head, but she was not sure if it was a denial or a refusal to discuss the matter. He said nothing.

"I am glad," she said, "that she is happy, that good has come out of evil." His stepmother must have thought that the world had come to an end when she found herself with child by a lover and when that lover cruelly abandoned her though she loved him. She must have wanted to die. At Chalcote. Two years ago. But good had come of it. There was the blond and blue-eyed Elizabeth and the new home and country. And the new beau. Perhaps good would come out of the ending of her world too, she thought.

"Yes," he said. "How would we live with ourselves if we could not feel the assurances that that does happen?"

She wanted to comfort him, Jennifer realized suddenly. She wanted to reach out to touch his hand and to assure him that though he had done a terrible thing, all would be well after all. Until she remembered everything she had lost. Lionel—oh, dear God, Lionel. Her reputation. She remembered that humiliating and painful caning her father had given her just three evenings ago. No, he did not deserve to be forgiven so easily or so soon.

"Will you come with me to the library to write our letters after all?" he asked. "I would like you to introduce yourself to Catherine, and I would like to boast about you and tell her what a fortunate fellow I am."

"Yes." She got to her feet. Catherine had a blond, blue-eyed child. Her own children might have been blond and blue-eyed. But now they would probably have dark hair and dark eyes. She wanted children, she realized, even if they could not be Lionel's. Even if they must be Gabriel's. She hoped she would bear him a son first. She wanted a son.

Something nagged at the edges of her consciousness again as he tucked her arm through his and led her in the direction of the library. She had the same feeling as she had had last night that there was something there just waiting to leap into her conscious mind. But maddeningly it evaded capture.

*   *   *

Samantha had had a night of broken sleep. Her heart went out to her cousin and the wedding night she was now spending with the man they had called the devil from the first. She wondered with a shudder if he would mistreat Jenny. Surely a man who was capable of such ruthless cruelty as the sending of that letter to Jenny's betrothal ball was incapable of tenderness.

Poor Jenny. Samantha felt terrible guilt for listening with such eager hope to Lionel's protestations of regard and for the elation she had felt at first when she had realized that the betrothal was at an end—an elation that had got all nightmarishly mingled up with horror. Poor Jenny had suffered dreadfully—and innocently, it seemed. First the exposure at the ball, then the beating from Uncle Gerald. He had been persuaded not to send out for a whip, but she and Aunt Aggy had listened at the library door after they had been dismissed. Before fleeing in a panic, Samantha had heard both his command that Jenny bend over the desk and grip its far edge and the first swish of his cane.

And now—and now perhaps at this very moment that man, Lord Thornhill, was subjecting poor Jenny to unknown indignities. Samantha was not really sure what happened in a marriage bed, but whatever it was would be dreadful indeed with a man one had been forced into marrying.

But not all of Samantha's sleepless thoughts were of her cousin. Some were of the evening just past and the dreadful pain she had felt at seeing Lionel with Horatia Chisley. It was worse—far worse—than seeing him with Jenny had been. At least that had been an attachment that had preceded his acquaintance with her and one that he was trapped in. And at least Jenny was someone she loved dearly. Seeing him with Miss Chisley felt like a dreadful betrayal.

Except that he could not possibly show his true feelings just yet. It would be in dreadfully bad taste. He could not sever his relationship with Jenny one day and escort her cousin to the theater two days later. Not under the circumstances of that severance, anyway. He would have to wait a while. Perhaps a few weeks. Or a month. Or—heaven forbid—he might feel honor-bound to stay away from her for the rest of the Season and start afresh next year.

He would tell her. He would seek her out and make some arrangement with her. She must be patient. She must agree with what he had decided. He was so much older than she— seven years. Sometimes she felt her youth as a dreadful handicap. Sometimes she felt that she knew nothing. She would leave it to Lionel to be wise.

He would let her know. He would arrange a meeting with her somehow at Lady Truscott's ball tomorrow night.

The thought was soothing. And perhaps if the Earl of Thornhill had wanted Jenny so very badly, he would treat her kindly after all. Perhaps all would be well with Jenny. And she would not have been happy for long with Lionel. Sooner or later she would have discovered that he had felt trapped into marrying her by a promise he had made when he was too young to know quite what he was doing. He had been two years older than Samantha was now.

Tomorrow she would talk with him. He would arrange it.

She slept, comforted by the thought.

Chapter 16

The Earl of Thornhill and his new countess had appeared at the theater the night before and had driven in the park this afternoon, both times accompanied by the eminently respectable Lady Brill and by Miss Samantha Newman, cousin of the countess and one of the more lovely of the new faces of the Season.

On both occasions the newly married couple sat as close as propriety would allow, her hand on his arm, his hand covering hers. And on both ocasions they smiled and looked happy. Almost radiantly so, the more kindly disposed were inclined to say. One sour dowager christened them the hussy and the rogue, and her names for them were whispered about and nodded over and chuckled at.

And yet there was something almost romantic about the description. And something almost romantic—though shockingly improper—about the reckless manner in which the earl had wooed and won his bride. Had they fled the capital in shame and humiliation, as they really ought to have done out of deference to decency, they would doubtless have been universally condemned, and the word *romance* would not have occurred to even the most fanciful of minds.

But they had not fled. And they were undoubtedly a young and an extraordinarily handsome pair. And titled and fashionable and wealthy. And apparently happy with what they had so shamelessly accomplished.

Yes, the *ton* whispered with collective reluctance, there was certainly something romantic about the new marriage. They had undoubtedly been extremely naughty and should by rights be expelled from decent society for life. But even the *ton*, jaded as it was as an entity, recognized that young

love did sometimes triumph. And the *ton* felt a collective
envy to go along with the reluctance.

The *ton* was prepared—with great caution and many reser-
vations—to begin to take the Earl and Countess of Thornhill
back to its collective bosom.

Though there was, of course, the fact that the earl had
been in deep disgrace even before this scandal.

And there was the fact that Viscount Kersey was nursing a
broken heart and was being very brave about it. One might
have expected that the poor gentleman would disappear to
the country or even overseas to avoid the embarrassment of
such public rejection. But he stayed and conducted himself
with quiet dignity in company with other gentlemen and with
a sweet smiling sadness in that of ladies.

The ladies might have been disdainful of any ordinary
gentleman who had been abandoned by his betrothed. But
Lord Kersey, with his blond and shining hair and his bluest
of blue eyes and his very manly figure, could never be an object of scorn. Especially not with that new air of tragic dignity. He could only be an object of maternal pity to older
ladies and one of longing to young ladies and even to many
not so young.

The *ton* was constantly a prey to boredom during the Season. Despite the dizzying round of social pleasures, really
there was much of a sameness about most of them, and one
saw much the same faces wherever one went. Anything even
a little out of the ordinary was pounced upon with well-bred
glee, especially if there was also something a little scandalous about it. What about this strange and fascinating tri-
angle of three such handsome and—yes—romantic figures?
They had all stayed in London. Would Lord Kersey demand
satisfaction of Thornhill? Would the countess regret her decision? Would . . . ? Oh, the possibilities were endless. And
the chance to watch their development was quite irresistible.

Lady Truscott, whose annual ball was never one of the
main squeezes of the Season, was suddenly in the enviable
position of seeing her home and her ballroom become the
arena for the first formal appearance since their marriage of
the Earl and Countess of Thornhill and for the first real encounter of the three protagonists since the scandal broke
three evenings before.

Lady Truscott had the unutterably pleasurable gratification of seeing her ballroom so crammed with guests before the dancing even began that it was positively bursting at the seams, as one portly gentleman was heard to remark. Everyone should be paired with someone else, another wag declared in a voice of fashionable boredom, so that they could arrange to take turns breathing.

Lady Truscott's cup of joy ran over.

"Smile," her husband had commanded her as soon as he handed her out of the carriage. It was a reminder he did not need to give. She had smiled at the theater last night until she had thought her face would crack, and she had smiled in the park this afternoon so steadily that she feared some might think she must be an imbecile. She would smile tonight even though she must expect no partners except Gabriel. Unless they were turned away from the house, of course. She did not believe she would be able to hold her smile if that happened.

She had a horrible memory as she entered the ballroom on her husband's arm of the last time she had been in a ballroom—just three evenings before. It felt like a lifetime ago. In that ballroom she had been betrothed to Lionel. Now she was married to Gabriel. The unreality of it made her feel slightly dizzy.

She was fully aware, as she had been at the theater last night, of the near hush and then the renewed rush of sound when they entered the ballroom. She was less aware of the unusually crowded nature of the ballroom. She smiled warmly up at her husband and looked determinedly about her.

There were hundreds of eyes she might have met. And perhaps she did meet some of them fleetingly, though most of Lady Truscott's guests were too well bred to be caught gawking at her. But the pair of eyes she did consciously meet, across the full width of the ballroom, were those of Viscount Kersey.

Her heart performed a painful somersault and for many frozen and agonized moments she could not look away. Lionel! As handsome and as elegant as ever. Her Lionel. Her love. The dream that had sustained her through five long and dreary and rather lonely years.

And then she wrenched her eyes away and looked down at the hand she had rested on her husband's arm. She was quite unaware, in her distress, of the intense satisfaction the *ton* was drawing from the scene, though none gazed openly.

The earl took her hand in his free one and raised it to his lips. He was, as she expected, smiling at her with an admirable imitation of adoration in his eyes. She felt a strong wave of hatred again and fought not to let it show.

Someone was bowing before her. Someone was willing to acknowledge her. She looked up in surprise and saw those blue eyes at far closer range. He reached for her hand, and she took it from her husband's and set it in his, without realizing quite what she did. He lifted it and placed his lips against the exact spot where her husband's had just been.

He had never before looked at her like this, one part of her mind told her. With such softness and warmth and tenderness. Never. Oh, he never had, though she had yearned for it and told herself that it would happen as soon as their betrothal had been announced or as soon as they were married.

"Ma'am," he said, his voice soft, though she knew that several people around them, apparently involved in other activities and conversations, would hear what he said, "I would like to offer my sincere good wishes on your marriage. You must know that your happiness has always been my chief and my only goal. I hoped that you could find it with me, but I am glad that you have found it even at the expense of my own. You must not feel guilt." His smile was warm and sad. "Only happiness. It is what I wish you for the rest of your life."

He released her hand, bowed deeply to her, turned away rather jerkily, and hurried from the ballroom.

"The devil!" her husband muttered close to her ear. And then his hand was firm at the back of her waist, propelling her forward. "At last. The first set is to be a waltz, I hear. Come, we will dance it."

She wanted nothing more than to flee into the ladies' withdrawing room and hide in its farthest corner. She stepped forward onto the dancing floor, surprised that her legs would obey the command of her brain.

"Put your hand on my shoulder." His voice was almost

harsh as his arm came about her waist and he took her other hand in his. "Now look into my eyes."

She obeyed him woodenly. She rather thought she might entertain the *ton* by fainting in front of them. It was unthinkable.

"Now," he said, "tell me you love me. And when you have done that, smile again."

"I love you," she said.

"Once more." He looked down at her lips. "And with a little more conviction. And then the smile. Your pallor will be understandable under the circumstances, but it might be misconstrued if it continues."

"I love you," she said and smiled at him.

"Good girl. Keep looking into my eyes for a while," he said.

It was ludicrous. Telling him that she loved him, smiling into his eyes, while both of them knew that she was almost fainting from love of another man. Lionel had been so kind and so very—noble about it. She would have expected him to cut her completely for the rest of her life. He had wished her happy. Even at the expense of his own happiness, he wished for hers. Did he not realize that her heart was aching for him?

Except that treacherously, gazing into her husband's face, she felt that physical pull toward him that she always seemed to feel. And looking at his lips, she thought about his way of kissing and the strange effect the touch of his mouth against her own had on her whole body. She always felt it as much in her toes as on her lips. Her smile broadened with amusement despite herself. And despite herself she found herself thinking about last night, their wedding night, and becoming a little breathless at the knowledge that it was to be repeated tonight. Every night, he had said. At least once and sometimes more if he desired it and she permitted it.

And then her thoughts shifted suddenly and unwillingly to three evenings before and the reading of that letter. Lionel had been with his father. He had been absent from the ballroom with his father, no doubt planning with him what they were to do about the intercepted letter. He had walked at his father's side back into the ballroom and up onto the dais, where he had stood quietly while his father read.

He desired only her happiness, he had just said. How could he have done that, then? How could he have exposed her to such cruel treatment? Even if she had been guilty, it would have been ghastly and unusual punishment. They might as well have stripped her and confined her to a pillory and whipped her. She had felt that helpless, that exposed, that hurt. Of course, the whipping—or the caning—had come later in more privacy.

Even assuming that that letter had shocked and hurt Lionel, how could he have acquiesced in what his father had done? How could any gentleman have done such a thing? Especially a gentleman who had just professed to desire her happiness.

He had just made a gesture so noble that she had almost fainted. But was it really so noble? He had not apologized for his cruelty and lack of gallantry. He had merely—he had made himself look like a gallant martyr to everyone who had watched and listened. She had no doubt that a vast number had watched and that a significant number had listened. His words were probably known to every guest in the ballroom by now.

No, she was doing him an injustice. It was Lionel she was thinking of. Lionel. Her love.

"It was kind of him," she said hesitantly. "It was nobly done."

"It was pure theater," her husband said softly. "He won the hearts and the sympathy and the deep respect of all of fashionable society, Jennifer. He put you entirely in the wrong."

"But he wished me happy," she said.

"He does not care the snap of two fingers for you," he said. "There is one love and one love only in Kersey's life— and that is Kersey himself. If you did but know it, Jennifer, you are a thousand times better off with me."

She looked at him, startled, her smile slipping for a moment. There was quiet venom in his voice. She would have expected him to feel some shame at the wrong he had done Lionel. But perhaps it was natural to hate the person one has wronged.

And then it was there, full-blown and startlingly unexpected and unbidden—that thought that had been nudging at her consciousness like a maddening irritant. Lionel had been with his sick uncle at Highmoor House two years ago. Catherine, at nearby Chalcote, had had a secret lover two years ago. She had been seduced by youth and beauty and charm, as she had put it in her letter. Her daughter was blond and blue-eyed—like her father. Gabriel, when she had asked if the child's father was in London now, had not really answered her question. Gabriel hated Lionel.

The tumbling thoughts so terrified her that she tried to push them from her back to the place where they had only irritated her.

"Who was your stepmother's lover? Who is Eliza's father?" Horrified, she heard herself whispering the questions.

"No." His hand tightened somewhat at her waist and he twirled her about a corner and then twirled her again. "This is neither the time nor the place, my love. We are dreadfully much on view."

She felt enormous, knee-weakening relief that he had refused to answer, yet she knew that she would not be able to leave it alone. She knew that when they went home she would ask again and that she would not rest until she had heard his answer. Though she knew what the answer would be. And denied it to herself with panicked vehemence.

The set was almost at an end. But it did not end quite soon enough to save her. Even as the music drew to an unmistakable end, the final thought opened the door into her conscious mind and stepped through.

Gabriel hated Lionel. Because Lionel had been Catherine's lover and had abandoned her and denied paternity of her daughter. *Do not seek revenge*, Catherine had written.

But he had sought it.

And he had achieved it, too.

In the crowded and stuffy and stifling hot ballroom, Jennifer suddenly felt freezing cold right through to her heart.

Lady Brill had been very afraid that her one niece's notoriety would reflect on the other. She had feared that Samantha would have no partners at Lady Truscott's ball. She had been quite prepared to use all the power of her influence in order to prevent the disaster of her niece's being a wallflower. The situation might well be irreversible if it once happened. And so Samantha, just like Jennifer, was instructed as soon as she stepped from her uncle's carriage to smile.

But Aunt Agatha need not have worried. Her usual court was about her almost before she had settled in one spot inside the ballroom and she had promised the first three sets. Even some gentlemen who did not normally crowd about her did so this evening. Samantha guessed that she was somehow benefiting from Jennifer's disgrace. Perhaps a few of them hoped that she would say something to feed their thirst for gossip.

She smiled and danced and chattered to gentlemen and to other young ladies of her acquaintance. And she noted with pleased satisfaction that Jenny was not being shunned but that she danced each set. But she could not feel happy. She had witnessed the incredible spectacle of Lionel crossing the ballroom—he had not walked around the edge of the dancing floor as people usually did but right across its emptiness—and kissing Jenny's hand and saying something to her and bowing to her and then hurrying from the room.

While her heart had gone out to him for his courage and nobility in doing something so very difficult to do, the scene had also depressed her. He truly cared for her. She heard those words or words to that effect all about her as people discussed the incident.

Perhaps Lionel had loved Jenny after all.

She watched unhappily for his return to the ballroom and felt mortally depressed at the strong possibility that he had left the house. But he had not. During the second set he returned. He spoke with a group of ladies and danced the third set with one of them.

Samantha waited for him to approach her. Or if not that, for him at least to glance at her. For some sort of signal to pass. Surely he would give some sign. A smile, perhaps. An inclination of the head. Some private promise that he would speak with her openly at a more opportune time.

But there was nothing. He was being very discreet.

Or she was being very foolish?

She could stand it no longer when supper was over and she could see that Lord Graham was about to ask her for the next set. Lionel was standing close to the doorway, talking with two other gentlemen.

"Excuse me, please," Samantha said, and she hurried away after murmuring to Aunt Agatha that she was going to the ladies' withdrawing room. She did not stop to listen to the exasperated question of why she had not gone there when she was passing it a few minutes ago on the way back from the supper room.

Her heart beat painfully as she approached the doorway. She had never in her life contemplated anything so brazenly improper. She bumped awkwardly against Lord Kersey as she hurried past him and stammered an apology as he caught at her upper arms.

"Let me speak with you outside," she whispered, and hurried on past.

A moment later she would have given anything in the world to have those words and that collision back. How could she? Oh, how could she? She stood uncertainly, fanning herself, and decided that after all she would rush for the ladies' room. He would think he had imagined what she had said.

But he came strolling from the ballroom while she still hesitated.

"Ah, Miss Newman," he said, making her an elegant bow and taking her hand to raise to his lips. "I am charmed to see you here. I trust you are enjoying the evening?"

"Oh, yes, my lord, thank you," she said breathlessly, looking anxiously into his face. Let him speak without delay, she thought. There was nothing improper in their exchanging civilities for a few moments. But a few moments were all that propriety would allow.

He was looking at her politely, his eyebrows raised. There was . . . amusement? in his eyes. "Yes, Miss Newman? How may I be of service to you?"

How unspeakably mortifying. Except for that look in his eyes—that knowing look—he might have been addressing a stranger.

"I thought—" she said. "That is— When you were still betrothed to Jenny you said— I—"

He leaned his head a little closer to her as if trying to make sense of a child's meanderings. "I believe," he said, "your extreme youth has led you into a misconception, Miss Newman.

You are a lovely young lady, and I have always appreciated loveliness. Perhaps I expressed some gallantry that you misinterpreted?"

She stared at him in disbelief and horror. And realized in a painful rush everything that her extreme youth had led her into. She had been disturbed by his willingness to speak secretly of love to her when he was promised to Jenny. And she had once suspected that he wanted her to try to end the betrothal by speaking with Jenny. She had been quite right—though she had mistaken his motive. Oh, yes, she had. It was so crystal clear to her now that she felt mortified at her own stupidity. Or at her own childish refusal to listen to her own doubts.

"You wanted your freedom from Jenny," she whispered. "You tried to use me. Oh!"

"My dear Miss Newman." His look was one of avuncular concern. "I believe the heat of the ballroom has been too much for you. May I fetch you a glass of lemonade? And help you to a chair first?"

But another ghastly thought had struck her. Jenny had denied those indiscretions that the letter had listed, and Samantha had known it was almost impossible for her to have had clandestine meetings with the Earl of Thornhill. And Jenny had said the earl had denied writing the letter. Lionel had done nothing to protect Jenny from that dreadfully public disgrace. He might have confronted her privately, put her away from him quietly. But he had not. And now she knew why.

"You wrote the letter." She was still whispering.

"I believe," he said—he was chafing her hand— "I should summon your aunt, Miss Newman, and advise her to take you home."

"No." She snatched her hand away, brushed past him with ungainly haste, almost collided with the Earl of Thornhill, remembered where she was, and hurried toward the ladies' withdrawing room.

The music had come to an end before she came out again. She would decide tomorrow whether or not she should tell Jenny and Lord Thornhill what she now suspected, though really it was more than suspicion that she felt. Yes, she should tell them. But in the meantime there was the remainder of a ball to be enjoyed and partners to be danced with, and perhaps—yes, perhaps a husband to be chosen.

Although she had been in the ladies' room for only half an hour, she felt as if she had grown up at least five years in that time. She was no longer a naive and innocent girl. She felt quite like a cynical woman of the world.

Never again would she allow herself to be so deceived.

Never again would she love.

Chapter 17

The Earl of Thornhill had been deeply affected by the letter from Switzerland. The very fact that it had absolved him in Jennifer's eyes of at least one of the charges against him was no small matter, of course. But it was not just that. There were two particular points in the letter that had impressed themselves deeply on his mind.

She had begged him not to seek revenge. Her plea had come too late, of course. He had already sought revenge and failed to get it. He had helped rather than hurt Kersey, he firmly believed. Kersey had been quite happy to rid himself of the encumbrance of an unwanted betrothal. But the attempt at revenge had not been without result. Far from it. It had hurt two people—Jennifer and himself.

And he had been contemplating further and more vicious revenge. He had been half planning Kersey's death—by provoking him into a duel, perhaps. And yet Catherine's plea had somehow made him realize that hatred merely breeds hatred and violence. He had made himself every bit as bad as Kersey in the past month. Yes, every bit.

It was a chilling realization.

Especially in view of that other thing Catherine had said. *I was the winner of that encounter.* She really had been. It was true that she had suffered dreadfully, but the experience had matured her, and it had led her to find for herself the place and the life that would make her happy. She was about to remarry, it seemed. And most important, she had Eliza, whom she adored.

Yes, Catherine had gained in almost every way, while Kersey was still selfish and rootless and very possibly unhappy.

I was the winner of that encounter. The words had haunted

him all day. In his efforts to get some measure of revenge, he had severed Kersey's betrothal to Jennifer and had been tricked and trapped into marrying her himself. Was he the loser of the encounter? Was he? Or was he the winner, as Catherine had been?

Was it in fact, in both their cases, a matter of loser take all?

It was a severe provocation when Kersey came to speak to Jennifer at the start of the ball. It was so obviously a well-calculated move. And the Earl of Thornhill would not have been human had he not felt furiously angry and even murderous. But he chose to make his wife his chief concern throughout the evening. He could never atone for what he had done to her in the past. But he could and would do everything in his power to protect her interests and look to her security and contentment in the future. It was all he could do.

He was relieved to find that she was not after all to be a social pariah. Frank, of course, came to pay his respects as soon as the first set had ended and led her into the second set. And at the end of that Bertie brought his blushing and timid betrothed to present—with her mother's permission, Bertie had whispered when the earl had raised his eyebrows and looked pointedly at him. Bertie danced the next set with Jennifer while the earl was forced to lead out the terrified Miss Ogden. It took all of his charm and all of five minutes to draw the first smile from her and another two minutes to draw a giggle. When she relaxed and smiled, she was almost pretty, he thought. She certainly had a considerable amount of sweetness. He must remember to commend Bertie on his choice.

When that set was ended, Colonel Morris strolled over to talk and then bowed in courtly manner to Jennifer and asked for the honor of a dance. And after that the crisis seemed to have passed. It apparently became the fashionable thing to dance with the notorious new Countess of Thornhill.

Such was the fickleness of the *ton,* her husband reflected, watching her and not even trying to hide the admiration in his eyes. He had watched her with deliberate admiration while he had been seeking his revenge. Well, now it had become very real.

And yet all was not perfectly well. Of course it was not. It was only amazing that the evening was proceeding as well as it was. The earl danced the supper dance with her himself even though he had seen two other prospective partners approaching her. He was not quite sure of what would happen at supper and preferred to be at her side to protect her if necessary.

He was very glad he had had the forethought to do so. He had seated her at a table with Bertie and Miss Ogden and two other couples of their acquaintance. The table adjoining theirs was empty, but three older couples were approaching it, among them the Earl and Countess of Rushford. And then the countess, who must have been in the card room all evening, saw them and froze.

"Rushford," she said after a significant pause and in a very distinct voice, "find me another table, if you please." She lifted her head and sniffed the air delicately. "There is something—putrid in the vicinity of this one."

Rushford led her away and the other two couples trailed after them while the Earl of Thornhill lowered his head to his wife's, made some mundane remark to her, and smiled. She smiled back at him.

Before supper was over, everyone in the supper room, and doubtless everyone else who had not come there, would have heard what the countess had said. Many would applaud her wit.

No, all was not yet perfectly well. And it was going to be difficult to forget about revenge when his wife was likely to be the butt of other sallies of wit like that one during the week before he would take her away to the peace and safety of Chalcote.

Henry Chisley danced with her after supper while the earl watched as usual. She was a woman of great strength of character, he thought with an unexpected twinge of pride. She was holding up wonderfully well under circumstances that would have given most other women the vapors long ago and sent them into a permanent decline. Jennifer, he suspected, would not go into a decline even when the full reality of what had happened to her in the past few days finally hit her.

He remembered suddenly her asking him who Catherine's lover had been, who Eliza's father was. Was she suspecting the truth? He drew a slow breath.

But his attention was distracted.

He had been half aware of the fact that Samantha had left her aunt's side and was approaching the doorway. There was nothing very strange about that, but his attention was caught when she stumbled against Kersey of all people. She hurried on past him and out through the doors, but no more than a few seconds later Kersey turned and left too.

The earl frowned. He had not had the chance yet to become well acquainted with Samantha, but she was Jennifer's cousin and even younger than she. He did not see why Kersey would want to have anything to do with Samantha when he had just rid himself of Jennifer. But if he did decide to turn his charm on the girl, her youth and inexperience would doubtless make her easy prey.

He hesitated and looked back to his wife, who was still dancing with Chisley and saying something that had him chuckling. He hesitated a moment longer and then slipped from the room himself.

Yes, Kersey had accosted her and they were talking. He could see only Kersey's back, but she looked considerably agitated. She appeared not to notice him as he strolled closer just in case he was needed. Perhaps he had given up the idea of revenge, but he was not going to stand by while Kersey seduced an innocent young girl.

" . . . a lovely young lady," he heard Kersey say, "and I have always appreciated loveliness. Perhaps I expressed some gallantry that you misinterpreted?"

The earl watched agitation give place to horror in Samantha's face. "You wanted your freedom from Jenny," he heard her say, though she spoke almost in a whisper. "You tried to use me. Oh!" The final exclamation was agonized.

It did not take a great deal of intelligence to understand what had happened. Kersey had obviously been playing two games at the same time in the hope that if he did not win the one, he would succeed with the other. And in the process he had quite heartlessly hurt two innocents.

The Earl of Thornhill felt again the murderous urge to get even. He stood where he was until Samantha pushed past Kersey, almost collided with him, and hurried on in the direction of the ladies' withdrawing room. Kersey turned a moment later, a look of amusement on his face. The look disappeared when he saw the earl standing no more than a few feet away.

"Ah," he said, "a soft-footed spy. Must I be looking over my shoulder wherever I go for the rest of the Season, Thornhill?"

"It might be arranged if I thought it would give you a few sleepless nights," the earl said pleasantly. "I will have a word with you now, Kersey."

"Will you?" Viscount Kersey smiled, at his ease again. "I believe I can be expected not to consort with the man who is responsible for my broken heart."

"I shall wait, then," the earl said, unruffled, "for you to return to the ballroom and then slap a glove in your face in defense of the honor of my cousin by marriage, Miss Newman."

"You would simply make an ass of yourself," the viscount said contemptuously.

"We will put it to the test." The earl smiled at him. "I have very little to lose, after all. When reputation is gone, there is nothing much left to guard from public scorn, is there?"

Viscount Kersey looked nettled. "Well?" he said. "What do you have to say?"

"A few things," the earl said, looking about him, "which I would prefer to say in some privacy. By a stroke of good fortune I see that the first anteroom is at this moment being vacated. Shall we go there?"

"Lead the way." Viscount Kersey made him a mocking bow and extended one hand in the direction of the anteroom.

The Truscott mansion had been carefully built for social occasions. There was a whole series of small, cozy anterooms opposite the ballroom, all interlinked by doors that could be closed for privacy or left open for greater sociability. The understanding was that some guests would wish for a quieter place than the ballroom at some point in the evening and yet would be uninterested in cards. The understanding was too that young couples who were involved in the marriage mart, as so many were during the Season, would perhaps wish a moment in which to steal a kiss without being observed by half the *ton*.

Closed doors were not the rule. Closed doors suggested clandestine goings-on and might arouse scandal if left closed for too long a time.

The Earl of Thornhill closed the door into the corridor outside. Viscount Kersey turned to face him, amusement in his face again.

"It is a pity gentlemen gave up the fashion of wearing dress swords a few decades ago, Thornhill," he said. "We might have had a spectacular clash of arms in here, might we not?"

The earl stood just inside the door. He set his hands at his back. "I have to thank you, Kersey," he said, "for making it so easy for me to acquire my wife. She is, I believe, the greatest treasure any man could hope to find."

Lord Kersey laughed. "That good, is she?" he said. "Perhaps I should have tried her out for myself a few times, Thornhill. Broken her in for you and all that."

"Have a care." The earl's voice was very quiet. "Be very careful, Kersey. The lady has been made to suffer indescribable humiliation, for which we are both responsible."

"Come," Lord Kersey said, still laughing, "you must admit that I was a better player than you, Thornhill. The letter was masterly. At least, in the humble opinion of its author it was. I did not expect you to take on a leg-shackle with her, though. That fact will afford me amusement for many a long day."

"I will be brief," the earl said. "I came to say this, Kersey. You debauched my stepmother, you ruined the lady who is now my wife, and you have cruelly toyed with the affections of her cousin, another and even younger innocent. You have nothing to fear from me as I have discovered to my cost since my return from Europe that I have merely reduced myself to your level by seeking to punish you and have hurt innocent people in the process. But if you come near any lady within the sphere of my protection or affection ever again, or if you say or do anything calculated to cause them public humiliation, I will slap that glove I spoke of across your face in the most public place I can find. I will not ask if you understand me. I do not believe imbecility is among your faults."

Viscount Kersey put his head back and roared with laughter. "I am in fear and trembling, Thornhill," he said. "My knees are knocking."

"If they are not now, they will be before this night is out."

Both men turned their heads sharply to look in astonishment at the door to the next anteroom, which now swung open and crashed against the wall behind it. It must not have been quite shut, the Earl of Thornhill realized.

The Earl of Rushford stood there, his eyes ablaze, his face almost purple. Behind him Thornhill had a brief glimpse of the shocked face of the countess. The two gentlemen with whom they had taken supper were hastily ushering their ladies out through the other door into the corridor.

"Father!" Viscount Kersey said.

A well-rehearsed melodrama could not have played itself out with half as much precision, the Earl of Thornhill thought. Well, so much for private rooms and private conversations. He wondered irrelevantly if the sound of a kiss carried from one anteroom to another.

"Rushford," he said curtly, inclining his head. "Ma'am." He did likewise for the countess. "I have had my say here. If you will excuse me."

He turned and left the room, closing the door quietly behind him. The music was just ending, he could hear. Jennifer would need him in the ballroom.

She knew herself for the coward she was before the night was out. Those questions she had asked him during the first waltz, the ones that had gone unanswered, had repeated themselves in her mind over and over again through the rest of the evening. Not that she really needed to have them answered. But as long as they were not, as long as she could not hear the answers in his voice, then perhaps she could convince herself that they were still merely questions, that she did not know the answers.

She would ask again as soon as the ball was over, she decided. And yet she did not ask in the carriage on the way home. They were alone together, and they traveled in silence. It was not that she had no opportunity to ask. But she did not. He sat as far to the right of the seat as he could and she sat as far to the left as she could. But he took her hand in his and held it so tightly throughout that silent journey that her mind became wholly focused on her pain. Or so it seemed. She welcomed the pain because it gave her mind something to focus on.

She would ask him as soon as he came into her bedchamber, she decided when he had escorted her into the house and left her at the door of her dressing room after kissing her briefly and telling her he would be with her shortly. But she did not do so. By the time he came to her she was in her nightgown, and her newly loosened and freshly brushed hair was comfortable against her back, and she could feel only anticipation and desire. If she asked now, a treacherous part of her mind told her, everything would be ruined and he would not make love to her. Or if he did, she would not be able to enjoy it.

And so she decided to ask him afterward, before they fell asleep. But making love took a good deal of time and even more energy. And making love reminded her that she did not want any of it to be true. Any of it, including what she knew beyond all doubt was true. She did not want it to be true because she wanted to love him. And she wanted to be free to enjoy this for the rest of her life. She did not want to have to cringe from him at the once nightly performance of her duty. She did not want it to become nothing but a duty.

"My love," he murmured against her ear when they were finished at last and she should have been the one talking. "My love, I have not overexhausted you?"

From Aunt Agatha's description and her own previous knowledge, she had not expected it to take longer than a few minutes at the most. And she had expected only a little discomfort to herself, certainly no expenditure of energy. But it had taken many times longer than a few minutes and yes, he had exhausted her and she had exhausted herself. She had not an ounce of energy left with which to utter even a single word. She sighed deeply, cuddled closer, and slept. She was asleep even before she could hear his answering chuckle.

There was a strong suggestion of dawn light in the room when she woke again and realized that it was his lips feathering across one temple and down her cheek that had changed her dream into an erotic one and then waked her. She sighed sleepily against his chest and stretched her legs along his. They were strong, very masculine legs, she decided, and remembered how they felt against her inner thighs.

All right, she told herself firmly as full consciousness returned. *This is it. Ask him now. Get it over with. There will be no peace until everything is in the open.*

And then perhaps none ever again!

But the questions must be asked. She took her face away from his chest and tipped her head back. He was smiling at her.

"Good morning, my love," he said. "I did not wake you by any chance, did I?

"Yes, you did," she said. "What do you mean by it?" *I am smiling,* she thought helplessly. *I am smiling at him.*

"Only to ask humbly," he said, his smile becoming knee-weakeningly tender, "if I might make love to you again, my wife."

"Oh." The body had a frightening power over the mind, she thought briefly. She never would have suspected it before her body had been awakened to pleasure—just last night. Every part of her now leapt into instant arousal. She wanted him. She wanted to feel him—everywhere.

"Only if you wish," he said. "You must say no if you do not."

She realized suddenly and in total amazement that she was seeing his face through a blur. And then she felt a hot tear roll diagonally down her cheek to drip onto his arm.

"Oh, Gabriel," she said, "I do wish it. I do. Make love to me."

When it was over, she said nothing, though she did not immediately sleep and neither did he. They might have talked, but instead they kissed warmly and drowsily with their eyes closed. And she marveled at what she had learned—that he could make love to her with his hand and his fingers and bring her to madness and ecstasy over and over again so that when he came inside at last for his own satisfaction she could be a soft and relaxed cradle for his driving hardness and finally for his seed.

She would ask him the questions tomorrow, or rather later this morning. Not now. Now was going to be one of the precious memories of her life. She was going to remember tonight as the night she had loved totally. She was going to re-member it as the night before love died forever.

But that was tomorrow. This was now. She slipped an arm about his waist and pressed her breasts more comfortingly against his chest. Their kiss was broken for a moment, but they opened their eyes, smiled lazily, and joined mouths again.

Chapter 18

He was gone again when she woke in the morning. Though it was not as late as it had been the day before, she was ashamed of the fact that she could sleep so late and had not even stirred when he left her bed.

She felt very married this morning, she thought as she dressed and as her maid styled her hair. It was a curious thought. She had been just as married yesterday morning. Except that yesterday morning she had been embarrassed about meeting her maid's eyes and embarrassed about having to leave her rooms to be seen by other servants, who would know. And except that this morning that somewhat tender feeling in her breasts and the slight soreness—though that was not quite the right word—between her legs, denoting that there was now a man in her life, were more familiar to her. And pleasant. She liked the feeling.

Her eyes, reflected in the looking glass, seemed larger, dreamier. It would be wonderfully pleasant, she thought, to have a marriage free of troubles. She would enjoy having a man as companion and friend during the day and lover during the night. She would love having children of such a marriage.

Lionel. She sighed inwardly and remembered what he had done last night, how his gesture had seemed sadly noble at first until she had analyzed his possible motives for doing such a thing. And until she had begun to wonder about his past. Somehow—and the thought was frightening because it broke a habit of thought she had developed over five years—somehow she did not know if it would ever have been possible to have had Lionel as a companion and friend. There had never been any sort of closeness between them. Whereas with Gabriel . . .

With Gabriel she had always found it easy to talk and easy to listen. If only circumstances were different, they might have been friends. Of course, they already were lovers at night. It was far more wonderful than she had ever imagined it could possibly be. Probably they would continue to be lovers. He had said that he would insist she perform that duty once each night. Except that they would not really be lovers, merely a man exercising his sexual rights and a woman being obedient.

If she was correct, that was. If she asked him again.

She knew she was right.

She was not so sure this morning that she would ask him again. Why not just keep quiet about her knowledge, or her suspicions anyway? Why not let it all slip silently into the past and hope that they could build something of a future at Chalcote? Perhaps she could bring him to love her. She knew he found her desirable already. And she knew he felt responsible for her. He had married her, had he not? And she knew that she loved him.

The admission caught her unawares, and she found herself playing absently with her hairbrush after her maid had set it down. Yes. Oh, yes, it was true.

She drew a deep breath and got to her feet. There was no point in planning what she was going to do or not do. She should know from experience by now the power that Gabriel's presence had on her. She would not know until she was with him again whether she would be able to live with unanswered questions forever festering in her mind or whether she would find it impossible to ask those questions again even if she wanted to.

There was a tap on the door of her dressing room and her maid answered it. His lordship was requesting the presence of her ladyship in the downstairs salon at her earliest convenience, a footman explained.

The downstairs salon was used for visitors, Jennifer had learned the day before in a tour of the house. Who? Aunt Agatha and Sam? It was a little early in the day for them, especially the morning after a ball.

The same footman who had delivered the message and run lightly down the stairs ahead of her, opened the salon door, and closed it behind her when she stepped inside.

The room was silent even though it had four occupants. The Countess of Rushford was seated to one side of the fireplace, with her husband standing behind her chair. Viscount Kersey was standing before the fireplace, his back to it. Jennifer turned instinctively to the fourth occupant of the room. Her husband was standing at the window, his body turned toward it, though he had looked over his shoulder at her entrance. She fixed her eyes on him as he hurried toward her.

"My dear." He took her hands in a strong clasp and raised one of them to his lips. He looked as pale as if he had seen a ghost. "Come and have a seat."

He seated her on a chair at the other side of the fireplace and then moved away from her—to stand behind her chair, she believed, though she did not look. She fixed her eyes on the carpet a short distance in front of her feet. They would present what would look like a carefully arranged tableau to anyone now coming through the door, she thought irrelevantly.

"Ma'am." The voice was the Earl of Rushford's. "It was good of you to grant us some of your time. My son has something to say to you."

There was a long silence, which might have been uncomfortable if she had allowed herself to think or to feel atmosphere. And then Viscount Kersey cleared his throat.

"I owe you a deep apology, ma'am," he said. "I did not have the courage to tell either you or my father that a promise made five years ago was no longer appealing to me."

He stopped again and Jennifer thought of that poor naive girl with her dreams of beauty and love and forever after. That girl who had been herself.

"I tried to win my freedom in another way," he continued. "I saw your interest in Thornhill and his in you and I decided to help along your—courtship. I was the author of that letter, ma'am."

His voice was stilted and cold. Jennifer wondered how his father had persuaded him to come and make this confession. Power of the purse, perhaps? Had he threatened to cut off Lionel's funds?

"And the other matter too, if you please," his father said now.

Lord Kersey cleared his throat again. "While I was unofficially betrothed to you, ma'am," he said, "two years ago, I was unfaithful with another lady—with the Countess of Thornhill."

"An ugly reality with which we would not have burdened you, ma'am," the Earl of Rushford said, his voice harsh, "except that it concerns your husband, and you should know that he is not the dishonorable man you might have suspected him of being."

No one filled the silence that followed. The viscount shifted uneasily from one foot to the other.

"We will not distress you further by prolonging our visit, which is not, after all, a social call," Lord Rushford said at last. "We have to make another call, on Viscount Nordal, your father. But you must know, ma'am, that I deeply regret my part in what happened four evenings ago."

"And I mine in what happened last evening," the countess added hurriedly and breathlessly.

"You may be sure," the Earl of Rushford said, "that the *ton* will be informed quite as decisively as they were four evenings ago of the truth of the matter. And you may rest assured that you will not have to suffer the embarrassment of setting eyes on my son for at least the next five years. He will be leaving the country within a few days."

She did not raise her eyes from the carpet as they left, accompanied by her husband. Or after they had gone. Every part of her felt frozen. Mercifully so.

He held up a staying hand when his footman would have opened the salon door to admit him again. He needed to catch his breath and order his thoughts. He had known that something very similar to this was going to happen. There had been those questions she had asked him at the ball last night. He had known that she would ask them again. He had been thankful that she had not asked them last night. He had wanted last night in which to give her something that she might remember as tenderness after the crisis was over.

But he had known that it would come today. Or tomorrow. Or some time soon.

Well, it was now. He nodded briskly to the footman and stepped inside the room again. He heard the door close quietly at his back.

She was sitting where he had left her. She had not moved. She looked as if she had been turned to marble.

"You had suspected?" he asked her quietly.

"Yes." A mere breath of sound. She did not look up.

"Jennifer," he asked, staying close to the door, clasping his hands behind him, "do you love him? Is your heart quite shattered?"

"I loved the thought of him," she said, addressing the carpet at her feet, almost as if she were merely thinking aloud. "He was so very handsome and fashionable. He represented the dream of love and romance and exciting living that I suppose most girls who live in the country dream of. For five years he was my life, or at least my hope and my dream. It is shattering, yes, to know that in all that time he did not care for me at all and that this year he was so desperate to be free of me that he would resort to lies and cruelty. It is shattering to feel so very unloved."

"Jennifer—" he said softly.

"It is amazing," she said, "how in the space of a few days one can grow up all in a hurry so that one was a girl one day and is a woman the next. I thought Lionel loved me. I thought you were so obsessed with me that you would resort to dishonorable trickery in order to win me." She laughed softly and at last moved in order to press one hand over her mouth.

"Jennifer, my dear—" he said.

"It was revenge, was it not?" she asked. "You had returned from being with your stepmother and you saw Lionel here and you discovered that he was newly betrothed and you thought to end the betrothal and embarrass and possibly hurt him. That was it, was it not?"

He inhaled slowly. "Yes," he said. He watched her eyes close and then clench tightly above her hand.

"The best way to do it was to make me fall in love with you and break off my own betrothal," she said, "or perhaps cause Lionel to cast me off. And to do it in a rather public manner so that he would look something of a fool. That was it, was it not?"

"Yes."

"I did not matter at all to you," she said. "I was a mere tool. Tools do not have feelings. It did not matter to you that I would be disgraced and probably hurt."

"At first," he said, "I persuaded myself that you would be better off without him. Your life would have been hell with him."

"And now," she said, "it is heaven? You might have written that letter, Gabriel. You were both playing the same game. You might have called it 'Cast-Off-Jennifer.' Perhaps you did. But you were both playing it. He outmaneuvered you. He thought of writing that letter before you did. But you might have done it, then or later."

"I might have," he said quietly. "But I did not. I could not."

"Why not?" she asked.

"Because after that . . . kiss," he said, "at the Velgards' costume ball, guilt would no longer allow me to use you. I had come to know it was a person I was using as a pawn. I had come to realize what I was doing to you—and to myself."

"Ah," she said, "the loser's excuse. The noble explanation. And so all must be forgiven. At the last possible moment you had an attack of conscience and put an end to your dastardly scheme. You would have allowed my reputation to recover."

"What I did was inexcusable," he said. "It will be on my conscience until I die, if that is any consolation to you, Jennifer. I can find no excuse whatsoever for what I did. I can find no redeeming feature in my behavior that would give me any right to beg your forgiveness. There is nothing I can say or do."

"You married me." She laughed again and looked at him at last. Her eyes coming to rest on his felt like the flailing of a whip. "You will be able to carry around your guilt for the rest of your life, Gabriel. It will be there every time you look at me. Will you ever make it up to me, do you think?"

"No," he said, "never. And so you must tell me what you wish, Jennifer. If you wish for my protection and perhaps for

. . . children, then we will continue to inhabit the same house. I will give you as much freedom as you desire. Or if you would prefer never to set eyes on me again, I will set up a home for you with everything you need and access to a man of business who will handle your concerns so that you will not need to have any dealings with me. Think about it for a day or two or for as long as you need. It will be entirely as you wish."

He turned to the door and set a hand on the knob. He wished that he could set her free so that she would not have to bear his name for the rest of her life, so that she could look for a husband to love. He wished it especially now that her name would be cleared in the eyes of the *ton*.

But there was one thing more he must say to her. He turned his head to look back at her. "I suppose for the rest of your life," he said, "it will be a toss-up in your mind which you hate more, Kersey or me. Or perhaps we will be equal in your low esteem. But I must say this, Jennifer. You feel unwanted and unloved. You feel that both men you thought cared about you did not but merely used you. You are wrong. You are both wanted and loved. I did not even realize it until after I had married you. I thought I married you to save you from ruin, and perhaps that was a part of it. But only a part. You are eminently lovable. I love you more than life."

He left the room, directed a footman to see to it that his horse was at the door within ten minutes, and took the stairs up to his dressing room two at a time.

Samantha called during the afternoon, bringing a maid with her. She was wide-eyed with the news that the Earl and Countess of Rushford and Viscount Kersey had come during the morning and been closeted with her uncle for all of half an hour. Aunt Agatha had been summoned after they had left. Jennifer's name—and Lord Thornhill's too—were to be publicly cleared, it seemed.

But Sam still looked unhappy even after hugging Jennifer and telling her how glad she was. And finally she disclosed what she said she had been planning to say today anyway. Lionel had pretended an attachment to her and she had fallen in love with him and then she had discovered how he had used her.

She did not know if Jenny would be able to forgive her.

Jennifer was beyond being hurt more than she had been hurt already. Feeling seemed quite dead in her. Except feeling for the cousin who had been her closest friend for several years. She did not blame Sam at all. Men were such evil creatures and so powerful when they had looks and charm to combine with ruthlessness and experience.

They walked in the park during the quiet part of the afternoon, arms linked, reflecting on what a difference a few weeks in town had made to their lives—but not at all in the way they had expected.

Jennifer dined alone after word had been brought that her busband would eat at his club. She sat in the dining room feeling the silence, feeling the presence of the servants, eating her way determinedly through at least a small helping of each course.

She spent the evening alone in her private sitting room, stitching at some embroidery. She would have to make an appointment to speak with him, she supposed. She had a feeling that he would keep himself away from the house as much as possible until she had done so and told him what she wanted.

What did she want?

I love you more than life. She did not believe him.

She did not know what she wanted. She did not want to think about it yet. At the moment the burdens were too heavy to allow for rational thought. He would have to wait for her decision.

She went to bed early. She was bone-weary. She needed an early night. And so she lay staring up into the darkness, wondering when he would come home and if he would come home—until she heard quiet sounds coming from his dressing room. She had left the door into her own open. And then the sounds stopped. Perhaps it had been only his valet in there.

She could not sleep. For twenty years she had slept in a bed alone. For two nights she had shared her bed. Now she did not know if it would be possible ever again to sleep alone. She could not sleep. She must have been lying in bed for two hours or more.

She sat up and lit a candle. And hugged her knees and stared into space while it burned half down. She could not sleep. Yet she could not get up the energy to pick up one of her books from the shelf below her nightstand. She did not want to read.

There really was only one thing to do. She acknowledged the fact eventually with a sigh and swung her legs over the side of the bed. She left the candle where it was.

She did not knock. She just opened the door quietly and stepped inside. She was not even sure that he had come home or that, if he had, he had not gone back downstairs. The curtains were drawn back from the windows, making the room quite light. He was standing by one of the windows, wearing his dressing gown, looking back over his shoulder at her. She walked across the room until she was standing quite close to him.

She could speak only what was in her heart. She had not thought out any plan of what she wanted. But some things were best spoken without prior thought.

"I want our marriage to continue," she told him.

"Very well." His tone was cautious. "It need not take long. Just a few minutes. Shall we do it here? You can go back to your own bed then. With luck and nightly effort I will have you with child very soon. Then you need see me less frequently."

"That is not what I meant," she said.

He stood quiet and still, waiting, looking at her.

"Did you mean it?" she asked him. "Please. Please, please, Gabriel, it must be the truth now. If you said it only because you knew I needed to hear it, and if you say it again now, I will know soon enough. Better by far merely to say that you wish me well and that you want to work with me to a mutually comfortable arrangement. Did you mean it?"

"I love you more than life," he said again.

"Do you?" She set her head on one side and looked closely at his face in the darkness. She had given him a way out without his having to be cruel. But he had said it again. "I think we can make it work, then, Gabriel, because I love you too, you see. I know that I do because you have offered me a comfortable alternative to living with you but I know that I want to go on with you."

He turned his head to look down into the square. It took her a few moments to realize that he was crying.

"Gabriel." She touched his arm, horrified. "Don't."

But he shook his head and turned it even farther from her until he had got control of himself. "You cannot possibly be willing to forgive me for what I did to you, Jennifer," he said. "It would be there between us for the rest of our lives."

"There you are wrong," she said, and she stepped boldly forward to set both arms about his waist. "We say it at church every Sunday when we recite the Lord's Prayer, don't we? But we rarely realize quite what we are saying. But we are all thoughtless sometimes and ride roughshod over the feelings of others. And we all use other people sometimes for our own ends. It is a regrettable part of being human. We are all in need of forgiveness over and over again throughout our lives. The measure of our goodness, I suppose, is the strength of our consciences. I think yours is strong. And apart from the fact that you are hurting now and filled with self-loathing, I am glad all this happened, Gabriel. If it had not, I would have married Lionel and been miserable with him. And I would never have known you or loved you. When I said I wanted our marriage to continue, I meant in every possible way."

His hands were gripping her shoulders. He leaned forward now to rest his forehead against hers. His eyes were closed.

"If it is what you want, of course," she said, suddenly timid again.

"If—" She heard him drawing a deep and slow breath. "I have just spent a day accustoming myself to the thought that I had very probably lost you, wondering how I was to live without you. Hoping that at the very least you would want a child of me before leaving me."

"Ten, please, Gabriel," she said, tipping her head back so that for a moment their mouths met.

"Be careful that I do not take you at your word," he said, chuckling unexpectedly. "And I have been hoping, Jennifer, I must confess, that the begetting of a child would take a long time."

"For shame," she whispered to him, and she feathered kisses along his jaw to his chin. He must have shaved before coming to her last night and the night before, she realized. He had not shaved tonight.

"I know," he said. "I am incorrigible. Don't do that any more, Jennifer, unless you mean it."

She started along the other side of his jaw. "I have been trying for hours to sleep," she said. "You have done a terrible thing to me, Gabriel. You have spent two nights in my bed and now I do not believe I can sleep without you in it."

"Are you sure it is sleep you have on your mind?" he asked. His hands were at work on the buttons of her nightgown.

She dropped her arms to her sides with a sigh of contentment and a little shiver of something more. "Well, perhaps after and between," she said.

"After and between what?" His hands stilled.

"After you have made love to me and before you do it again and after that before you do it once more and so on," she said.

"Good Lord," he said, "do you want to make an invalid of me?"

Suddenly, amazingly, they were both laughing—with genuine and prolonged amusement and with a deeply shared affection. They wrapped their arms about each other as if they would never let go. They continued to cling together when they were finally quiet again.

"Lord God," he said, sounding shaken. "Oh, dear Lord God."

"Amen," she said. "It really was a prayer, was it not?" She laughed softly.

"Yes," he said. "It really was."

She rubbed her cheek against his.

"I think perhaps," he said, "we should get started, my love. Making love and loving and living and being married in every way it is possible to be. Will my bed do?"

She nodded and gazed up into his face as he nudged her nightgown off her shoulders and slid it down her arms and then dispensed with his dressing gown.

"As long as you are in it with me," she said as he guided her over to the bed and laid her down on it.

He lay down beside her, slid an arm beneath her shoulders,

and turned her against him. "That was definitely the idea," he said. "Clever of you to perceive it, my love."

She felt him along the length of her body. She felt the warmth of his mouth against hers and the promise of passion. And she knew she was where she belonged, where she wanted always to be, and where she would not be had it not been for a certain dastardly game.

Life was a strange phenomenon.

But philosophy soon died under the onslaught of passion.